# THE DUKE'S LANCE

## The Duke's Guard Series
## Book Twelve

## C.H. Admirand

## ARE YOU SIGNED UP FOR DRAGONBLADE'S BLOG?

You'll get the latest news and information on exclusive giveaways, exclusive excerpts, coming releases, sales, free books, cover reveals and more.

Check out our complete list of authors, too!

No spam, no junk. That's a promise!

### Sign Up Here

www.dragonbladepublishing.com

*Dearest Reader;*

*Thank you for your support of a small press. At Dragonblade Publishing, we strive to bring you the highest quality Historical Romance from some of the best authors in the business. Without your support, there is no 'us', so we sincerely hope you adore these stories and find some new favorite authors along the way.*

*Happy Reading!*

*CEO, Dragonblade Publishing*

# Additional Dragonblade books by Author C.H. Admirand

## The Ladies of the Keep Series
Liberating the Lady of Loughmoe (Book 1)
Bargaining with the Lady of Merewood (Book 2)
Rescuing the Lady of Sedgeworth (Book 3)

## The Duke's Guard Series
The Duke's Sword (Book 1)
The Duke's Protector (Book 2)
The Duke's Shield (Book 3)
The Duke's Dragoon (Book 4)
The Duke's Hammer (Book 5)
The Duke's Defender (Book 6)
The Duke's Saber (Book 7)
The Duke's Enforcer (Book 8)
The Duke's Mercenary (Book 9)
The Duke's Rapier (Book 10)
The Duke's Man-at-Arms (Book 11)
The Duke's Lance (Book 12)

## The Lords of Vice Series
Mending the Duke's Pride (Book 1)
Avoiding the Earl's Lust (Book 2)
Tempering the Viscount's Envy (Book 3)
Redirecting the Baron's Greed (Book 4)
His Vow to Keep (Novella)
The Merry Wife of Wyndmere (Novella)

## The Lyon's Den Series
Rescued by the Lyon
Captivated by the Lyon
The Lyon's Saving Grace

# Historical Cookbook
Dragonblade's Historical Recipe Cookbook:
Recipes from some of your favorite Historical Romance Authors

# Dedication

For DJ, we always had each other's backs, and I was never afraid as long as you were with me. I miss you, babe.

# Acknowledgements

*A special thank you to my wonderful editor Arran McNicol! I am so grateful for his attention to detail, innate ability to find unnecessary words, and his all around "nitpickery." Confession time: my books have hidden nits that I didn't even realize needed to be picked!*

*For my loyal readers, and new-to-me readers, thank you for reading my books and letting me know how much you love The Duke's Guard Series and my handsome-as-sin Irishmen. Now that Eamon O'Malley's book has been published, there are only four more stories in The Duke's Guard series...the Flaherty brothers. Then it's on to a new series, Wyndmere's Warriors. Although I should have expected it, it was still a surprise when I look back and realize that every one of the heroes in my next series have already appeared in the duke's guard books! Lieutenant Gryffyn Tremayne, Captain David Bayfield, Colonel Iain Masterson, and Lieutenant Daniel Hennessy. Men!*

# CHAPTER ONE

E AMON O'MALLEY WONDERED when he'd hear the full story of what had happened to the duke's ward Emily Montrose and her maid Helen on their journey from London to the Lake District. A fortnight ago they'd arrived at Wyndmere Hall under the protection of his cousin Aiden Garahan, and two of Captain Coventry's men assigned as added protection.

He whispered a few words of greeting to his gelding before gaining the saddle to head out on patrol to the village and back. The day was still cool in the early hours just before dawn. He enjoyed the invigorating temperature, knowing soon enough the air would warm as the sun climbed in the sky. As he rode by the open fields, he scanned his surroundings, though the chance of a sharpshooter being able to stay hidden in the openness was slim.

His mind returned to Garahan's arrival. It had been obvious to anyone with eyes in their head that Emily and Garahan had developed feelings for one another during the time she was under his protection. The men in the duke's guard were honorable, and no one would ever question that anything untoward would happen on their journey.

What had caused the initial uproar—and heated discussions on both sides—upon their arrival at Wyndmere Hall had been their physical appearance. Garahan and Emily had arrived looking bruised and battered, worse for wear. This was, apparently, due to circumstances revolving around the rumored murder of Emily's father, and the wager in White's betting book involving her dowry and sudden inheritance. There had been more than one attempted ambush before the outright attack on Emily and Helen at an inn not far from the duke's estate.

His horse whickered, and O'Malley responded, "Exactly what I'd been thinking, lad. Though as soon as I wheedle the particulars out of Garahan, I'll share the tale with ye." He patted his gelding's neck and added, "Sure and there'll be tales of blows exchanged. Though from what I've overheard, more than one of Garahan's injuries were caused by his new bride."

Settling down into the ride, he braced for the end of the open fields and the thick, forested area a mile ahead. Knowing he had the time before reaching the area known to draw sharpshooters, he wondered if Garahan had been prepared to meet the woman destined to be his wife. O'Malley had been raised to believe that the other half of his heart was somewhere out there just waiting for him to find her. He grinned recalling Emily's arrival. She'd stepped down from the carriage and stumbled, and Garahan's immediate reaction had been to sweep her into his arms. Aiden was in love with the lass and fighting it. As luck would have it, she felt the same for his cousin.

A few days later, Emily and Aiden had married by special license. The only outward indication that anything untoward had occurred were the fading bruises on Emily's and Helen's cheeks. 'Twas obvious someone had struck them in anger. His gut roiled at knowing Garahan's wife had been injured and threatened. Had her ebony-haired, violet-eyed maid been threatened too? O'Malley needed to know!

The outward sign of the women's suffering triggered his need to find the blackguard and exact retribution. There had been a moment when Helen had looked up and their gazes met. The turmoil of emotions in her expressive eyes had O'Malley feeling gut-punched, a moment before his protective instincts clicked into place, and his heart whispered... *Mine!*

The trees on both sides of the road blocked out the rising sun, chilling the air considerably. His eyes searched the deep forest hemming him in on both sides as he rode. A man could easily lie in wait and ambush the unsuspecting—and had. But he and the other members of the duke's guard were aware and took precautions. These next few miles of road leading into the village were rife with hiding places.

As he passed through the first of several areas where an ambush could occur, his mind returned to the disturbing thought that something far worse had happened to the women when they'd been surprised by the attacker lying in wait in their bedchamber at the inn. While he understood Emily's decision not to speak of it, what he did not understand was her need to gloss over what had happened.

Advancing along the road, he reached the section where the trees began to thin out, and knew no one would be springing an attack on him this morning. "All's well, lad. Let's pick up the pace a bit to a fast trot."

O'Malley's mount obeyed, and he let his thoughts circle back to Helen and the most recent encounter with her etched on his brain. He had been on patrol by the stables, passing near to the back of the herb garden, and come upon Helen and Emily speaking quietly. Not wishing to alarm them, he intentionally scuffed the sole of his boot. They both jumped at the sound and turned around in time for him to see the shattered look in their eyes, quickly banked.

Eamon had a knack for healing, though not to the same degree as his cousin Emmett O'Malley, who was stationed at the duke's town house in London. Eamon had an inherent ability to sense an injury and to prevent further damage, until the physician could be summoned. Oftentimes an emotional injury occurred simultaneously with a physical one. Especially in the case of what happened to Emily and Helen. His fraternal twin Thomas was adept at picking up on emotional injuries.

He smiled, thinking that his brother had found the other half of *his* heart when he rescued Caroline Gillingham. Thomas's last missive had had Eamon grinning. Caro had captivated his brother from the moment she stumbled out of the bedchamber she'd been locked in and landed in Thomas's arms. The couple had married recently, as had Emmett. That left Eamon as the last of the Wexford and Cork O'Malleys to wed.

Up ahead was the last section of deep woods. He slowed his mount and cleared his thoughts, opening his mind and his heart to his surroundings. A soft swirl of wind brushed his cheek. A hawk shrieked as it took flight from deep within the forest lining the road. O'Malley inhaled and caught the scent of the sun-warmed pines and clear, crisp air—scrubbed clean by last night's storm.

The hairs on the back of his neck stood up. He slid his rifle off his shoulder in time to hear a metallic click echo through the suddenly still air.

Attuned to the sound, he took aim and fired into the trees. A gasp of shock was followed by breaking branches and a groan of agony as a sharpshooter fell from his perch. O'Malley quickly loaded and primed his rifle as he nudged his horse toward the downed ambusher, reining in a few feet from the now-unarmed man, who was writhing and moaning as if dying.

O'Malley snorted. Anyone with enough energy to moan like that was nowhere near taking his last breath. "Who are ye, and why in the bloody hell did ye take a shot at me?" The man stopped moving and opened his eyes. The shock of recognition was one-sided. O'Malley demanded, "How do ye know me? Who sent ye?"

The blackguard clamped his jaw shut, refusing to answer. Well, this would not be the first time O'Malley had had the pleasure of beating an answer out of someone who'd tried to kill him...or one of the duke's family under his protection. Faith, it wouldn't be the last.

He dismounted, told his gelding to wait for him, and walked toward the man. The closer he got, the younger the man appeared. *"Shite!* Ye aren't even old enough to grow whiskers!" O'Malley grumbled. "What in the bloody hell were ye doing up in that pine tree?"

The younger man closed his eyes again. This time a telltale trickle from the corner of his eye had O'Malley cursing. "I'll take ye to the physician in the village and see that ye're patched up."

"You'll let me go?" The hope in the lad's voice was laughable.

"Nay. Our next stop will be the constable. Ye can cool yer heels there while I finish me patrol and report to His Grace."

"You really are *the* O'Malley." The voice held a hint of awe.

"Is that why ye took a potshot at me?"

But the young man wasn't listening. He was staring at O'Malley's face, his eyes glazed over. "My aunt told me how you helped them when my uncle was imprisoned because of…"

His voice trailed off, and O'Malley prodded him, "Because of what?"

"My uncle had fallen on hard times and needed to find a way to put food on the table. My cousins were little, and my aunt was due to have another babe."

O'Malley sensed what the youth did not say. "A strong man does whatever he has to do to feed his family. Me uncle and me da were imprisoned on trumped-up charges." He didn't share the rest of his story, or the fact that his uncle Patrick O'Malley had fallen ill just as he and Da were cleared of any wrongdoing. It had been too late… Uncle Patrick died in Da's arms.

Sympathy for the injured man had O'Malley pulling him to his feet with less force than he would have used otherwise. Inspecting the younger man's shoulder, he whipped the spare black cravat from his waistcoat pocket and wrapped it around his upper arm, tying it tight. "What's yer name?"

"Burrows."

"Well, Burrows, 'tis but a graze. Ye may need threads to hold it together, or if ye're lucky, only a hot blade to sear the flesh."

His prisoner's legs went out from under him. O'Malley grumbled, tossed him over his shoulder, and laid him across his horse. "We'll be taking him to see the constable, laddie." He swung into the saddle, decided there wasn't enough room, and eased Burrows over his shoulder once more. "There's an extra cup of oats and an apple for carrying the extra load."

The high-pitched whinny of delight had O'Malley chuckling.

A few miles farther, the village was in sight, and Burrows regained consciousness. "O'Malley?"

"Be still, else ye'll spook me horse." The young man immediately obeyed. Pleased that he'd listened, O'Malley told him, "If I slide ye off me shoulder and set ye behind me, are ye planning to hang on to me or black out again? The chances are good that ye'll fall off me horse and land on yer hard head."

The snort of laughter wasn't what he'd thought to hear, and for some reason it pleased him. He was starting to like the lad, and wondered what the rest of his story was, which of the O'Malleys—one of his three brothers or four O'Malley cousins—had helped the lad's uncle. He intended to find out later. "Now then, which is it: hang on to me, or fall off on yer head?"

"I can hang on."

O'Malley took him at his word and eased him off his shoulder and onto the back of his horse. "Ye've a strong grip. We'll take it easy, just a few more buildings to ride past. There it is, on the right. 'Tis the stone building set back from the others."

His passenger tensed, but did not try to leap off the horse. There must be more to the story. O'Malley dismounted and helped Burrows off. "Now then, ye're to tell the truth. No prevaricating. Understand?"

"Aye."

O'Malley had a feeling Burrows's future would be tangled with his. Just when he'd met the woman he felt a bone-deep attraction to, a lad, who couldn't be more than seven and ten years old, ambushed him and had O'Malley feeling responsible for him. No one in the O'Malley clan ever backed away from a challenge or ignored someone in need.

They walked to the door together. O'Malley knocked, and it

opened wide. He motioned for Burrows to follow him into the building. "Constable, I've someone who's been dying to meet ye."

The constable shook his head. "It's been a month or so since you've brought me a guest for my gaol." The older man's sharp eyes didn't miss the blood-soaked cravat wrapped around the prisoner's arm, nor the terrified expression on the young man's pale and pasty face. "Have a seat and tell me what happened."

✦◈◇◈✦

# CHAPTER TWO

HELEN LANGLEY GLANCED around where she and Emily stood, halfway between the kitchen and the rear entrance to the building. They were alone. Worry that her mistress would think she was abandoning her, Helen rasped, "You don't understand, Miss Emily. I feel useless here after serving you for so long. Your father, Lord Montrose, was the best of men—he changed my life when he hired me on to work as your companion and lady's maid."

Emily smiled. "Neither one of us knew just what that entailed at the time, did we?" When Helen shook her head, Emily frowned. "And you're still calling me miss even though I have asked you not to."

"Forgive me. Mrs. Garahan."

Emily's bright laughter soothed the worry that had been so hard for Helen to hide.

"While I do count my blessings, having married Aiden Garahan, I would ask that you please call me by my first name."

Helen wrinkled her nose. "Very well, but only in private." She sighed, knowing she had to at least try to explain. "I feel so insignificant here in the presence of the Duke and Duchess of Wyndmere."

"Hasn't Her Grace made you feel welcome?"

"Well, yes, but—"

"And hasn't His Grace done the same?"

Helen wished she dared to tell Emily what was really on her mind. After their perilous journey from Montrose House in London to the duke's estate in the Lake District, her friend had blossomed overnight, after receiving the duke's blessing to wed one of his trusted guard. They had married by special license and were gifted one of the cottages the duke had built just for the men in his guard who married. Not that she were jealous, but Helen admitted that she felt a smidge of envy. Would she ever find someone to love who would love her back?

"Yes, of course. His Grace has been magnanimous."

"There, you see?" Emily said. "You are very much appreciated by Their Graces and welcomed by the rest of the staff. As I have been."

Helen had to admit that she had been.

Emily continued, "You seem so happy, watching the twins in the nursery."

"They are such dear little ones. They have taken a liking to me," Helen admitted. "It is fortunate that the twins do not seem to mind that their nanny Gwendolyn O'Malley, Patrick's wife, brings their two-month-old darling Deidre, to the nursery with her."

"Richard and Abigail are such darling children and seem quite taken with Deidre," Emily agreed. Until she had started to help out in the nursery too, Helen had not realized that deep down, she longed to marry and have a family of her own.

Emily reached for Helen's hand and squeezed it. "I may not have said it enough, but you have always been more than a companion or maid. You've been my friend." Releasing Helen's hand, she frowned at her and said, "Which is why I'll ask you again, why are you leaving me? What will I do without you?"

"You don't need me any longer. You no longer live at Montrose House. You have a cozy cottage that is just the right size for you, Aiden, and any little ones that come along." When Emily flushed, Helen continued, "You are newly married and should be spending the time getting to know your husband and becoming accustomed to your new circumstances as his wife, and as a member of Their Graces staff."

"You are a valued member, too," Emily reminded her.

Helen hesitated a moment, then confided, "I'm so grateful Her Grace offered the position assisting Mrs. O'Malley in the nursery, but I feel like I don't belong here. Everyone seems to know their place and is comfortable with it. I feel as if I'm extra baggage… A burden."

"You are not a burden!" Emily insisted. "Her Grace would not have hired you if she did not feel you would be an asset to her staff. Have you noticed that everyone who works for Their Graces are happy? Constance confided that it is because they are treated as more than staff… They're treated as if they are family."

"But I'm—"

"Being unreasonable," Emily said. "Can you not see that?"

Helen did not feel that she wasn't being unreasonable, so she said the one thing that always had Emily changing the subject. "You are being stubborn again."

Emily's mouth gaped open for a heartbeat, then she slowly closed it. Finally, she replied, "You are right. I'm being stubborn because I don't want to lose you. Can you not understand? You have been my closest friend and confidante for years, and it would devastate me to lose you."

Helen absorbed the words, and knew Emily spoke from her heart. But she had to make her see reason and understand. "I do not want to get in the way of you and your handsome husband while you are building your life together. And before you contradict me, think about it. You and Aiden deserve to be happy. I need to find my place now that you've found yours."

She wasn't sure where she belonged, but she knew it wasn't as a third wheel in Emily and Aiden's life. Helen had put off telling Emily about the position as a companion she had applied for and was waiting for a response. Best just to tell her.

"I'm expecting a reply any day."

"Reply for what?" Emily asked.

"A position as companion in the Borderlands."

"You're leaving the Lake District?"

"If the dowager agrees to meet with me, and hire me, yes."

"What if I put my foot down?"

Helen shook her head. "You're being stubborn again."

"I need particulars. After what we've been through these last few weeks, I cannot just let you go off on your own. What if you run into another man such as Baron Hardwell? Are you prepared to fight him off, like you fought Hardwell to save me?"

Heart aching at the thought of losing their friendship, Helen said what Emily needed to hear: "If I have to, yes."

"Aiden and Masterson won't be there to break down the door and rescue you," Emily reminded her.

"I know, but I need to do this for me."

"What if there was another way?"

"Such as?" Helen asked.

"Well…" Emily seemed to be desperately trying to think of something to convince her to stay. "What if you were to marry?"

It was Helen's turn to gape. "I haven't been here long enough to meet an eligible man to marry. And beyond that, who in the world would marry me, just to ensure that I stayed on at Wyndmere Hall?"

"That would be me, lass," a deep voice rumbled from behind her.

⤜⤜⤜⇥⇤⤛⤛⤛

HELEN SPUN AROUND, hand to her ample breast, and rasped, "Eamon?"

"I'm pleased that ye remembered which O'Malley ye're talking to."

Her face lost every ounce of color, yet she managed to ask, "Why would you marry me?"

He took a step closer and stared into her upturned face. "Are ye wanting a list of reasons, or just the most obvious one?" Her eyes welled with tears, and his gut clenched. "I did not mean to make ye cry, lass. Forgive me." He pulled the handkerchief from his waistcoat pocket and gently dried her tears. "Don't cry. If I tell ye all the reasons, will ye stop crying?"

The lass didn't answer—truth be told, she seemed to have lost the ability to speak. Knowing he needed to say his piece and not *feck* it up, O'Malley pressed the now-damp handkerchief into her hand and took hold of the other. With a tug, she landed against his chest, and he slipped an arm around her. "With yer ebony hair and violet eyes, ye bewitched me from the moment ye stepped down from the carriage. Yer beauty takes me breath away."

Instead of melting against him, as any one of the fair lasses he'd wooed before he was hired on to work for the duke would have, she stiffened. Wondering what had caused the reaction, he slipped his other arm around her, fitting her generous curves to the hard planes of his body.

By God, she fit as if she were made just for him!

A soft voice from behind him asked, "Are there any other reasons?"

He belatedly realized he was making a fool out of himself in front of his cousin's wife, and nodded. "Aye, Emily, if ye wouldn't mind giving us a few moments of privacy, I'll be telling the lass meself."

"I do not think that would be wise."

Surprised that Aiden's wife would not do as he asked, he turned to stare at her. "I asked ye nicely."

"And I answered nicely. If you do not have a care for Helen's reputation, I do." Hands on her hips, Emily frowned at him. "You need to let her go. If anyone were to find you standing here holding Helen, there would be plenty of talk. You do not want her to be the brunt of innuendo or speculation from those on the staff and in the village, do you?"

"Of course not." O'Malley's heart was torn. He didn't want to let go of the lass, who felt as if she were a piece of the puzzle that had been missing in his life. He didn't want to cause her to suffer because his heart had overruled his head just now when he took the lovely lass in his arms.

"Ye know I wouldn't want that. I'm after protecting Helen, not harming her."

"Are those the only reasons you want to marry me?" Helen asked. "Because of the way I look and to protect me?"

At a loss as to how to answer, O'Malley asked, "Aren't those reason enough?" The lone tear streaking across her cheek tore at his heart. "What other reason does a man need?" Helen struggled against his hold, and he released her. "Are ye refusing me offer?"

"Are you going to ask me?"

His head began to throb. "Ask ye what?"

Helen put her hands on her well-rounded hips. His hands still tingled from having a hold of her womanly curves. "If you do not know, I'm certainly not going to tell you." She whirled around and hurried toward the servants' staircase at the end of the hallway by the rear entrance.

O'Malley scrubbed a hand over his face and blew out a breath. "What just happened?"

Emily's lips twitched, as if she were trying not to smile. "You didn't ask Helen to marry you."

"For the love of God! Of course I did, and she turned her back on me."

Emily sighed. "Are all of the men in the duke's guard as stubborn as you and Aiden?" When he stared at her, she shook her head. "Your exact words—in answer to her question as to who would marry her to keep her at Wyndmere Hall—were 'That would be me, lass.' You did not mention her name or ask her to marry you."

"Bloody *fecking* hell."

"I've heard that expression before, and it is not what Helen needs to hear right now either. If you really, truly want to marry her, the first thing you need to do is apologize. The second thing you should do is ask her, properly, to marry you. And the third thing—"

"Three things?" O'Malley could not believe the conversation he was having. Was Aiden's wife as daft as her former maid? And why couldn't Helen stay on as nursery help or maid to the duchess? Everything had seemed to be going along fine until just now. Damn and blast, he'd thought he would have plenty of time to woo the lass, make her aware of him and his feelings for her.

"Yes, Eamon. Three things," Emily said. "She needs to know the other reasons you want to marry her. Beauty fades over time. Isn't there anything else about her that would have you wanting to marry her?"

"Aye, but ye wouldn't approve of that reason either."

Emily frowned. "I see. She has applied for a position as a companion in the Borderlands and expects to hear any day now. As much as I wish she would remain here, I cannot stop her from trying to make a life for herself somewhere else. Now that I am married, and no longer in need of a maid, she feels she is free to entertain the idea of finding a husband herself."

Gutted at the very idea, but loath to admit it, he watched Emily rush after Helen, closing the door to the servants' staircase with more force than necessary. Raking a hand through his hair, he grumbled, "What in the hell is wrong with women?"

Flaherty entered the building in time to hear the question, snicker, and reply, "Where do ye want me to start?"

O'Malley turned around and muttered, "They're put on this earth to drive us mad."

"I won't be arguing that point with ye." Flaherty stared at him and shook his head. "Ye aren't after joining the rest of them, are ye?"

"The rest of who?"

"The eleven *eedjits*—yer three brothers, and our eight cousins—who have all fallen for a pretty face and gotten leg shackled."

O'Malley's heart ached. Had he bungled his chance? A chance he hadn't been anywhere near ready for. Was it to be his only opportunity to ask the lass to marry him? He struggled to speak past the tautness in his throat. "She said no."

Flaherty swore beneath his breath. "Ye're late for yer shift guarding the perimeter." He shoved past O'Malley and stepped over the threshold, back outside, slamming the door on his way out.

For once in his life, O'Malley was at a loss for words. That almost never happened. Drawing in a breath, he held it in for a moment, then exhaled. "Maybe me head will clear once I'm outside."

"If it's a woman that's weighin' heavy on yer mind," a familiar voice said, "I doubt it. Ye're late, Eamon."

*Patrick O'Malley.* Just what he needed, his eldest cousin—the head of the duke's guard—tracking him down to remind him he was late for his shift. "I'm surrounded by experts."

"About being on time, aye," Patrick agreed. "About what's in a woman's mind, I couldn't begin to speculate. Unless I'm kissin' the breath out of me wife."

O'Malley snorted with laughter. "That's where I went wrong. I had the lass in me arms and didn't kiss her."

Patrick clapped a hand on Eamon's shoulder. "One kiss—if it's the right woman—and ye'll be losin' sleep until ye can convince the lass to marry ye."

"Is that what happened with Gwendolyn?"

Patrick nodded. "Aye. After that first kiss, I knew I'd never get her out of me system. I needed her in me life. She's the best thing that ever happened to me."

O'Malley nodded. He had to speak to Helen again, make her understand what he was thinking and what he felt for her...it was so much more than being captivated by her beauty and curvaceous form. Never mind the fact that his head had been in a spin since that first moment he saw her. Forget how quickly he'd fallen under her spell. None of that would matter if she left Wyndmere Hall, never to return.

He was on a mission. A mission he could not fail. His heart, and their future, hung in the balance.

✦✦✦

# CHAPTER THREE

ELEN SIGHED AS she heard light footfalls coming up the stairs behind her. She did not want to argue with Emily, nor did she want to be swayed from her decision to seek a position elsewhere.

"Wait, Helen! Please?"

She paused, gathered her slipping composure, and turned around. "If you are going to continue to batter me with reasons why I should stay on at Wyndmere Hall, please do not. Can you not understand the reason why I feel uncomfortable being a part of Their Graces' staff?"

"Honestly...no."

Helen rubbed her forehead, but it did nothing to alleviate the ache this conversation—and situation—had caused. "I know in my heart that I do not belong here. Your father rescued me from starvation after my parents died. If not for his kindness and offer of employment, I would not be standing here today."

"What does that have to do with working for the duke and duchess?"

"I am not like you, Emily. My father did not earn his title for bravery on the field of battle. He was a laborer, and Mum took in laundry just to put food on the table. Before he died...he left us for another woman. When we heard that he had died..." Helen could not bring herself to continue. Tears welled up and threatened to spill over. She bit the inside of her cheek to keep from crying, or else her composure would completely shatter. She refused to let that happen.

Emily slipped an arm around her. "We grieved together for your parents and my mum. Now you're helping me grieve for my father, who loved you too. No one else here knew him. You and I are the only ones. Have you forgotten how we shored one another up, one day at a time? We shared our grief. I'm afraid I won't be able to cope alone."

A few tears escaped, but Helen ignored them. "You were so wonderful to share your father with me. I loved him too. But you are not alone any longer. You have a man who loves you and would move mountains for you, if you asked him to. Lean on him in your sorrow, Emily—Aiden is strong enough to bear the weight of it."

The expression on her friend's face warned Helen that Emily was going to change directions in order to convince her to stay. She had to forestall her friend. "We both know there is no set time to grieve."

Though the others had been gone for some time, Emily's father's shocking death had happened a little over a month and a half ago. The Bow Street Runners and the duke's men stationed in London were still in the process of locating another witness to what they now knew was *not* an accidental death.

"Society encourages us to dress in mourning for a year before we go into half-mourning," Helen said. "How can Society be so cruel as to expect us to wake up months after we've lost a loved one and tell ourselves, 'Today is the last day I will grieve'?"

Emily shook her head. "I know it seems easy for some, yet harder for others."

Helen had to agree. "I suppose you are right. It has been years now, but I'll never stop missing them."

"Neither will I." Emily tugged Helen toward the nursery. "It will be so difficult knowing that we are apart and grieving, when we could be together, reminiscing over a pot of tea, sharing our stories of what was so special about our parents."

Helen rubbed a hand over her heart. It actually ached. "I promise I will write to you."

"A very poor substitute," Emily rasped.

"Better than to lose contact altogether," Helen reminded her.

"I suppose."

"Ladies! I am so glad you are here." Gwendolyn stood in the doorway to the nursery with her babe in her arms. Two excited little voices, in what sounded like a foreign language no one else understood, babbled behind her.

Emily apologized, "Sorry to be late, Gwendolyn."

"It was all my fault," Helen said.

Patrick's wife smiled at them. "No matter. You're here now. Come in—the twins are ready for story time before we build castles with blocks."

Smiling at the notion, Helen and Emily stepped into the happy atmosphere that always managed to lighten their hearts and restore their faith in humanity.

Squeals of delight and more babbling had Helen wondering—was her decision to leave in order to find her happiness too hasty? What if her happiness *was* here, and she left and no one else offered for her hand? Who then would marry her?

A broad-shouldered, handsome-as-sin Irishman's voice sounded in her head. *"That would be me, lass."* But would it? Could she change her plans and stay on at Wyndmere Hall? If she left and came back, would Eamon O'Malley still marry her?

"I don't even know the man," she whispered to herself.

Gwendolyn's knowing expression was unsettling. "Which one of the duke's guard are we talking about? Rory Flaherty or Eamon O'Malley?"

Helen bit her lip to keep from blurting out Eamon's name. She could have saved herself from a fat lip, because a heartbeat later, Emily cheerfully answered, "Eamon."

Patrick's wife's eyes positively danced with mirth. "That one will run you ragged and badger you until you accept him. He *did* ask you to marry him, didn't he?"

"Not exactly," Emily and Helen said at the same time.

"Once an O'Malley makes up his mind to marry, nothing, and no man, will stop him or stand in his way. You'll have to tell me all about it over tea after we put these darlings down for their morning nap."

Helen had a feeling there was no escaping the conversation. Patrick's wife was known to be as stubborn as Emily. There was no getting around it. She sighed and scooped up Abigail, while Emily picked up Richard. "Let's read a story."

PATRICK O'MALLEY STOOD in the hallway digesting the snippet of conversation he'd overheard. So his cousin Eamon was finally ready to own up to what everyone else had noticed from the moment Garahan and the others arrived with the duke's ward. His younger O'Malley cousin had fallen arse over his blockhead in love with the lass. If anyone asked, he would have to admit that Helen was lovely, with curves almost on par with his wife's. But it was not her looks that had his cousin's attention. Eamon had no doubt noticed what Patrick had—Helen was loyal and fiercely protective of Emily.

Once Garahan had shared what occurred during their journey to Wyndmere Hall, Patrick was ready to welcome Emily to their extended family with open arms. At least he had, after sorting out the situation with Garahan. It was a bit complicated when Garahan confessed he'd given his heart to Emily, but had not been ready to fight for her because of his vow to the duke and position within the guard. What was it about his brothers and cousins that had them falling so hard and fast in love that they had difficulty accepting it wasn't just the physical attraction?

Mayhap it was time to give Eamon a push toward the dark-haired lass. He could start with the fact that Helen intended to leave Wyndmere Hall. That just might force his cousin to take action instead of being thickheaded, holding back his feelings for the lass.

There was a lull in the conversation. *Perfect time to interrupt.* He knocked on the partially open door and was bidden to enter.

Gwendolyn was in the rocking chair with their babe snugged up against her shoulder, rubbing her back. He was sorry to have missed the soothing sight of his wife nursing their babe. He thanked his good fortune, and his perseverance, in chasing after Gwendolyn when she thought she had to leave the duke and duchess's employ after falling in love with Patrick. A situation similar to Aiden and Emily's.

Patrick's gut told him that if Eamon let Helen go, he would regret it for the rest of his days. Not willing to let that happen, he walked over to his wife, bent, and pressed a kiss to her cheek and another to the wisp of hair on top of their daughter's head. Deidre promptly burped. The duke's twins jumped up from where they sat on the floor playing with blocks, giggled, and started clapping.

The joy on Helen's face as she joined in their cheers decided for him. He was going to interfere.

# CHAPTER FOUR

THE DUKE'S MEN filed into the library. Patrick—the duke's right-hand man—was the first to enter, followed by Garahan and Flaherty, with O'Malley bringing up the rear.

"Shut the door behind you, Eamon." As soon as he complied, the duke put his hands behind his back and paced to the window overlooking the gardens. O'Malley and the others waited, knowing the duke was gathering his thoughts before speaking. When he turned and walked toward them, his frown was fierce.

*Trouble,* O'Malley thought—he'd best bring up Burrows to the duke before His Grace launched into whatever reason he had for calling the meeting. "If I may have a moment, Yer Grace, I haven't had a chance to tell ye about the sharpshooter I winged today on me patrol to the village."

All heads turned toward him.

"Sharpshooter?" Patrick and the duke said simultaneously.

"Aye. Though he needs a bit more practice, if ye ask me."

"Tell us the particulars, O'Malley," the duke said. "I need to inform everyone about a missive I received."

O'Malley frowned. He shouldn't have interrupted the duke before the man had a chance to speak. "Forgive me, Yer Grace. It can wait."

"Not if it's a sharpshooter," Garahan grumbled. "The potential for the man not acting alone is too great."

"Aye," Flaherty agreed. "Best to tell us now."

Patrick nodded. "We can add to the guard if the situation warrants it."

"I was riding past that last bit of thick trees on the way into the village when the breeze died and a metallic click echoed in the stillness," O'Malley said.

"Did ye shoot first, or wait to return fire?" Flaherty asked.

"What do ye think?" O'Malley replied.

"Well then," Patrick interjected, "'tis a fine thing that ye heard it, fired first, and winged the man."

O'Malley wondered if he could get through the telling before his cousins interrupted and tried to recount the story for him. "Not one of ye were there, and His Grace has a missive to discuss with us."

The duke said, "Hold your comments, men. Finish it, O'Malley."

"The long and short of it is, after I coaxed him out of the tree, he recognized me as an O'Malley and said he was waiting for either Patrick or meself. Though he did not say why, he mentioned his uncle was down on his luck and was helped by one of the O'Malleys previously in London."

"We'll get to that later," the duke said. "Where is the man now?"

"Cooling his heels in the constable's gaol. Oh, and the constable agreed after hearing Burrows's tale that—"

"Who is Burrows?" Flaherty asked.

"The sharpshooter," O'Malley answered.

"What did the constable agree to?" the duke asked.

"That he'd send for the physician to take care of the wound where me lead ball grazed the young man."

The duke's expression was neutral. "Why was he waiting for you? Did he mention a connection with either Baron Hardwell or any of the other blackguards we have been dealing with lately?"

"He did not," O'Malley replied. "Only that his uncle had turned to other ways of putting food on the table when he'd fallen on hard times. O'Malley was the name his uncle spoke of."

"Why in the bloody hell would he be shootin' ye, then?" Patrick demanded.

"I shot *him*," O'Malley reminded his older cousin.

That had Patrick clamping his jaw shut.

"So ye dropped him off with the constable," Flaherty said.

"In the hopes that he would be questioned, and reveal the reason he was watching for ye," Garahan added.

Patrick picked up the thread of the conversation. "In a dense bit of forest along the road ye were patrolling. 'Tis best that he's safely tucked away, should any of Hardwell's lackeys show up thinking to finish the business with Garahan, his bride, or her maid."

A splitting pain shot across O'Malley's forehead at the thought of any of the women being at the mercy of that blackguard again. "'Tis a possibility."

"You'll need to check in with the constable," the duke told him.

"Ye can switch shifts with Flaherty," Patrick said. "Find out whatever the constable has learned. Burrows may know something vital." He looked to the duke, who inclined his head.

"Now then, on to other matters," the duke said. "I received a missive from Gavin King a short while ago. Apparently someone has finally come forward regarding the incident involving Lord Montrose." The duke paused and held Garahan's gaze for a moment. "Yes, it is the person Michaela identified as the one who not only witnessed Lord Montrose being pushed in front of that carriage, but who carried Montrose away from the scene. We must still use caution and never mention Michaela's account of what she witnessed that night. It would put her in danger and jeopardize her ability to continue her good works in London rescuing those who have no hope left."

The duke turned and told Patrick, "I am confident your brother Emmett is more than capable of protecting his new wife while continuing to head up my London guard. But Michaela may be in even more danger, if a connection is made between Emmett and the rumors surrounding the identity of the Angel of the Streets."

"Will King continue to monitor the situation and see that Michaela is protected?" O'Malley asked.

"King and Coventry are both committed to protecting her. However, I will send a missive to the both of them regarding Burrows, and the possibility that someone is out to kill one of the O'Malleys."

Garahan's anger was palpable. "We need to end this now! Me wife tries to hide her tears from me, but I've come upon Emily weeping at odd moments of the day."

Patrick placed a hand on Garahan's shoulder. "Be thankful she's grieving. Gwendolyn held the double loss of her first husband and unborn babe close to her heart for years. I've been coaxing her to trust me with a bit more of what happened since we married. I think the miracle that she was pregnant, and then shared worry with me that she would be unable to carry our babe Deidre to term, drew us closer together. I encouraged her to let me share her grief."

"There are nights when Persephone's nightmares take hold of her," the duke rasped. "And I know she's in the ballroom at our town house in London when that madman burst in and held my sister at knifepoint, claiming that I was dead. I stopped wishing I had been there, instead of following a false lead, and concentrated on encouraging her to tell me her dreams. Sharing her pain has helped."

O'Malley waited for Garahan to add his situation and how he was helping his wife handle her volatile emotions and grief, but his cousin remained silent. O'Malley had never asked, but sensed that Patrick and the duke knew the full story of what happened to Garahan's wife, and her maid. Not just the ambushes along the route to Wyndmere Hall, but the attack at the last inn they'd stayed at. He knew Garahan still blamed himself for not anticipating that the blackguard would somehow get the key to Emily and

Helen's bedchamber and lie in wait for them.

His cousin had not spoken openly about what happened, and O'Malley had been hesitant to push Garahan to tell him. But now that he'd accepted what his heart already knew—Helen Langley was the woman he had been waiting for—O'Malley needed to hear the whole of what happened during the attack. He planned to be the one to help Helen conquer her nightmares for the rest of their lives. He wanted to be the man she clung to in the night when fear overwhelmed her. Needed to be the one she held on to when the grief over the loss of her family at a young age was too much to bear. He could not do that if she avoided him.

Garahan clenched his jaw and gave a brief shake of his head. "'Tis like pulling teeth to get me wife to share the depth of her worries. I'm hoping this new information will ease at least one of her nightmares—that she would never seek justice for her father's murder."

Garahan acknowledged Patrick's direct gaze. "Did ye ever wonder if it was our destiny in life to use our God-given talent with our fists, and all manner of weapons, to protect the greater good?" Garahan paused and nodded to the duke. "The greater good being yerself and yer family, Yer Grace." Looking at Patrick again, Garahan added, "And once we found our purpose in life guarding His Grace, we'd meet the other half of our hearts?"

"Never in me wildest dreams," Patrick answered before turning toward the duke. "The pieces of what must have been God's plan fell neatly into place when ye asked if I had any suggestions for adding to the guard."

The duke slowly smiled. "I believe you mentioned you had three brothers working in and around London."

"Don't forget me eight cousins." Patrick frowned, then said, "Though it might have been Coventry that I mentioned me eight cousins to."

The tension in the room eased a notch at the recounting of how the duke's guard had been formed. O'Malley said, "Getting back to meeting yer future wives, I'm thinking that was part of

His plan too, as it happened in a heartbeat—to all of us." All eyes were glued to him as he continued, "Yer eyes meet, and ye recognize the lass, though ye've never met her before. The women who have captured our hearts are valiant, fearless, stubborn, irritating, and beautiful, with bruises on their hearts that only we can heal."

When O'Malley sensed that every man in the room was staring at him, he shrugged. "I'm not as stubborn as the lot of ye, who didn't see what was right in front of him, nor recognize that the woman was his destiny, until he'd nearly lost her." He grinned at Patrick and Garahan. "I'm not afraid to follow me heart."

"We still recognized what was happening before ye did," Flaherty told him. "And for the record, no woman has turned me head yet."

"Eamon is the last of the O'Malleys to fall," Patrick said. "'Twill either be yerself, Rory, or one of yer brothers, Dillon, Seamus, or Fenton, who'll be the first of the Flahertys to fall."

Flaherty grunted. "It won't be me."

O'Malley shook his head. "We'd best get back to the topic at hand. Pardon us for straying from the topic, Yer Grace."

"Indeed. Now, as I was saying," the duke continued, "apparently the witness feared for his family if he came forward."

"Why now?" Patrick asked. "What has changed? 'Tis been nigh on two months since Lord Montrose died."

"Murdered," Garahan corrected him.

"Aye," O'Malley agreed. "Was it a guilty conscience?"

Garahan swore beneath his breath. "Nay. I'm thinking it had to do with me wife's harebrained plan. God help me, I couldn't understand why Emily didn't realize if she did what she intended, she may end up paying to hear a pack of lies."

Patrick looked from Garahan to the duke and back. "Are ye sayin' that yer wife offered a reward for news of her father's death? How did she manage it without any of us knowin'?"

"Aye. She admitted she wasn't going to tell me at all, but she kept giving me worried looks when she thought I wasn't paying attention." Garahan shook his head. "I charmed the information out of her."

Flaherty snorted. "Ye mean ye wore her down until she confessed."

Garahan ignored his cousin. "She contacted King. We had talked of the possibility of doing so, but I thought she and I would speak of it further before she went ahead and sent a missive to Bow Street."

"Tell us everything," the duke said.

"Apparently Emily decided to offer coin from her dowry as a reward for any information regarding the night her father was run down by that fast-moving carriage."

The duke listened intently, then asked, "Is that all?"

Garahan's pained expression had O'Malley and the others guessing there was more. "Nay. She offered a large portion of her dowry if any witnesses to the incident contacted Gavin King directly."

"And she heard back from King?" Flaherty asked.

The duke's gaze never left Garahan's when he answered, "Aye, and he mentioned they had a witness, but that was all, Yer Grace."

"Ah, so the witness's guilty conscience for not coming forward got the better of him," O'Malley remarked.

"If not for the witness's wife falling ill from a fever, and lack of coin to pay the physician and the apothecary, he might never have come forward."

Patrick's frown was fierce. "Did his account of what happened match Michaela's?"

"Aye," the duke replied, "along with a detailed description of the person who rushed from the shadows into the lamplight to shove Montrose in front of that coach-and-four."

"Emily was right," Garahan rasped. "He was murdered, though he did not die until a few hours later."

"Has King found the culprit?" Flaherty asked.

"His men are combing the city," the duke told them. "He feels certain it is only a matter of time before they find the man."

"That could take months…years," O'Malley murmured.

"Aye, if not for one fact," Garahan said.

"What might that be?" the duke asked.

"Hardwell is in King's custody."

"'Tis been a few weeks since ye arrived," Patrick said. "Do ye think King has enough reason to detain the baron?"

Garahan exuded confidence. "Aye, that I do. One of the young men who worked for Lord Montrose had been hired by Hardwell to infiltrate the Montrose household."

"Where is he now?" the duke asked.

"He accompanied Tremayne, Bayfield, and Greeves to London early this morning."

"Ah, Stark—isn't that his name?" the duke asked.

"Aye. Though he accepted coin from Hardwell to spy on Montrose," Garahan said, "when push came to shove, the lad couldn't go through with any of the other plans Hardwell had for Montrose or his daughter. His conscience would not let him."

"What of Masterson?" O'Malley asked.

"As I understand it—though correct me if I am wrong, Garahan," the duke said, "Masterson accompanied King's man Jackson, and their prisoner, Hardwell, to London from the inn where he attacked Garahan's wife and maid."

Garahan's expression was dark and forbidding. "The inn, where he nearly had his way with me wife, if not for Helen's quick thinking."

O'Malley's heart clenched, then swelled. He was proud of Helen for standing up to the blackguard in a bid to protect Emily, but her actions could have had the opposite effect had she been overpowered by Hardwell. "Helen's a brave lass."

Flaherty rolled his eyes. "'Tisn't a reason to lose yer head over a female, boy-o."

"If not that, what then?"

Flaherty snickered. "If I have to be telling ye—"

Patrick interrupted, "Enough. Was there anything else in the missive, Yer Grace?"

The duke inclined his head. "Apparently the description King received from Michaela, and the witness, matches the man Hardwell insisted instigated the incident that resulted in Lord Montrose's untimely demise—though the baron did not mention a name."

"How do ye know we can trust the baron's word?" O'Malley asked.

Garahan grunted. "Ye cannot."

The duke replied, "I beg to differ. There is an instance in which I believe we can trust Baron Hardwell's word."

"What might that be, Yer Grace?" Patrick asked.

"Another of Hardwell's contacts has come forward, a former soldier by the name of Poston…with information that Hardwell paid another handsomely to make it look like an accident."

"I might have known coin was involved," Flaherty muttered.

"Some men are ruled by it," O'Malley added.

"Others would sell their soul for it," Garahan mumbled.

Patrick asked the duke, "Did King supply a name along with a description of the man identified?"

"He did—Wilson."

"Too bad Stark left with Tremayne and Bayfield," O'Malley murmured. "He may have met Wilson in the short time he was employed by Hardwell."

The duke walked over to his desk, sat, and penned a brief note. After sanding it, he sealed it with wax and handed it to Patrick. "Ask Humphries to have this delivered via special messenger."

"At once, Yer Grace. With yer permission, I think it's best to have Humphries alert the footmen on staff who double as guards to stand ready."

"Excellent suggestion," the duke replied. "See to it."

"Aye, Yer Grace." With a nod to the men, Patrick said, "Back to yer posts and be prepared to give additional instructions to the footmen who'll be manning yer shifts with ye."

O'Malley knew that Garahan would be filling his wife in on their discussion. Emily would not breathe a word of it, as Garahan would no doubt swear her to secrecy. But what about Helen? Would Emily tell her maid? O'Malley decided it would be up to him to confide in Helen so she would be aware of the possible danger headed their way. He had to speak to her alone. "I'll protect ye with me life," he murmured. But first he had to take Flaherty's patrol to the village and speak to the constable. There may be other facts he uncovered while Burrows was in custody.

O'Malley strode toward the stables. The sooner he went out on patrol, the sooner he could return and speak to the lass. *Time to get to it.*

# CHAPTER FIVE

HELEN SMILED OVER the rim of her cup at the conversation Emily and Gwendolyn were having about babes. Emily had mentioned hoping to have a family just the other day. No wonder, given the fact that she was newly married and head over heels in love with her husband.

Taking a sip, Helen wondered what it would be like to be so besotted with another that a person would stare off into space and forget what they were saying, only to blink and smile and blithely go about their business. Helen had never met anyone who had distracted her the way Aiden Garahan distracted Emily. During the time she had been with Emily, her mistress had not seemed interested in any of the gentlemen who had called upon her.

Lord Montrose had teased his daughter about being too selective, and Helen quietly agreed. After the sudden death of Emily's father, their lives were forever changed with the solicitor's reading of the will and the shocking news that her mistress was now a ward of the Duke of Wyndmere. Further shocking was the stipulation that, as the duke's ward, she would be under the protection of one of one of the duke's private guard—plus two others! Three men, none of whom Emily, nor Helen, had ever met!

Helen smiled listening to the talk of the volatile emotions that were part and parcel of the nine months spent carrying a babe in one's belly. When Emily's hand drifted to her abdomen, Helen's heart warmed. Emily would be a wonderful mother. The perilous journey to the Lake District had changed Emily, who no longer had a tendency to speak her mind without regard to how it impacted those around her. Helen was pleased with her friend's transformation. Emily was happy. Loved. Settled. In her heart, she knew that Emily would make a wonderful mother.

"What do you think, Helen?"

Gwendolyn's question caught her off guard. "I beg your pardon, I was woolgathering. What did you ask me?"

"I think we are boring poor Helen," Emily said. "All this talk of babes and swollen ankles and bellies."

"Not at all," Helen replied. "I was listening, but then thought of something."

"Don't you mean *someone*…with broad shoulders?" Gwendolyn asked.

"Over six feet tall, with grass-green eyes and blond hair," Emily teased.

Helen felt her face flush with embarrassment. She needed to steer clear of any discussion involving Eamon O'Malley. "I was recalling the upheaval Garahan, Bayfield, and Tremayne caused the day they arrived at Montrose House claiming to have been sent by His Grace."

It was Emily's turn to blush. "Aiden was high-handed and arrogant."

Gwendolyn laughed softly. "Sounds like every man in the duke's guard. What happened?"

"Once he explained the situation, I still was not convinced there was a need for protection, although I had to admit I had paid attention during the reading of my father's will."

"Tell her about the callers," Helen said.

"It was so odd," Emily mused. "They arrived in droves, and were exceedingly ill-mannered, trying to force poor Wilcox to allow them entrance."

"Wilcox?" Gwendolyn asked.

"Our butler. I had no choice but to change my mind and accept their protection."

Helen missed the kindly butler, the cook, and the housekeeper too. They had always treated her—and the others Lord Montrose opened his home to—well. Saved them from starving with the offer of a home and employment. "And that's when everything seemed to happen at once," she added.

"Must we go over these events again?"

"You asked what I was thinking about, Emily."

Gwendolyn had a mischievous glint in her eyes. "Was that *all* you were thinking about?"

Helen did not want to encourage Patrick's wife, but knew she could not hold out against the woman's patience, so she gave in. "I was thinking what a wonderful mother you will be someday, Emily."

Tears welled in her friend's eyes and spilled over. Without missing a beat, Gwendolyn rose from her seat and pressed a large handkerchief into Emily's hands. "Do you always carry a man's handkerchief?" she asked.

Gwendolyn answered, "Yes, I do, on the sage advice of my husband. I was prone to tears while carrying Deidre, and was always trying to mop them with one of my much smaller, lace-edged handkerchiefs, to no avail."

"I think I may borrow one of Aiden's."

"Just a word of warning—if he has not already done so, your husband may start making a point of asking you how you are feeling, if you're getting enough rest, and whether or not you are putting your feet up," Gwendolyn predicted.

"Whyever would he do that?"

Helen lifted her teacup and sipped her lukewarm beverage, waiting for Gwendolyn to answer.

"I would venture to guess that his older and wiser cousin—my husband—would have warned him to watch for certain signs."

"Signs?" Now Emily sounded totally confused.

"Shall I tell her?" Helen asked.

"Tell me what?" Emily demanded. "And how would you have any idea what a husband would say to his wife?"

Helen did not want Emily fretting. "I listen, and observe those around me."

"When have you ever been around a newly married couple?"

"Never," Helen replied. "But I noticed the times my father paid very close attention to my mum before it became obvious she was increasing."

Emily blew out a breath tinged with frustration. Helen was actually happy to see it—she wanted her friend to be happy, while at the same time retaining her confidence and a bit of her independent attitude. "Forgive me, Helen. I don't mean to be so sharp with you."

Before Helen could reassure Emily that she understood, Gwendolyn said, "Emotional upheaval and an uneasy stomach when you wake will be something else your husband will be watching for."

Emily's face drained of color, and Helen jumped to her feet at the same time as Gwendolyn. Between them, they were able to keep Emily from falling forward and smacking her head on the table as she fainted.

"Easy now, Emily," Gwendolyn crooned. Turning to Helen, she said, "Help me settle her on the settee." Frowning, she added, "I should not have been so blunt. At times I forget not everyone is acquainted with the vagaries, and changes, a woman endures while expecting."

Helen helped shift Emily's legs up onto the seat. Patting the inside of Emily's wrist, she wished she had thought to remind Emily to bring her reticule—if not that, then simply the vial of hartshorn. Her mistress had been more prone to lightheadedness since her father's death.

"I'll be right back. I'm going to fetch Emily's hartshorn."

"She's coming around," Gwendolyn said. "Don't sit up," she

told Emily. "Lie still for a few minutes."

"I was about to fetch your vial," Helen said.

Emily blinked and sighed. "I'm sorry. I don't know what came over me."

Gwendolyn's light laughter felt like a hug. "You have been married for how long now, Emily?"

"A fortnight, but what does that have to do with—" Emily clamped her mouth shut and closed her eyes. "This is all Aiden's fault."

Helen put a hand over her mouth to keep her laughter inside.

Gwendolyn didn't bother to hide hers. "In his defense, I am not certain that he could help that his dark eyes and devastating smile have kept you awake when you could have been sleeping."

Emily's mouth gaped open. For a moment she sat frozen...and then she laughed. "I refuse to let you bait me into responding."

Gwendolyn just smiled. "You don't have to. The smug, satisfied look on your face speaks volumes."

While Helen had not been married, she was well aware of what happened in the marriage bed, having been invited to listen when the Montrose's housekeeper and cook warned Emily what to expect during her first Season. Gentlemen did not always act as such when spirits were involved... Some were wolves dressed in Weston's finest frockcoats and waistcoats.

Their frank discussion had eased Emily's—and Helen's fears when they hinted at having been happily married and enjoying the special attentions of their late husbands. Helen noted that some women seemed to welcome their husbands' attention, while others seemed to regard it as their duty. From snippets of conversations she'd overheard since arriving at Wyndmere Hall— and the looks Aiden and Emily, and Patrick and Gwendolyn, shared—both couples were happily married and enjoyed their time alone together. Thinking of the happily married couples, she could not forget the way the duke fawned over his duchess. He would visit the nursery at various times of the day to hug his children and spend time with his wife. Though quite busy, the duke always made the time to be with his family. Those times, Gwendolyn quietly ushered Emily and Helen from the room to give them privacy.

With shining examples of marital bliss, was it any wonder that Eamon O'Malley's handsome faced popped into Helen's head? One thing led to another, and she wondered what it would feel like to be held in his arms.

"Helen, would you mind retrieving my reticule?"

She heard muffled voices, but her mind was elsewhere, while she imagined herself pressed against Eamon's broad chest, his strong arms wrapped around her as he brushed his lips to hers. Her heart began to pound as a question slipped into her mind: would he boldly mold his mouth to hers and—

"Helen!"

Startled from her reverie, she blinked. "Yes? What is it?"

"Emily asked if you would please fetch her reticule." Gwendolyn studied her intently, and Helen wondered if Patrick's wife had somehow guessed the direction of her thoughts.

"Right away." She hurried to the door and dashed down the hallway to the bedchamber Emily had been using before she and Aiden wed. It was easier to have a few things close at hand in case Emily needed to stay the night. "Do not think about that man," she chided herself. "O'Malley is lethal to your concentration!"

After retrieving the reticule, she rushed back to the nursery, out of breath and out of sorts. Intent on her mission, she did not notice her path was blocked until she ran into an all-too-familiar wall of muscle.

Strong arms caught her. "Whoa there, lass, where are ye headed in such a hurry?"

Tilting her head to meet Eamon's gaze, she couldn't seem to form the words. His eyes distracted her while he held her captive. The hand he slid around her waist to steady her seared through her gown, branding her. Did the man have any idea what he did to her?

"I… er…" Lecturing herself silently, she finally held up the reticule and nodded toward the doorway at the other end of the hall. "Emily's waiting for this."

"Take a moment to catch yer breath." Studying her closely, he added, "Ye seem winded." His tone changed from concerned to scolding. "Ye should have a care running in the house. There are others who are moving about His Grace's home that might not be expecting a whirlwind such as yerself plowing into them."

She felt her face flame, but ignored it. "Emily fainted. I need to get her hartshorn to her right away."

O'Malley shifted her against his side, looped her arm through his, and strode toward the nursery. "Why did ye not say so? I'll speak with her at once. Garahan will need to know if she's not feeling well. Depending on what Emily tells me, we may need to summon the physician."

When she stumbled, O'Malley lifted her off her feet, still plastered to his side. A moment later, he set her on her feet beside him and knocked on the nursery door. It opened immediately.

"Helen, what kept—Eamon!" Gwendolyn's expression was guarded. "I did not know you had returned from your patrol. Does Patrick know you are back?"

O'Malley tugged on Helen's hand, urging her forward. Instead of answering the question, he said, "Tell me what happened to Emily, then I'll ask her a few questions. Garahan'll expect an accounting from me before the physician arrives."

Helen was mesmerized by the command in his tone. It reminded her of Aiden when he took charge in London and on their journey north to the duke's estate.

O'Malley glanced over his shoulder at her and let go of her hand. "Have a seat next to Emily, lass. She'll be needing that hartshorn and the comfort yer presence gives her." He then asked Gwendolyn for a glass of water.

After a whiff from her vial and some water, the color returned to Emily's face.

"There now," O'Malley said, studying her closely and approving. "Ye'll do. Helen, I need to be asking Emily a few personal questions—would ye mind stepping into the hallway for a moment?"

"What about Gwendolyn?" Helen asked.

"Gwendolyn is married, and she'll understand what I'll be asking."

Emily placed her hand on Helen's arm. "If she doesn't mind, Eamon, I'd like her to stay."

"Of course, I would be happy to stay."

O'Malley hesitated. "Don't be blaming me if yer tender sensibilities are injured."

She was taken aback for a moment. Were all men as high-handed as those in the duke's guard? Lifting her chin, she met the uncalled-for censure in his gaze. "I won't."

O'Malley raked a hand through his hair, as if agitated. But was it because of the questions he said he needed to ask Emily, or Helen's staying in the room? Did her presence unnerve him as much as his did her? Not that she feared the man. Nay, his nearness had her wondering about things no virtuous woman should think about!

Burying her thoughts deep, she repeated, "I won't."

Given his expression, O'Malley did not believe her. "I'll be telling Garahan ye fainted, Emily. Now then, 'tis a delicate question, and I'm trying to think of the proper way to ask ye without Aiden threatening to knock me teeth down me throat."

Gwendolyn came to O'Malley's rescue. "Emily and I were discussing the possible reasons for her faint while we waited for Helen to return with the vial."

The frown lines between his brows smoothed. "I see. Yer eyes are clear and ye don't seem to be suffering from megrims—"

"My head isn't paining me," Emily replied.

"When was the last time ye ate?"

Emily's belly gurgled, and she placed her hand on it. The faraway look in her eyes and gentle way she kept her hand on her abdomen, as if protecting what lay sleeping beneath it, gave

O'Malley pause. He clenched his jaw and seemed to be bracing himself to ask a question, then changed his mind about it. "Do ye think there's a chance ye could be carrying Aiden's babe?"

Helen could tell from the uncomfortable expression that flitted across his face that he may have considered asking Emily about her monthly courses. She was greatly relieved that he had not. It was not a topic men discussed with women. By skipping that question, which would no doubt have been cause for Garahan to pummel his cousin, O'Malley had kept his teeth intact.

Emily's cheeks pinkened. She glanced at Helen before responding, "Er…yes, actually. A very good chance."

O'Malley cleared his throat. "Well then, I do not think there's any reason to summon the physician. Although Garahan may have a different opinion after I tell him there's no cause for concern, other than ye fainted."

"Thank you, Eamon," Emily rasped. "I suppose there's no chance you could hold off telling him?"

O'Malley snorted. "Not a one. I'd best see to it now, as I have to speak to the duke." He bade the women goodbye, but paused on the threshold. "Ye'd best lie down, Emily, until Garahan sees for himself that ye aren't at death's door. And Helen, I'd like to speak with ye after I meet with His Grace."

"I will be in the nursery reading to the twins."

His eyes held hers for a long moment before he added. "'Tis important, lass."

"So is the time I spend with Richard and Abigail. They love to be read to, and with Her Grace feeling poorly these last few days…" Her voice trailed off as worry speared through her heart. Though she did not ask, for the sake of the duchess, Merry and Constance had taken her and Emily aside to confide that the duchess's health was precarious after her miscarrying of a babe during the winter. She was building her strength back and had seemed to be doing well until a fortnight ago. They recognized the signs of pregnancy, but were worried, as it was only five months since Her Grace's miscarriage.

"Whatever it is ye're worried about, lass, we can speak of it after I meet with the duke."

"As you are familiar with most manners of healing, I would appreciate it."

He stared at her, started to speak, then changed his mind. "Until later." He bowed, stepped out of the room, and quietly closed the door behind him.

When Helen turned around, she noticed Emily's hand to her belly and an expression of wonder in her eyes. "Gwendolyn, is it possible for it to happen so soon?"

"Before I answer, I need to ask the question I believe O'Malley was about to but changed his mind. It is personal but important."

Emily waited. "What do you need to know?"

"When was the last time you had your monthly?"

Emily was silent for a few moments before she slowly smiled. "A few weeks before Aiden and I married."

"And you haven't had it since then?"

"No, though I should have last week."

Gwendolyn smiled too. "Then it is definitely possible. From your tremulous smile, I can see that the possibility is welcome. Do not fret if it doesn't turn out to be the case. Trust in the Lord's plans for you and Aiden. You'll know for certain soon enough. Rest now. I need to check with the duchess's maid and see if the babes are still sleeping."

"I'll go," Helen offered.

"Stay with Emily," Gwendolyn said. "You're a comfort to her. She'll appreciate it when Garahan comes stomping up the stairs demanding to know why she isn't in bed resting."

"He wouldn't do that, would he?" Helen asked.

Gwendolyn laughed. "If he's anything like Patrick, he will. Close your eyes and rest now."

Emily was still smiling a short while later when heavy foot-steps echoed from the servants' staircase.

Gwendolyn appeared in the doorway to the sitting room adjacent to the nursery. "Brace yourself."

The three women were facing the door when Garahan approached, hesitated, then asked, "May I come in?"

"Of course—Emily is waiting to speak with you. Helen and I are needed in the nursery."

Without another word, Gwendolyn linked her arm with Helen's, tugged her from the room, and closed the door behind them.

## CHAPTER SIX

"Eamon." The duke nodded as O'Malley stood in the doorway. "Where are the others?"

"On their way, Yer Grace."

"Excellent. Before they arrive, I must ask, did your meeting with the constable and Burrows in any way involve Her Grace?"

O'Malley curled his hands into tight fists until they ached, thinking of the duchess, Garahan's wife, and Helen, all of whom could be affected by what he'd learned. He slowly relaxed his hands at his sides. "Indirectly."

"I see. Is this tied to the sharpshooter's connection to the O'Malleys?"

"Aye, 'tis possible, but then again, it could be a carefully orchestrated rumor as a distraction."

"Distraction?"

"Aye, to keep Bow Street from discovering the whereabouts of the man who pushed Lord Montrose."

The duke's expression turned grim. "Then my wife is in as much danger as Emily and Helen."

"Aye."

The duke walked over to his desk, picked up one of the ledgers from a stack, leafed through it, then set it back down precisely where it had been. The movement struck O'Malley, because the duke was not normally restive. He was cautious and controlled.

Obviously something worried him.

O'Malley was about to speak when the duke asked, "How did you find my wife when you spoke with her earlier today?"

"Her Grace's spirits are up, though she seems exhausted." O'Malley relaxed at the change in topic, studying the duke, noting his hand shook when he picked up the same ledger a second time. The duke was worried about his wife. O'Malley needed to assure the duke, "It is normal in the first few months of pregnancy to feel drained. I know the physician and midwife have been to speak with Her Grace. Have they hinted that anything is amiss?"

"Nay, quite the opposite. I trust them implicitly, but I trust and weigh your observations more, as you see my wife on a daily basis."

"Other than what I've already told you, I have not noticed anything. In case you are wondering, I have delivered a foal—and a few calves—in my time, Yer Grace. Never a babe. So don't be doing yerself and Her Grace a serious injustice by not putting yer faith in the doctor and the midwife." O'Malley paused for a beat. "I have wondered, is there a chance that she may be carrying a worry or two?"

The duke's shoulders slumped for a moment, allowing O'Malley to see the full weight of the responsibility the man carried: the tenant farmers, villagers, the staff at his London town house and estates, the wives and children of the married men of his guard, Her Grace and their twins, and his family. "Persephone was despondent after what happened a few months ago."

It was no secret among the men in the duke's guard. They had been informed that the duchess had lost the babe she carried early in her pregnancy. The men needed to know, as did certain members of the staff, so no one mentioned the babe, causing the duchess further distress. "I've known a family or two who have dealt with the emotional and physical pain caused by a miscarriage, Yer Grace. Me own ma for one. Encourage Her Grace to share her grief with ye—it may be that she hides it from ye because she feels she is somehow responsible."

"I've told her many times it was not her fault." The duke appeared lost in thought. "We grieved together."

O'Malley knew from personal experience that grief could seem to fade, but then weeks or months could go by, and it would sneak back and tear your heart out all over again. "For how long, if ye don't mind me asking?"

The duke stared at him, then raked both hands through his hair. "A fortnight. I wondered why it had not been longer, but after two weeks, she no longer spoke of what happened. I thought it rather a short time, but did not want to ask her and run the risk it would have her hiding in our bedchamber with the drapes closed again."

"She could be hiding her grief from ye, Yer Grace."

"Why in the bloody hell would she do that?"

O'Malley's heart went out to the man. The duke always strove to have a handle on any and all situations that could crop up on any given day. He needed to learn to trust his estate managers with more of the running of his estates, so that he could spend more time with his growing family. Especially now.

O'Malley answered truthfully, "Because she loves ye, Yer Grace, and wouldn't want ye worrying."

"I cannot believe she'd keep something like this from me. I thought we had come to an understanding after I returned from London—and that fiasco caused by not confiding in one another—a few months ago, before we realized she was expecting."

"'Tis plain to every one of us in yer guard that Her Grace loves ye and would do anything for ye...including protect ye."

The duke narrowed his eyes. "She promised she would not hold back her worries from me."

An ebony-haired lass filled O'Malley's mind and his heart. What was Helen holding back from him? Garahan had told of her strength, and her conviction, trying to protect Emily when the women had been attacked.

O'Malley realized what the duke needed to hear. The truth. "Her Grace would do anything to protect yerself and yer babes."

Blue fire flashed in the duke's eyes. "That is *my* job, not hers."

Further discussion on the topic ended when the rest of his men filed in behind the head of the guard, Patrick O'Malley.

"Sorry to be late, Yer Grace." Patrick hesitated in the doorway for a moment, then entered the room. "What is this I'm hearin' about Her Grace protectin' ye?"

"Do you believe that Persephone would do anything to protect our children?"

"Aye," Garahan replied.

"In a heartbeat," Flaherty answered.

"And yerself as well, Yer Grace," O'Malley said.

Patrick continued, "Ye knew when ye married Her Grace that she was strong-willed."

"Indeed."

Garahan added, "Strong-minded."

The duke snorted.

Flaherty was not to be left out. "Brave."

His Grace smiled.

Patrick nodded. "Aye, with a heart of pure gold. She would not hesitate to stand beside ye to defend yer babes, yerself, and yer home, Yer Grace."

The bluster went out of the duke. "Her heart holds so much love, yet it always seems to expand to hold more. Why doesn't she see that it is my job to protect her?"

The pained expression on Patrick's face smoothed into a neutral one. "I nearly lost Gwendolyn to me pride."

O'Malley waited for the duke to say something…anything. Finally the man rasped, "Why couldn't I have fallen in love with a biddable woman?"

The men snorted, while Patrick snickered. "Instead of one wearing a bilious-colored gown and borrowed spectacles?"

"'Twas obvious she was meant for ye by the way she fell backward into yer arms," O'Malley said with a nod.

The duke smiled. "At the time, I had no idea it was part of her bluestocking disguise, and that she could not see through the lenses, or I never would have touched the tip of my finger to her spectacles to straighten them."

O'Malley had heard the story many times over. "Was that when ye knew?"

"Aye. I tried to ignore the voice inside my head when our eyes met, but couldn't." As if the duke knew what O'Malley wanted to ask, he added, "Don't ignore that voice."

"I won't, Yer Grace." O'Malley cleared his throat and changed the subject. "Now that everyone is present and accounted for, I'll be telling ye 'twas an interesting meeting with the constable and Burrows."

"Every one of you have spent time guarding my London town house, which is where I assume this Burrows's uncle met one of the O'Malleys. Does the name sound familiar?"

Patrick answered, "Nay. Depending on when the uncle met one of us, it could easily have been Sean, Michael, or Emmett."

Garahan's expression suggested he may have an idea, but the duke motioned for him to wait, while O'Malley continued with his report.

"Apparently whichever O'Malley it was left a lasting impression on Burrows's uncle, as the man was tossed behind bars for having been involved in breaking into Madame Beaudoine's shop—but before he was sent to the gaol, O'Malley offered to look after the man's wife and family until he was released."

Garahan grunted. "It had to be Sean. He was there after the break-in, and rescued Mignonette, one of Madame Beaudoine's seamstresses who had been staying at the shop."

"Wasn't she instrumental in saving Sean's arm?" Flaherty asked. "Before she married our cousin?"

Garahan grimaced. "Aye, along with Emmett O'Malley, and Lieutenant Sampson." He paled. "Emmett was the one who heard the commotion and found him outside... From the description, 'twasn't an exaggeration—his arm *was* flayed to the bone."

"Now that we've solved the mystery of which O'Malley," the

duke said, "why would Sean's helping the man's family have Burrows taking aim at *you?*"

O'Malley sensed the duke's patience was nearing its end. "He wasn't taking aim at me, he was protecting me. 'Twas meself who fired before giving whoever it was a chance to explain himself."

Garahan and Flaherty found O'Malley's suggestion humorous—which irritated him. "I had other concerns on me mind, and did not think beyond the fact that it was happening again and that I had to stop the sharpshooter."

While Flaherty snorted with laughter, Garahan said, "Ye should have pressed the man with his rifle aimed at ye…while ye were on patrol."

The duke asked, "What else did you find out from Burrows?"

"Apparently, rumor is rife through the bowels of London that someone has put a price on O'Malley's head—which we have just decided is Sean," O'Malley said.

The duke cleared his throat, and the men fell silent. "Do you have any other information about *who* is behind this threat, which you have already said could be a distraction?"

O'Malley glanced at Garahan before answering, "There's scuttlebutt that it's tied to the death of Lord Montrose. Which is why I have the feeling it is a distraction."

"Bloody *fecking* hell!" Garahan spun on his heel and made for the door.

Patrick blocked his way. "Ye gave yer word, Aiden."

"This involves me wife! How would ye feel if it were Gwendolyn?"

"The same way I would feel if it were Persephone," the duke calmly stated. "Go soak your head, Garahan. Flaherty, go with him to make sure he doesn't do anything rash."

"I'll make the man spill his guts," Garahan vowed. "'Tis me wife that's in danger."

"And Helen." O'Malley could not get past the worry that Helen would be in the middle *again.*

"Persephone and Gwendolyn could be in the cross-hairs of whoever is heading our way to exact revenge, too."

"We'll protect them all by doing what we've done in the past," Patrick said. "Draw back, keep a close eye on the women, and add to our number."

The duke nodded to O'Malley. "Eamon, tell Humphries that I'm preparing an urgent missive to be delivered to Bow Street."

"Aye, Yer Grace."

"You'll need to speak to Gwendolyn," the duke told Patrick, before turning to Garahan. "You will speak to Emily. Your wives will stay here at the hall until the danger is over—not in your cottages. That is an order and not open for discussion."

"I'll tell Humphries about that, too," O'Malley said. "Between yer butler, cook, and housekeeper, we'll stand prepared to meet the foe as we have done before." He was confident they would handle whatever was coming their way. "Yer Grace, the feeling in me gut is getting stronger—this distraction is planned."

"A salient point, O'Malley. We will not disregard any and all possibilities. Our wives and families, staff, and tenants depend upon us."

"Aye, Yer Grace." O'Malley dug deep to bury his concern. He would see to Helen's safety personally because he'd already decided she would be his wife. She just had to become accustomed to the idea.

Not for the first time, he wished that they had insisted the lad Stark had stayed on a bit longer at Wyndmere Hall. He may have been able to identify any strangers in the village as those working for Hardwell. But wishes didn't answer questions or point out those working for blood coin—money that paid for the elimination of another. The uneasy feeling that the newest threat was connected to the murder of Lord Montrose was not one he could ignore.

*Bugger it!* He'd forgotten to ask Garahan for the details of the attack on the women at the inn, and if there was any other information about Hardwell that may help lead them to the source of this latest threat. The niggling thought that therein would lie the reason Helen wanted to leave Wyndmere Hall, where she was safe within his sight, roiled in his gut.

Was she somehow involved in this? As soon as the thought occurred, he dismissed it. He'd taken the measure of the lass, and added it to what he'd learned by observing her in the short time she'd been at Wyndmere Hall. She would never be involved in anything that would harm another. Though why she was so determined to leave was something he planned to find out.

He needed Helen Langley to be safe. He also needed her in his arms and in his bed. But he wanted more than a quick tumble—he wanted forever, and her vow to cleave unto him and him alone.

O'Malley slowly smiled. All he had to do was convince the lass that she couldn't bear to part from him. And he knew just how to begin convincing her, but it would have to wait until the next shift change. He knew just where to find her, too. First, he needed to catch up to Garahan.

He found him a few minutes later, about to follow Flaherty out the rear entrance. "Garahan, I need a word."

"I've a horse trough with me name on it. Can it wait?"

Flaherty stood on the other side of the door. "I'll make sure there's plenty of water in it. Ye have five minutes before I come and haul yer *arse* out to the stables."

"I'll be there," Garahan told him. "And we can go a few rounds." Garahan turned back to O'Malley. "What's wrong?"

"I need to know what happened."

"Ye need to be more specific. A *shite*-ton has happened I since fulfilled me duty, escorting Emily to her guardian."

O'Malley felt his hands curling into fists and relaxed them, reining in his anger at the same time. "At the inn where the attack happened. Helen and Emily arrived with identical deep bruises on their cheeks. They were struck by the same person. Was it Hardwell?"

Garahan scrubbed a hand over his face. "Aye."

"What else happened?" When his cousin hesitated, O'Malley groaned. "Can ye not understand that I cannot fix what I do not know?"

"Aye, but can *ye* not understand how difficult it is for me to speak of it?"

O'Malley placed a hand to Garahan's shoulder, gave it a squeeze, and let go. "I do. I know ye interrupted Hardwell's plans. Can ye tell me where he was, and where Emily and Helen were, when ye and Masterson kicked in the door?"

"The first thing I saw was Hardwell straddling Emily on the bed. The bloody blackguard backhanded Helen—the brave lass was clinging to him, trying to get him off Emily."

"Emily wasn't—" Half the question slipped out before O'Malley could stop himself. "I'll be planning me form of retribution when I get me hands on Hardwell, not because I would think less of yer Emily if the worst had happened to her."

Garahan's eyes darkened, and O'Malley knew his cousin had his own plans in mind when he finally got Hardwell alone. "We may not have the opportunity to do what we're planning for some time, as he's behind bars." He shook his head. "We got there in time, and they had been threatened, battered, and bruised, but we stopped the buggering baron before he could violate either Emily or Helen."

The knowledge lowered O'Malley's lethal anger to a manageable level. "If I know ye, ye got a few blows in before someone stopped ye."

"Aye. You should know Helen was the one to tell me what happened. She said the baron sprang out from behind the door, bashing Brewster—one of the Montrose footmen assigned to help protect the women—on the head when he opened it."

"He's young yet, and will have learned from the experience to be ready for anything," O'Malley replied. "Did the lass say anything else?" What she'd told Garahan was enough to give her nightmares.

"Helen told us that Hardwell grabbed Emily, tossed her on

the bed, and threatened to do unspeakable things to her. We didn't ask her to go into detail."

O'Malley's heart began to hammer. "Anything else?"

"Aye. Helen said the bastard told Emily no one would care—or have her—when he got through with her. 'Twas then that Emily finally spoke up. She told me he planned to ruin her for her inheritance, and would force her to marry him."

O'Malley's gut iced over like the pond behind their barn back home. "Whenever ye're ready to ask His Grace to grant ye leave to take a few days off, I'll do the same. We can be in London in fifteen or so hours, less if we push it."

"Fifteen?"

"Aye—are ye forgetting the record set in Scotland a number of years back?"

Garahan frowned. "I am. How far was it again, and how many changes of horse?"

"One hundred and five miles and eight changes of horse in seven hours. I've estimated twice that time, as London is double the miles, plus a bit more."

Garahan grabbed hold of O'Malley's arm. "I'll be wanting the pleasure of gutting the man, though I will wait until ye get in a few blows first."

A sense of rightness settled over O'Malley. "I'll hold yer coat, so ye won't get his tainted blood on it."

Garahan let go of him and grinned. "Ah, what a ride that would be, what a satisfying revenge. But…"

O'Malley understood without asking what the "but" was. "His Grace would be displeased with us."

Garahan snorted with laughter. "That he would, but I'm thinking he's kept track of the number of times we've been shot, clubbed on the head, and stabbed, and it could count in our favor."

O'Malley sighed. "Aye, but that would not balance the scales, as I'm thinking a man doesn't recover from being gutted."

"'Twas an ingenious suggestion, and a good plan. Too bad we

cannot act upon it."

"Thank ye for confiding in me, Aiden. I know it pained ye to speak of it."

"I should have told ye before now, as it's Helen that yer heart has decided on. 'Tis clear the lass's heart calls to yers as well."

"She's stubborn," O'Malley admitted.

"The best ones always are."

The men parted to see to their assigned tasks. O'Malley hoped he could convince the lass that he would never hurt her or treat her as she had been treated by that bleeding bugger Hardwell. His mind made up, he decided he'd start paving the way to convince her to trust him and accept his offer of marriage.

# CHAPTER SEVEN

HELEN WISHED SHE did not feel such a kinship with the women working for the Duchess of Wyndmere, whom she had the utmost respect for. Her Grace had treated Helen as if she mattered from the moment she and Emily stepped down from the carriage at Wyndmere Hall. Though she had planned to leave the duke's estate as soon as Emily married Garahan, the duchess had convinced her to stay on and continue to work in the nursery.

Between the duke and duchess's eighteen-month-old twins, and Patrick and Gwendolyn's new babe, there was plenty to keep the four women busy. Gwendolyn, Emily, the duchess's maid Francis—who had been sharing nursery duties before being elevated to personal maid to the duchess—and Helen shared the duties. As the duke's guard rotated positions, so did the women, ensuring the pregnant duchess, and the two married women, got plenty of rest. Francis and Helen shared most of the overnight duties, as they were single, not married and expecting.

Helen had to speak with Emily again and explain her desire to seek other employment. It would free the woman from the need to watch over her, which she had done since Lord Montrose brought her home—though he had never told Emily how he met Helen. Emily had promised her father that she would always look after those he brought home to join his staff. She had kept her word.

With the help and guidance of Montrose's butler, housekeeper, and cook, they had formed a ragtag family. Every last one of those Lord Montrose had saved from starvation—or worse, Newgate Prison—were loyal to him. After his death, they turned to his lordship's staff for direction.

Helen knew that Emily would always look out for them...even though she had no plans to live there permanently. But Emily should no longer *have* to look after her. They weren't children anymore. They were both of age—well, Emily was a few years older than Helen, who would be nineteen in a few months. Most young women of the *ton* were either engaged to be married or married at that age.

*You're not a member of the* ton, *remember?*

She sighed deeply. It was beyond time to cut the cord, and childhood vows, binding them. Now that her friend was pregnant, Helen had to free her from the obligation so that Emily could lavish her attention on Garahan, and their babe when it arrived. Helen was confident that between Garahan and the rest of the duke's guard stationed at Wyndmere Hall, Emily would be well protected and live the fulfilling life she deserved.

"A letter just arrived for you, Miss Helen."

Helen paused in her task of helping Constance set out the accoutrements for the duchess's midmorning tea. "Thank you, Humphries." She hoped it was news from Mrs. Minnover—she had recently written to the Montrose's housekeeper. Turning the letter over, she paused to stare at the neat handwriting, noting it had not originated from Montrose House in London, but Flemington Gatehouse in the Borderlands.

"Good news from Montrose House?" Constance inquired.

Helen glanced up at the kind face of the duke's cook. "Er...no."

Constance brushed her hands on her apron and placed a comforting hand on Helen's shoulder. "If there is anything I can do, please let me know."

"Thank you, I will. Do you mind if I take a moment to read my letter?"

"Not at all. We have a bit of time before we need to fill the teapot and add the sweets to the tea tray." The cook made a shooing motion toward the hallway. "Why don't you use the room by the pantry? It's quiet right now, and you can have the privacy you need."

"Thank you, Constance." Helen hurried toward the room by the servants' staircase at the end of the hall. She closed the door, sat in the chair by the cot, and broke the wax seal.

Hands trembling, she read the note twice before blowing out the breath she'd held.

She pressed the note to her breast and breathed a sigh of relief. "This is what I want. Emily can devote all of her time and attention to Garahan and the babe she carries."

She read the note for a third time.

*Dear Miss Langley,*

*Your qualifications meet my requirements. I have rigid standards that my elevated station in life requires in a companion. Present yourself at Flemington Gatehouse in a sennight for a personal interview.*

*Dowager Duchess Flemington*

Folding the note, she slipped it into the pocket of her apron, rose to her feet, and opened the door. Head down, mind in a whirl, she was walking one minute, and on her backside the next.

"Miss Helen!"

She blinked and looked up at a footman she did not recognize, but must have bumped into. "I beg your pardon. I was preoccupied, not looking where I was walking."

"Forgive me." The young man held out a hand and helped her to her feet.

She bit her lip to keep from grimacing. It would not do at all for the footman to ask if she'd suffered an injury…given what part of her anatomy hit the floor. Ignoring the twinges of discomfort, she thanked him and stiffly walked away.

Constance was filling the teapot when Helen stepped into the kitchen. The cook's smile faltered. "Unexpected news?" When Helen did not answer right away, Constance asked, "Anything we need to advise Emily?"

"Er… No. Not unexpected, nor anything to bother Emily with. Simply a response to a letter I sent."

The cook did not try to wheedle more from Helen, for which she was grateful. Mrs. Minnover would have dragged Lord Montrose's cook into the mix. Between the two of them, they would try to extract every last detail of Helen's letter.

The tightness between her shoulder blades eased when the questions did not begin, but she winced as a twinge of pain shot from her backside to her waist, then breathed a sigh of relief that the cook had her back to her and did not notice.

"What's this I hear about ye falling on yer bottom?"

Helen spun around so quickly that she hit her backside on the edge of the table. Biting her lip to keep from moaning, she glanced up at the last man she would never admit her clumsiness to.

O'Malley stood in the doorway. "Did yer fall affect yer ability to hear?"

Constance smothered her laughter, and Helen watched as the cook turned to grab another plate of sweets. She wished she could ignore the Irishman, but he closed the distance between them and was just too…well, too *everything*! Broad of shoulder. Irritating. Handsome.

He raked a hand through his hair. "Are ye in pain, lass?" Her eyes met his, but before she could answer, he grunted and swept her off her feet and into his arms. "Not a bloody word."

She heeded his warning and bit her bottom lip.

"And don't do that," he practically growled at her.

"Don't what?"

"Don't be biting yer lip like that."

Startled by his request, she stammered, "I...I b-beg your pardon?"

"Yer lip, lass. Don't be calling attention to it by biting it."

She informed him, "It is a habit I have had since childhood."

He grunted again. And what in the world was that sound supposed to signify? Before she could ask, he strode into the room she had just left and deposited her on the cot. "Lie down."

She got off the cot as soon as he stepped back. "No!"

O'Malley's mouth hung open for a moment before he snapped it shut and gently placed his hands on her shoulders. "Ye need to lie down before ye fall down."

"I have no intention of sitting." Or telling the stubborn man that it was too painful to sit at the moment. Maybe when the sting in her bottom subsided a bit, she could.

His eyes widened, and he shook his head. Slowly, he set her free. "Ah, forgive me for not understanding." He slipped an arm around her waist and leaned close. "I can ask one of the footmen to bring ye a pillow to sit on." Her face flamed in response, and he chuckled. "Yer blush reminds me of me ma's roses."

"Do you make a habit of discussing such personal topics with women you barely know?"

His green eyes sparkled with devilment as he drew her alarmingly close. "Ah, but I know you, Miss Helen Langley, former maid to Mrs. Emily Garahan, ward to the Duke of Wyndmere. Ye're a welcome sight of a morning, with yer black-as-ebony hair coming loose from its pins, and yer entrancing violet eyes alight with joy."

O'Malley brushed the tip of his finger along the curve of her cheek. Her knees wobbled at his touch. She stiffened her legs and tried to add distance between them. When the backs of her knees pressed against the edge of the cot, she realized she had nowhere else to go.

"You are being far too familiar, O'Malley."

"I stated me intention the other day. Ye've yet to give me yer answer."

Helen struggled to keep her temper in check. "Your memory is faulty."

"Is it now?"

"Yes, it is. You did not ask me a question, therefore I do not owe you an answer."

He laughed, the sound reverberating off the walls of the small room. "Faith, ye're the only one for me, lass. 'Twas yerself that asked the question who would marry ye and offer protection to ye, and 'twas meself that answered, 'That would be me.' Have ye forgotten already?"

She clenched her teeth, gathered her composure, and whispered, "Have you forgotten that you did not ask me to marry you?"

⊱⊰

HE CLOSED HIS eyes and recalled the conversation he'd had with Emily that day. Actually, it wasn't a conversation—Garahan's wife had told him the three things she felt he needed to do if he truly wanted Helen to stay at Wyndmere Hall and marry him.

Three things he had yet to do. He'd start now. "Forgive me, lass, for not treating ye with the respect ye deserve." He ticked off the item in his head, then reached for her hand as he went down on one knee. *Now for the second.* Holding her gaze captive, he asked, "Will ye do me the honor of becoming me wife?"

She bit her bottom lip again, and the need to nibble on it distracted him.

"Are ye having trouble making up yer mind?"

"I'm sorry, Eamon. I'm leaving in a few days for the Borderlands." He stood and stared at her. A myriad of expressions flitted across her face. "If my life were different, Eamon..." She surprised him by cupping his face in her hand before lifting to her toes. Her lips brushed his clean-shaven jaw, the touch featherlight, but the feelings it roused inside of him were the exact opposite. He fought for control, grateful he'd taken the time to shave.

She lingered a moment before inhaling. "Mmm… You smell like the outdoors and sun-warmed pines."

He willed Helen to change her mind, and from the look in her eyes, he sensed she considered it. What was behind her need to leave? What did he not know?

She dropped her hand and stepped back. "I owe Emily for all that is good in my life. She deserves to be happy, now that she is married to Garahan and expecting. It would not be fair to distract her from her new life. It's past time for me to cease being a millstone around Emily's neck."

"Ye're right Emily will have her hands full—as will I if ye marry me, lass. 'Tisn't just yer beauty that has me asking for yer hand."

"No?"

"I just said it wasn't." He fought to hide the turmoil inside of him. "'Tis the twins' laughter I hear whenever ye're in the nursery, and I'm stationed on that floor. And ye have a way with Gwendolyn and Patrick's babe Deidre that warms me heart. Ye put all of yerself into whatever task ye undertake, lass. Constance and Merry speak highly of ye. Her Grace enjoys yer company, and she trusts ye with Richard and Abigail. I cannot think of a higher compliment."

Helen's eyes welled with tears, and he watched her struggle not to cry. "It sounds as if you would recommend me as a nanny or companion. Not a wife."

"Bloody hell, woman!" She flinched, and he fought his frustration. "Forgive me." When she stared at him, he reached for her hand. "*Please* say ye forgive me. Me ma would wallop me on the back of me head with her favorite cast iron pan for cursing in front of a lady."

"You are forgiven. I did not mean to upset you, nor do I mean to hurt you by refusing your offer of marriage. Please try to understand."

Gutted, he hid the pain inside him. "I can't say that I do. I'm offering ye the protection of me name, me position within the duke's guard, and me strength. I'd do anything for ye, lass. Can ye not understand that?"

Helen looked as if she were tempted. Then her expression changed to one of acceptance. Did she doubt his love? Did she not know that all it took sometimes was a glance to recognize the other half of yer heart?

"Emily and Garahan knew with one look," he said.

"I'm not Emily."

"I never thought ye were, lass." He lifted her hand and touched his lips to it. "Thank ye for accepting me apology. Me offer still stands, if ye find the position in the Borderlands isn't to yer liking. I'll be waiting for ye to come to yer senses and see that we're meant to be."

Helen seemed to be moved by his heartfelt declaration…until the part about coming to her senses. Her expression and stance changed. He should have left that part out. Women were touchy whenever men mentioned their senses.

"I cannot change my mind. But I will always remember the handsome-as-sin Irishman who offered the protection of his name and marriage."

He stepped to the side and motioned for her to precede him out of the room. As he watched her walk away, he noticed Flaherty standing by the rear door. Though his cousin's expression was neutral, he flinched in pain. O'Malley shook his head.

"I wish ye well, *Miss* Helen Langley. Don't be forgetting what I said."

"I won't."

"I'll be waiting."

"I wish you wouldn't."

"'Tis me choice. Ye have no say in what I do."

"As it is mine to leave. Goodbye, O'Malley."

"Goodbye, lass."

Flaherty placed a hand on O'Malley's shoulder in a show of comfort.

"Why can't she understand that I've offered the best of me—me name and me strength?"

"She could still change her mind."

"She won't."

Flaherty shoved O'Malley with his shoulder. "But she might."

"Bleeding bugger." O'Malley shoved him back.

They jostled one another as they strode outside, heading to their respective stations. It was going to be a long time before O'Malley's heart healed. He rubbed his palm over it and glanced down. "Not bleeding."

With a shake of his head, he drew in a breath, called on his steely control, and scaled the ladder to the roof. Time to remember the vow he'd sworn and his duty to the duke.

# CHAPTER EIGHT

MILY WRUNG HER hands and shook her head. "Tell me again what the dowager duchess said in her letter to you?"

Helen continued packing her portmanteau, but glanced up and sighed at the expression on Emily's face. Their relationship had changed over the years that she worked for Lord Montrose. It had been hesitant at first, gradually becoming more comfortable as they weathered the loss of Emily's mother together. In the last few months, Emily had confided in Helen her hopes and dreams, and Helen had been tempted to do the same. When she confided her dream of seeing her friend find happiness, and a husband worthy of her, before she left Montrose House, Emily had not accepted it, reminding Helen that she doubted she would ever find a man she would consider marrying.

Looking at her friend now, happily wed and pregnant with her first babe, gave Helen the hope that Emily would not continue to harp on her desire to find a position as a paid companion to a member of the *ton*. "The letter is in my reticule. Read it for yourself." After gently tucking the journal she had been keeping for the last six months, and her pencil, snug against the side of the leather bag, she closed it and turned around in time to see the frown on Emily's face. "What's wrong?"

Emily handed her the missive. "The tone of the dowager's letter, for one. She sounds condescending. You haven't had to deal with that before. Do you believe you can do so now?"

"I will have to, won't I?" Helen was silent for a moment before adding, "Remember, she is a dowager duchess. I wouldn't expect any less."

"The Duke and Duchess of Wyndmere have never been condescending to you and me," Emily reminded her. "I know it is not normal for members of the *ton* to treat their staff, and in the duke's case, his private guard, as if they were extended members of their family, but they do. Can you look me in the eye and tell me you will be able to work for a woman with such an elevated opinion of herself?"

Helen smiled. "You do not need to worry about me anymore. It's your new family where your concern should lie. I will be just fine."

Emily hugged her. "Are you certain you need to leave this afternoon? Why can you not wait until the morning?"

"The sooner I leave, the sooner I shall get there. I do not think the dowager is used to waiting."

"I should say not."

"Then we agree." To Helen's dismay, Emily's eyes welled with tears. Hoping to stem the flow, she asked, "Will you come with me to say goodbye to Her Grace?"

"Of course." Emily slipped her arm through Helen's and led the way to the sitting room adjacent to the nursery, where the duchess would be found this time of day.

Helen knocked on the door, and the duke opened it and held the door for them to enter. Had he been waiting for them? Helen was nervous as to what His Grace might say to her, but he immediately put her at ease, motioning for her and Emily to join them in the sitting room.

The duchess smiled and started to rise, but the duke shook his head. "Remember what the doctor said, love. Either rest sitting or in bed."

She rolled her eyes. "Fine, I shall sit." When Emily and Helen sat on the settee, she sighed. "Is it true then, Helen—you're leaving us?"

"Yes, Your Grace. It is an opportunity I cannot pass up."

Persephone glanced at her husband, who gave a brief nod. "Jared and I would like you to reconsider. Richard and Abigail have taken to you. They are quite selective, you know."

Helen smiled. She *did* know. "They were hesitant around me at first, too. They are such sweet, happy babes. It is impossible not to love them." But Their Graces' babes weren't the only ones at Wyndmere Hall that were impossible not to love.

*Eamon...*

Just like that, she remembered the look in O'Malley's eyes when she refused his offer of marriage. She had been half in love with him since the moment their eyes met that first day. But she didn't believe it was a feeling that could last once he found out about her past.

The duke put his hands behind his back and nodded to her. "If you decide the position is not to your liking, I sincerely hope you will send word. I shall have a carriage sent for you. You will always be welcome here at Wyndmere Hall. And not just by Her Grace and me."

His meaning was not lost on Helen. She had a suspicion that the men in the duke's guard, and possibly the staff, knew that O'Malley had proposed to her—and that she'd refused. What no one knew was why, and she wanted to keep it that way. She was not some silly miss whose head could be turned by broad shoulders, a firm jaw, and a handsome face.

O'Malley's face popped into her head, and she inwardly sighed. *Don't forget the power of his smile and brilliant green eyes,* her heart reminded her head. No, there was no chance that she would forget Eamon O'Malley. He would forever hold a place in her heart.

Forcing those thoughts aside, she smiled at the duke and duchess and thanked them again. Emily accompanied her back to her room to collect her portmanteau. They stopped in the kitchen, where Constance and Merry were waiting to say their goodbyes. Humphries nodded to them as he took her bag and opened the door for her. She stared at the shiny black coach-and-four waiting outside, wondering whom it belonged to—the duke's crest was not emblazoned on the side. But it wouldn't matter whom it belonged to. She was leaving.

"I'll just get out of your way." Helen started to walk toward the road to the village. She enjoyed walking, and looked forward to the time to think—mayhap it would help to purge Eamon O'Malley from her mind and heart.

"Wait, Miss Helen," Humphries called to her as a footman opened the door to the carriage.

"Does whomever is in the carriage wish to speak to me?"

Emily caught up with her, slipped her arm through Helen's, and steered her toward the coach. "His Grace is sending you to the Borderlands in one of his carriages."

Helen froze, ignoring when Emily tugged on her arm to get her moving. "Why would he do that?"

"I would imagine to ensure you arrived safely, Miss," Humphries replied.

"But he's only just met me," Helen protested.

"It has been some weeks," the butler reminded her.

"And the twins love you," Emily added. "Their Graces haven't given up hope that you will return to Wyndmere Hall."

"True, Mrs. Garahan," Humphries said. "You have been a welcome addition, Miss Helen."

"That she has."

Helen spun around and gasped. "How long have you been standing there?"

O'Malley's eyes swirled with too many emotions to name. "Long enough to add me hope that you will return not just to the hall," he rasped, "but to me."

Helen drew in a deep breath and slowly exhaled. She was weakening and couldn't. "Wish me well?"

He reached for her hand, brought it to his lips, and kissed it. "With all me heart, lass, until ye return."

When she moved forward, his confident look slipped. He quickly adopted a neutral expression and handed her into the carriage. When she was seated, he leaned into the carriage and locked gazes with her. "Be well, *mo chroí.*"

She blinked. Garahan and Patrick used those words when speaking to their wives. She wondered what it meant, and was about to ask, but O'Malley closed the door and stepped back from the carriage. She slumped against the leather squabs, ignoring the comfort, and closed her eyes. Why *was* it so important to throw away the promise of the love of a good man?

"Because he deserves a wife who never scrounged for food by picking pockets." The tears came, and she gave in and let them fall.

# CHAPTER NINE

HELEN WAS EXHAUSTED by the third time they stopped to change horses. Not that it took long. The hostlers at the inns were adept at hitching up the fresh teams in mere minutes. It was the tediousness of traveling that was a bit numbing and drained her of her enthusiasm for the journey. That and the unknown that lay ahead of her.

*A future without the man who turned your head,* her heart reminded her.

*He deserves far better than me,* her head insisted.

Her stomach rumbled, interrupting her thoughts. It was just after six o'clock, and she was looking forward to a hot meal, and beyond desperate for a pot of tea all to herself. She did not have to worry about navigating the inn yard, or the inn itself. It had both surprised and gratified her to discover at the first stop that the duke had made arrangements for the care and keeping of not only his team of horses but Helen, too. It was a heady feeling to discover that the cachet that accompanied the duke's name would be extended to her at his request.

She had given her circumstances a lot of thought as the miles passed. At each stop along the way, she had been treated as if she were a family member. Although the duke's carriage did not have his crest on the side, the footman, as well as the coachman he sat beside, wore the duke's livery.

Helen had remarked on the deep sapphire blue with thin, braided silver trim when she and Emily had first arrived. The duchess had smiled and remarked that the duke had given her *carte blanche* to select new colors for the servants' garments when they married. She'd chosen the deep sapphire blue to match her husband's eyes. It was a nice contrast to the unrelieved black the men of the duke's guard wore—from their cravats to their boots. The only hint of color was the embroidered golden Celtic harp over their hearts, and the emerald-green *Eire* embroidered beneath it.

She shifted her thoughts away from the duke's guard, and the man she'd left behind. She needed to think of something else—anything but brilliant green eyes and broad shoulders…

*Horses!* She tucked thoughts of O'Malley away and concentrated on the efficiency of the hostler and his men taking care of the teams of horses at the inns on the journey. It was a surprise at first that the duke kept horses stabled at a number of inns between the Lake District and London, the Borderlands, and Cornwall. Though it should not have been, given that he was rumored to have not only refilled his family's coffers, but amassed a fortune before taking on the mantle of duke after the shocking death of his elder brother.

Judging from the animals in his stables, he had a keen eye for horseflesh—further evidenced by the matched set of grays waiting to replace each team of horses along the way to the Borderlands. It was as if each successive inn along the road north expected her to arrive on a schedule. Had the duke gone to that much trouble on her behalf? Why would he? Was something less innocuous behind the royal treatment? Did it have to do with O'Malley's proposal?

She yawned, no longer thinking travel via coach was exciting. Hours on end spent in the carriage with only herself for company had cured her of that notion. As the coachman called to his team, and the carriage slowed to a stop, she tucked a few stray curls into place and smoothed the wrinkles from her gown. She was ready to disembark.

The duke's footman opened the door and held out his hand to help her step down from the carriage. She was a bit stiff from sitting, and smiled. "Thank you."

"My pleasure, Miss Langley." Though she recognized him as the footman she'd bumped into, Helen wished she could remember his name, but she had not been introduced to all of the duke's staff in her short time at Wyndmere Hall.

The hostler shouted to his stable hands as a trio of coaches rolled into the yard. No longer a novice regarding etiquette while traveling via carriage, she felt comfortable with the footman escorting her to the inn, where she was immediately greeted by the innkeeper. "Ah, Miss Langley. We have been expecting you. His Grace has arranged for your room tonight, and the choice of either having your meal in one of our private dining rooms, or in your bedchamber."

Unused to being fawned over, she hesitated a moment, then relaxed when the innkeeper smiled at her. No one was going to question why she was traveling in one of the duke's carriages, nor would they be questioning her ancestry, or ask what page her family occupied in *Debrett's Peerage* to see if she deserved such preferential treatment. She owed Their Graces for their kindness. Helen planned to pen a note of thanks to them after she settled into her new position. "Thank you. His Grace is so thoughtful."

"Would you care to go to your room first, or have tea?"

"I would love to freshen up, thank you, Mr....?"

"Edwards."

Helen liked the way the man's eyes crinkled at the corners, indicating he smiled often. "Thank you, Mr. Edwards."

He motioned for her to follow him. "This way."

Following in his wake, she wondered why he did not question why she was traveling unaccompanied. She'd thought of it because she had been Emily's companion, traveling with her whenever she left Montrose House. But she hesitated at the notion that her speaking up may negate the duke's instructions.

Though she was not related to His Grace, and did not work for him any longer, it was best not to speak out of turn. It would be far worse to gainsay the duke than to hold her tongue. Wouldn't it?

"Here we are." The innkeeper unlocked the door to her bed-chamber, then handed her the key. "Hot water should be arriving any—Ah, here it is now." He smiled. "There you are, Sally. Set the hot water over on the washstand."

When the servant did as he instructed, he turned back to Helen. "The duke advised that you would not be traveling with your maid, knowing that our inn would be more than happy to have one of our servants stand in. Sally will be serving you from now until tomorrow morning, when you are ready to leave." He bowed. "Whatever you need, His Grace wants you to have it."

"You have been so kind, Mr. Edwards. Thank you."

He nodded and left as Sally finished pouring hot water into the washbowl. "Do you need assistance washing?"

"Er… No thank you, Sally. It won't take me more than a few moments to wash my face and hands."

Soon, Helen was ready and descending the staircase to find the promised pot of tea and hot meal. She hoped the rest of her journey would be as pleasant as this.

Hours later, she lay in bed wide-eyed and worried. Why had no one questioned her closely? And why in Heaven's name was she concerned? She should be pleased that everyone seemed delighted to wait on her, instead of digging deep to discover her past and talent for lifting coin from the deep pockets of the *ton*. Would Sally mention how awkward Helen had been while attending to her? Did the young woman suspect that Helen was little more than a servant herself?

"If you don't shut your eyes now," she chided herself, "you'll arrive with bags under them instead of appearing fresh and eager to speak to the dowager."

Her thoughts awhirl, it was finally the deep, lilting voice of a certain Irishman telling her that he'd be waiting for her to return that lulled her to sleep.

➙➙➙❬❬❬

GARAHAN GRABBED O'MALLEY by the shoulder and spun him around. "Out with it! Ye are no good to us if yer head is up yer *arse!*"

O'Malley's fist connected with Garahan's jaw, snapping his head back. "Last time I checked, ye weren't the bloody boss of me!"

A deep voice from behind them rumbled, "That would be me."

O'Malley groaned. "'Tisn't what ye think, Patrick."

"I'm thinking ye're acting like a horse's *arse*. The lass has only been gone for a day." Patrick's eyes burned like hellfire. "Have ye forgotten that every last one of us is needed to guard the duke?"

O'Malley shook his head. "I haven't."

"Ye were just in the meeting where we received confirmation that one of Hardwell's lackeys was paid—and paid well—to make it look like an accident when he shoved Lord Montrose into the path of that carriage. Hardwell's man could be on his way here right now!"

O'Malley struggled to gain control of his anger. He'd taken an oath, the same as his brothers and cousins. "Ye're right, but ye don't understand—"

"*I bloody well do!* If Finn were here, he'd swear to the fact that I made an *arse* of meself. First by lettin' Gwendolyn leave after I'd been shot, then makin' a fool of meself shoutin' her name in the taproom, shaming her in front of everyone gathered at the inn in the village."

O'Malley had been patrolling the perimeter at the time, not there to witness Patrick's victorious return with the woman he loved enough to chase. Should O'Malley have done the same as his cousin? But what possible reason could he have had for going after Helen? What could he say to the duke in order to receive his blessing to do so now?

O'Malley asked Patrick, "What happened?"

"She agreed to return to Wyndmere Hall, but then gave me a piece of her mind. The lass couldn't help herself, proclaimin' her love for me. Finn bought a round for everyone in the common room, and that's when I tossed Gwendolyn over me shoulder, mounted me horse, and carried her back to Wyndmere Hall."

"I heard a slightly different tale," Garahan said.

"Ye weren't at the inn," Patrick grumbled. "Me brother was."

"And now Finn is married to Mollie with a babe of their own, living in Cornwall, protecting the duke's manor house and Penwith Tower."

"Aye. It has been too long since all of us have served under one roof," Patrick murmured.

"Do ye think there will ever be an occasion when we will all be together again?" O'Malley asked.

"Not without our wives and babes," Patrick replied. "Not a one of us would willingly be separated from them for long."

"I wonder what kind of occasion would warrant that?" Garahan mused.

O'Malley glanced from Garahan to Patrick and back. "A very special one." He waited a beat. "Garahan?"

"What the *feck* do ye want?"

O'Malley fought the urge to smile. "I'd like to tell ye that I'm sorry I tapped ye on the jaw."

Garahan snorted. "Ah, but ye aren't. I wouldn't be either. 'Twas a solid blow. Sneaky. Something I'd have done meself."

"Faith, I know it. Ye can owe me."

"Well now, O'Malley, that's an offer I cannot refuse: one free clip to your jaw."

O'Malley was wondering when his cousin would be taking him up on it when a short, sharp whistle had the three of them rushing to where Flaherty stood in front of the stables.

Patrick was the first to speak. "Trouble?"

"The duke just received an urgent missive from Baron Summerfield, regarding the Dowager Duchess Flemington. Anyone familiar with her?"

O'Malley's heart clenched in his chest. Patrick and Garahan weren't familiar with the name, but he was. Emily had given him the information hoping he'd follow after Helen. He rubbed at the pain in his heart. "'Tis the position Helen left me for."

Patrick stared at O'Malley for a moment. "Head inside, and see if we're needed. The rest of us will head to our posts."

"But it's yer job to be there with the duke—"

"And I'm sending ye in me place. His Grace knows ye asked Helen to marry ye. We all know." When O'Malley shook his head, Patrick gave him a shove. "That's an order. Move yer *arse!*"

O'Malley turned around and sprinted toward the back entrance. He strode down the hallway past the room where Merry and Constance kept their healing supplies, past the pantry, and in through the kitchen. He greeted Constance, but kept going. He had to find out if the missive from the dowager duchess had anything to do with Helen.

The hairs on the back of his neck stood on end as he approached the library. The duke was leaving it. "Ah, O'Malley. Just the man I need."

"Patrick will be along shortly, he's—"

"Summerfield sent word that it is urgent that I send someone to collect Miss Helen from Flemington Gatehouse."

"She was not hired?"

The duke's eyes blazed with anger. "Apparently the dowager has taken it upon herself to warn any and all of her acquaintances within the *ton* against hiring Miss Helen Langley. Adding the caveat that her reputation has been damaged due to her former post at Montrose House—which has been tainted because of Lord Montrose's murder. She is insisting Miss Langley is unfit to darken her doorstep—or that of anyone within her circle."

O'Malley let his confusion show. "The lass had nothing to do with the murder. Why would the dowager say such a thing?"

"I have no idea. I must speak with Persephone. She'll need to create the list of those within our circle of acquaintances—whether they are titled or not—so that we can stem this disastrous slander of Miss Langley. Lord Montrose trusted me as Emily's guardian and, by default, her maid Helen's guardian. Montrose took in young men and women—most times as children—to save them from the streets. Employing them gave them a sense of pride. Protecting them with his name gave them the sense of family. I will honor Montrose's request to continue to protect all those under his care. I will not let someone censure Miss Langley's good name because of some bacon-brained dowager's idea that it is her duty! I will not have it!"

The duke's words felt like a direct hit to O'Malley's heart. "I'm sensing there is more that I need to know."

"Miss Langley has no idea that the dowager sent out these missives days ago via special messenger, *before* she was to meet with Miss Langley." O'Malley swore beneath his breath, but the duke heard. "I could not have said it better. We cannot let the woman you plan to marry, become a victim of the dowager's slander."

O'Malley could not think of any response other than to nod his agreement.

The duke pinched the bridge of his nose. "My father never liked Flemington, or his duchess, for that matter."

"I'm not as familiar with the hierarchy of the *ton*. But I have to ask, is the duchess in the dower house because she did something to upset the duke who sent her there?"

"It means that the former duke—her husband—passed away, and their son is now duke. My sources informed me that the duke married six months past and Flemington Hall was not big enough for the new duchess *and* his mother."

"Where is Helen now?"

The duke clenched his jaw. "I have no idea. My sources informed me that the dowager sent Helen packing, and has the unmitigated gall to slander my name for offering a place on my staff to a woman of questionable reputation. She has no idea of the friends and acquaintances that I have reestablished a friendship with, or the new ones I have gained over the last three years. She does not wield one quarter of the power she thinks she does."

"Even if she did, why would she slander ye?"

Again the duke replied, "I have no idea."

O'Malley nodded. "What about yer carriage? Weren't the coachman and footman supposed to wait until Helen had spoken to the dowager before leaving?"

"Aye, but apparently, the dowager raised bloody hell and ordered them from the estate."

O'Malley's heart beat faster. "Do ye mean to tell me the woman kicked Helen out of her home and sent her on her way...on foot?"

"Aye. There's a good chance that my footman was in the servants' quarters waiting for Miss Langley, while the coachman will have waited far enough away from Flemington Hall that the dowager could not see the carriage. Then again, I would not put it past the disagreeable woman to have booted my footman out and sent one of her servants after my coachman to ensure he left."

"How long ago?"

"Earlier today. Apparently the dowager sent word to the inn that she would be meeting with Miss Langley before noon."

"A few hours ago!" His gut felt as if he'd swallowed shards of glass. "Even on one of yer best horses, the fastest I could get there would be—"

"I have Thoroughbreds stabled at inns on the road to the Borderlands, as well as teams, for emergencies such as this. Every one of my stallions has the heart of a champion and can run like the wind. You can push them to the limit, O'Malley... They'll thank you for it, as long as you see to it they are properly cooled down before giving them food or water. Make certain to warn the hostlers that it is an emergency and that you have my permission. With a few changes of horse, you can be there in four and a half to five hours."

"But Helen'll have been missing for—"

The duke reached into his waistcoat pocket and handed O'Malley a sealed, folded document. "You may need this, if things go awry."

"What is it?"

"A special license. I am giving you my permission and blessing to marry Helen. God forbid she is injured—because of your promise to protect her, I know you would refuse to leave her side. It could ruin her reputation. If you are married, it will not be a problem." The duke paused. "Summerfield is sending Flaherty to Flemington Hall. He'll meet you there."

"I won't need any help—"

"Consider it an order to accept Flaherty's help. Two heads are better than one."

Emotion had O'Malley's throat constricting for a moment before he cleared it. "Aye. Thank ye, Yer Grace. I will never be able to repay ye for yer kindness."

"You have already done so, tenfold. Now, go! I need to speak to my wife, or else she'll badger me because I did not confide this situation to her immediately. Then she'll tell me I completely botched it."

O'Malley didn't need to be told twice. He bowed to the duke, shoved the license in his waistcoat pocket, and sprinted down the hallway toward Humphries.

The butler was waiting for him. "Godspeed, O'Malley. We're keeping Miss Helen in our prayers."

"Thank ye, Humphries!"

# CHAPTER TEN

ELEN COULD NOT hide her shock at the vitriol the dowager spewed at her. "I beg your pardon, Your Grace, but I—"

"You were there, working in Lord Montrose's house. A man murdered! Did you think I would not uncover that information about you before I asked you to meet with me? Furthermore, Lord Montrose did not inherit his title—it was given to him on the battlefield!"

Confused, Helen stared at the formidable dowager. Normally she would never question the woman due to her high rank in Society. But she had traveled ten hours to be here, thinking that she would be offered the position of companion. "Why did you ask me to meet with you if you had such strong feelings about my situation?"

The dowager lifted her chin. The look of contempt was plain as day and had the breath snagging in Helen's lungs. How was what had happened to her former employer, and a dear man, a reflection upon Helen's character?

Before she could ask, the woman continued, "I have already contacted all of my acquaintances and warned them about you. You, Miss Langley, will never work for any member of the *ton*! Stevens!"

Helen could not form a thought, let alone speak. She did not move until the butler entered the room. "Yes, Your Grace?"

"Show this person out, and see that she removes herself from the estate immediately!"

"I beg your pardon, Your Grace. But you've already sent the duke's carriage away."

"I am well aware, Stevens. See. Her. Out!"

At the dowager's screeching tone, the butler's expression changed from concerned to dutiful. "This way, miss."

Helen rose from her seat, clinging to the last shreds of her dignity. Never had she been treated so shabbily. Did she not deserve to breathe the same air as the dowager?

By the time the butler opened the front door to show her out, Helen realized that she had no transportation waiting for her. She glanced at her feet and then at the butler. "I am to walk, then? What of the Duke of Wyndmere's carriage? Where will I find it?"

Stevens motioned for one of the footmen to take his place in the entryway, and gently grasped Helen's elbow and urged her outside. With the door nearly closed behind him, he pitched his voice low and said, "There is a cottage just past the entrance gates. I am certain that the duke's coachman will be concerned about you and wait for you there, just out of sight."

"What if the dowager had hired me? Would she have sent him away then as well?"

"I'm sorry, miss, but there was never a chance that she would offer you employment once she found out that you had not worked for what she considers to be a true member of the *ton*. The report Her Grace received indicated his lordship was a military man."

Helen lifted her chin. "Lord Montrose was honorable and given his title for bravery beyond the call of duty in battle. He was kind to me and the others who worked for him. That anyone would hold his untimely death against him shocks and saddens me."

"I wish I could be of more help, but she has all of us watched."

"The dowager?"

"Aye." The expression in his eyes softened. "I am close to being pensioned off and cannot do anything to lose the pay promised to me after thirty years serving here."

Helen understood. "I would not want you to. Thank you for telling me. I'll leave now so that she can see that I am walking down the long drive that will lead to the road…and the cottage you mentioned just beyond."

"Be safe, miss."

"Thank you for your kindness, Stevens."

He inclined his head and stiffly walked to the door. He opened it wider, slipped inside, and closed the door firmly behind him.

Helen did not turn around to glance over her shoulder, though she would swear she could feel the dowager's pale gray eyes following her every step as she increased the distance between the gatehouse and the wrought iron gate ahead. Just another quarter mile or so beyond the gate before she stepped onto neutral ground. Once she was through the gate and closed it behind her, she increased her speed until she was running toward the safety of the cottage she prayed was just out of sight. Tears blurred her vision. She never saw the stone jutting up from the packed earth until her toe caught on the rock, and she pitched forward, hands outstretched, scraping as she tried to stop her forward motion. Pain shot through her wrist a heartbeat before her chin connected with the ground.

Stunned, Helen lay there for a few moments before she was able to gather her wits. It took more effort than she anticipated to lift herself up onto her knees. Bracing her hands on the ground, she moaned when her wrist gave, and she hit her chin a second time.

She heard hoofbeats and sighed with relief. Someone had seen her fall and was rushing toward her to help.

Helen looked up into pitch-black, soulless eyes, and knew he meant to do her harm. She rolled away from him and braced her opposite hand to the ground to sit up, only to be grabbed from behind. A large, gloved hand covered her mouth and nose, cutting off her ability to breathe.

One-handed, she fought against the iron grip of her captor as dizziness set in and her vision grayed at the edges. Out of air, she felt her grip slacken a heartbeat before she lost consciousness.

Her eyes slowly opened, but the light from a window disoriented her. She blinked as she regained consciousness, immediately aware of the pain lancing through her wrist and chin. Awareness set in and she knew she had to escape! Bracing a hand beside her to sit up, she cried out when a hand grabbed hold of her injured wrist. She swore she felt the bones move. The pain was excruciating.

"I nearly gave up hope that you would awaken." The rough voice grated on her shattered nerves. It was not one she recognized.

Helen was afraid to speak, but afraid not to. "Who are you, and what do you want?"

"I have what I want—you."

"I don't know you. Why would you want me?"

"Finishing a job that I started. You will be worth your weight in gold."

Fighting to remain calm, she racked her brain to reason out what this dark-haired, dark-eyed man wanted with her. "You must have me confused with someone else. I have no family who will be searching for me."

His black eyes gleamed. "You have a connection to the Duke of Wyndmere through his ward."

Her heart fluttered in her breast at the mention of the duke and Emily. In that moment, she knew who the man worked for, and something inside of her snapped. "Baron Hardwell."

"You are not as lack-witted as you appear."

That comment had the rest of the fog in her brain clearing.

"He owes me and will pay handsomely when I turn you over to him."

That made no sense. Hadn't she heard that he was being held

until his trial? "But he's locked away at Newgate."

"I have connections. My orders were to capture you if I couldn't get my hands on the duke's ward."

Incensed that the baron was behind bars, but still had his sources searching for Emily, she demanded, "What do you want with her?"

"It isn't what I want *with* her." The tone of his voice and the expression on his face had her biting the inside of her cheek to keep from telling him anything more. Helen was more than aware what the baron wanted and why. She had helped to thwart his intentions when he sprang his attack on her and Emily, all the while shouting his vile threats.

Helen vowed in that moment that she would not give in to fear. She had been resourceful, living off her wits and quick hands before Emily's father rescued her from a life of crime. It had been years, but she would use what lay dormant inside of her to escape.

Emily's life depended on it!

O'MALLEY MADE GOOD time, thanks to the excellent horseflesh the duke had stabled at the inns between the Lake District and the Borderlands. As directed to by the duke, he made certain to alert each hostler that he had the duke's permission to push his mount to the limit. It was an emergency. Thankfully, no one questioned him.

As he rode into the last inn to change horses, he saw a tall, auburn-haired man dressed in black from head to toe speaking to the hostler. "Dillon!"

His cousin and the hostler turned around. "Ye made good time." Flaherty's eyes widened as O'Malley dismounted. "That's a fine bit of horseflesh ye're riding, boy-o."

O'Malley nodded, scratching behind the animal's ear. "I knew

His Grace stabled teams of horses for his carriages, but didn't realize he stabled stallions too. We had a good run, didn't we, laddie?"

The horse whinnied, and the hostler chuckled. "Here, I'll take him. I have a stallion waiting for you."

O'Malley and his cousin followed the man into the stables, where Flaherty filled him in. "His lordship was livid when he found out what happened to Miss Langley."

"Had the baron met her before?" O'Malley asked.

Flaherty grunted. "Nay, but word the from yer twin is that yer head was turned recently by the lass. The baron—as well as the duke—want the men in the duke's guard to find happiness. They feel we deserve it for putting our lives on the line daily."

"Have ye met *yer* match yet, Flaherty?"

His cousin snorted with laughter. "No, and I don't intend to."

O'Malley paused, then asked, "How would Thomas know that I may have had me attention snagged by a winsome woman?"

Flaherty laughed in his face. "Faith, did ye not know that the women who have married into our extended family keep up a steady correspondence with one another? There's no secrets between the O'Malley and Garahan wives."

"I see."

"I don't," Flaherty admitted. "Ye must have a better understanding of women than me. Why would they be confiding such to one another when they've only met through their letters?"

O'Malley didn't have the answer. "We'll have to ask Ryan's or Thomas's wife after I find Helen and bring her to Summerfield Chase. Do ye think his lordship would mind? It's closest, and I'd like the vicar to perform our wedding."

"Have ye asked the lass yet?"

O'Malley shrugged. "In a roundabout way."

"Has His Grace secured a special license for ye?" O'Malley patted the pocket of his waistcoat, and Flaherty laughed harder. "This is a tale I need to hear."

O'Malley thanked the hostler and mounted the stallion. "As ye've come to lend a hand, Dillon—not that I need it—I may be coerced into confiding in ye."

His cousin grinned. "We have a bit of time before we reach Flemington Hall. Start talking."

By the time they rode up to the wrought iron gates of Flemington Hall, O'Malley had confided that he'd thought he was answering the lass's question when she asked who would marry someone like her to protect her.

Flaherty, God love the man, agreed. She should have realized it was as good as a proposal. There were times when O'Malley and his Flaherty cousins were of the same mind...until they weren't, and then fists would fly.

He wouldn't mind going a few rounds with Flaherty, in fact. The man was built like a bull, but a few inches shorter than him. He'd have to guard his chin—Flaherty had a wicked uppercut.

As if his cousin knew what O'Malley was thinking, Flaherty nodded. "After we find yer bride-to-be and are back at Summerfield Chase, I'll be taking ye up on what ye're thinking."

O'Malley grunted and dismounted. Keeping hold of the reins, he led his horse to the gates. "Not locked."

"Foolish to close yer gates and not lock them," Flaherty commented as O'Malley opened them, mounted his horse, and rode through. Flaherty followed behind him, dismounted, and closed the gates behind them.

As they approached the gatehouse, a man rushed toward them from the stables. "Is the dowager expecting you?"

O'Malley decided that if she wasn't, she bloody well should have been. "Aye. Would ye mind giving our horses a bit of water? We have not come far, but 'tis a warm day."

"I'll let the dowager know you're here. What are your names?"

Flaherty dismounted before answering. Standing beside O'Malley, he crossed his arms over his broad chest. "Name's Flaherty. I'm an emissary from Baron Summerfield." He nodded to his cousin. "O'Malley here is an emissary from the Duke of Wyndmere."

"Baron? Duke?"

The man's inquisitive gaze moved from Flaherty to O'Malley while they waited for him to take the reins to Flaherty's horse. "We can find the way to the front door, if ye'd water our horses," O'Malley said.

"Be certain to let the dowager's butler know who you are and why you are here."

"We're here on behalf of Miss Langley. I'm to escort her to Summerfield Chase," Flaherty said.

"After she's enjoyed a visit with the baroness—the duke's sister—I'm to escort her back to Wyndmere Hall in the Lake District," O'Malley added.

The stable master's eyes widened. "I'd like to be a fly on the wall when you inform the dowager of that."

Flaherty's expression hardened. "Why is that?"

"Given the way—"

The door to the gatehouse opened, and a stoop-shouldered man in dark livery stared at them. "The dowager wishes to know who you are and what you are doing on her estate."

The stable master leaned close to O'Malley and Flaherty. "She watches out her parlor window to see who's coming and going. You'd best go speak with Stevens."

"The butler?" O'Malley asked.

"Aye." The stable master gave a brief tug on the reins, and both horses went along obligingly. "I'll take care of these fine animals for you."

Flaherty nodded. "Thank ye."

O'Malley was halfway across the yard to the gatehouse. He paused to wait. "I'll do the talking."

Flaherty shrugged and motioned for O'Malley to precede him.

O'Malley nodded to the butler. "Me name's O'Malley, and this is Flaherty. We're part of the Duke of Wyndmere's personal guard. I'm stationed at Wyndmere Hall. Flaherty is stationed at Summerfield Chase. We've come to escort Miss Langley to Summerfield Chase—from there, I'll escort her to Wyndmere Hall."

From the way the man's face paled, O'Malley wondered if, wherever Helen was, she was not being treated as she should be. "We'll not be staying for tea," he added. "We're only here long enough to collect Miss Langley."

The butler glanced over his shoulder and looked to the left and then the right before saying, "Miss Langley left hours ago."

"I didn't come across the duke's carriage at any of the inns on me way here," O'Malley remarked. "Is there another road that leads to the Lake District?"

"There is," Flaherty replied. "It is not as well traveled and will add at least an hour or two to your journey."

While O'Malley was digesting the news, the butler motioned the men closer. "Her Grace, the dowager, instructed the stable master and myself to order the duke's coachman to leave as soon as Miss Langley was inside the gatehouse."

O'Malley's anger roared to life. "Why in the bloody hell would she do that?"

The butler shook his head. "I have no idea. Those of us who have worked for Her Grace for a number of years have learned never to question her."

O'Malley's fingers flexed with the need to grab the man by the shoulders and shake him until he told them everything. Flaherty nudged him out of the way with his shoulder and asked the butler, "How did Miss Langley leave, if the duke's carriage was ordered off the property?"

The servant sighed heavily and confirmed what they already suspected: "On foot."

O'Malley closed his eyes and ordered himself to remember his vow to the duke. He could not react physically, unless a member of the duke's family—or extended family—were being attacked. In that moment, he was glad Flaherty had accompanied him. His cousin was a stickler for rules. O'Malley needed to clear his mind, to concentrate on finding Helen, the coachman, and the footman. He needed to get the lay of the land beyond the road he traveled to find her. "I noticed a cottage a quarter of a mile or so before I reached the gates. Who lives there?"

"The widow Dawson and her son. Though the dowager would not appreciate my telling you this, the woman is a healer, and has a fine hand with stitches."

O'Malley glanced at Flaherty, who gave a brief nod. "Thank ye." They turned and began walking toward the stables.

"O'Malley," the butler called out. "There is one more thing you need to know."

His gut clenched. "What might that be?"

"Her Grace sent out missives to all of her contemporaries within the *ton*."

"'Tis the reason meself and Flaherty are here. Baron Summerfield received one of the dowager's missives and sent word to his brother-in-law, the Duke of Wyndmere."

The expression on the man's face was definitely one of shock. Knowing the dowager would come to regret her ploy was the only reason O'Malley was able to keep his mind on the end goal—find the lass, sweep her away to Summerfield Chase, and marry her before returning to Wyndmere Hall.

The butler shook his head. "In Her Grace's words, Miss Langley's reputation has been ruined, her having worked in the household of a man who was murdered."

O'Malley saw red, and it took every single ounce of his considerable control not to lash out at the man. Flaherty intervened. "We understand ye're the messenger… *Not* the guilty party here."

"Thank you."

"Tell the dowager that I will be informing Baron Summerfield what she has done, and her slander against a man who fought for his country, defending its king valiantly. For his efforts, he was granted a title."

O'Malley struggled to keep the anger from his voice when he

said, "And I'll be informing His Grace, and his contact on Bow Street, of this atrocity and slander against the duke's ward. The dowager will be hearing from His Grace's solicitors."

The butler flinched. "I hope you find Miss Langley safe and sound at the cottage."

O'Malley gave a brief nod and continued walking to where the stable master had their horses ready and waiting for them. "Thank ye for yer help."

"I hope you find Miss Langley. She may not realize it, but the dowager did her a favor."

"Are ye daft?" O'Malley demanded.

Flaherty elbowed him. "Ye aren't seeing it from another perspective. I'd agree with him. Miss Langley is too kind to be working for a shrew like the dowager."

The stable master nodded. "Aye."

As they walked their horses toward the gates, O'Malley grumbled, "I didn't see hide nor hair of the lass on me way here."

Flaherty narrowed his eyes as they reached the gate, each pulling one side of it open. "From the description from Caro, yer brother's wife—"

"I bloody well know who Caro is."

Flaherty snorted. "As I was saying, I did not come across her either. I asked at the inn between here and Summerfield Chase. No one saw a woman fitting her description."

"As she was on foot, she must still be in the area," O'Malley mumbled.

"Aye. We'd best not trample any clues."

The men closed the gates behind them, and O'Malley paused for a moment, considering the best course of action. "We'd best search along the edge of the road for signs of a scuffle."

Flaherty agreed. "If we don't see anything in the next quarter mile or so, we can mount up."

O'Malley had spent a few minutes scouring the side of the road when Flaherty called out, "There!"

O'Malley walked over to stand beside his cousin, who had

been searching the road itself. He bent to examine the rock protruding from the road, and the way the dirt had been disturbed. "Do ye see that?" Flaherty asked.

"Aye."

Flaherty got down on one knee. "The stone's been loosened, and the dirt around it disturbed."

It looked to O'Malley as if something had scraped through the loose surface dirt. His heart nearly stopped. "See those indentations? Could someone have put their hands out to break a fall?

Flaherty stood and placed a hand on his shoulder. "Ye don't need to ask, because I do think it's the lass ye're seeking. She may have smacked her forehead after a fall, then come to and wandered off."

O'Malley studied the road a few moments longer. "Do ye see the large footprint?"

"Aye. And next to it could be the print from a knee."

The cousins had tracked enough men back home to read the signs. Whoever it was had to be at least O'Malley's weight, if not his height.

"From the direction of the footprint," Flaherty said, "the man must have stepped from the wooded area over there."

"And knelt beside where Helen tripped and fell." Had she been unconscious? Bleeding? O'Malley couldn't see any sign of it, but that did not mean someone hadn't wiped away any evidence. Who had taken her? And why? To lend aid, or for some nefarious reason?

"Do ye think Lord Montrose's murderer has been following Aiden and the others and latched on to Helen when he saw her leaving Wyndmere Hall?"

O'Malley fought against the need to vomit. *Dear God in Heaven, do not let the lass be suffering at the hands of the murderer!* "King said the man all but disappeared."

"If not him, it could be some other blackguard."

"What if it *is* Hardwell's lackey? What if the baron has a connection within Newgate Prison's walls and has offered coin to whomever finds the lass and brings her back?"

"It could be we're wrong." Flaherty's voice had dropped to a low pitch. "Mayhap it's someone who saw her in the duke's carriage and is thinking to hold her for ransom."

Flaherty's supposition bugged the ever-living *shite* out of O'Malley. He had to get word to His Grace, the baron, and the others, to alert them of the possibility that the murderer was on his way to Wyndmere Hall. Her Grace, and the women, needed to be protected at all costs!

O'Malley mounted, and Flaherty followed suit. They rode to the cottage in silence.

"We'll find her, Eamon."

"We have to."

No one answered the door. Expecting trouble, given that Helen was missing and a murderer could be in the area, O'Malley dismounted. Flaherty did the same. It took a few moments for him to plan what he would do next.

"Flaherty, scout out the outbuilding. I'll take a closer look at the cottage."

Flaherty walked over to the small structure, while O'Malley peered in the cottage windows. It was not large inside, but appeared homey.

His cousin returned to his side. "There's an empty stall, and ruts indicating a wagon or carriage. Do ye want to wait?"

O'Malley clenched his hands into tight fists. The need to relieve his frustration at coming up empty for the second time in less than an hour had him by the throat. His throat constricted as his mind came up with all sorts of dire reasons the lass was not at the cottage. "Where in the bloody hell is the coachman—and, for that matter, the footman?"

Flaherty shrugged. "We'll find them all! The lass, the men— the duke's carriage and team of horses. Wait here. I'll ride toward the inn and see what I find."

O'Malley hadn't waited long when he heard a wagon and

hoofbeats approaching. Flaherty was riding alongside an open wagon being driven by a gray-haired woman.

"I came across Widow Dawson on me way to look for the duke's coachman."

The widow asked, "Did the Duke of Wyndmere really lend his coachman, and carriage, to Miss Langley?"

Flaherty nodded at her. "Aye, Mrs....?"

"Widow Dawson."

Flaherty nodded. "His Grace is a generous man." Turning to O'Malley, he said, "I found the coachman, but not the footman."

"I was summoned to the inn to tend to the driver of the carriage." Her expression showed her concern. "He was attacked from behind and has a huge lump on the back of his head."

"Thank ye for taking care of him." O'Malley shook his head. "Are ye certain there was only the one man?"

She answered without hesitation, "Yes."

"What of the horses?"

"They were unharmed," the widow answered. "Flaherty tells me you are also looking for a footman and a young woman, a Miss Langley."

"Aye. She was not where she was expected to be." O'Malley ignored the acid bubbling in his gut. "Flaherty here has arrived to escort us to Summerfield Chase. The duke's sister is married to Baron Summerfield. When we find Miss Langley, she'll be able to rest at the baron's estate before I escort her back to Wyndmere Hall."

"Will her maid be your chaperone? It would cause talk otherwise."

O'Malley bit back what he was about to say. The woman had no idea what the duke and his family had been through for the last few years, and it wasn't his place to discuss it. But he would set her straight on one important point. "There will be no talk about me intended. His Grace secured a special license for us. 'Tis in me pocket. We'll be married by the vicar after Helen has a chance to rest. Then we'll return to Wyndmere Hall."

Flaherty snorted, then coughed to cover his laughter. O'Malley sent him a look that promised he'd be punching him later. Flaherty grinned.

"Flaherty advised that the both of you are members of the Duke of Wyndmere's private guard," the widow said.

"That we are."

"He also confirmed what you just said, that Miss Langley is your intended. I still say that without a proper chaperone there could be talk."

"Mayhap ye'd be obliged to help stem the talk. The lass has suffered enough."

"Given what I heard at the inn, I agree with you. The dowager has been bitter for many years. I am sorry to hear that she treated Miss Langley in such a way…but she is not the first young woman to seek employment at Flemington Hall or Flemington Gatehouse that has been ostracized and vilified. How long has she been missing?"

"Since earlier today," O'Malley replied. "From what we discovered halfway between here and the gatehouse, we have reason to believe she was abducted."

The widow frowned. "I have been at the inn for a few hours. Otherwise, I may have noticed Miss Langley walking this way. You may be right, because I cannot imagine how far she would get on foot."

O'Malley was encouraged by the sympathetic expression on the older woman's face. "Then ye'll help us counter whatever rumors ye hear?"

She nodded and stood up. "I will, but first you need to find her."

O'Malley held out his hand. "Let me help ye down, then we'll unhitch the horse for ye."

Flaherty dismounted. "If ye could wait here, in case she has been turned around and wanders back."

"Of course. Poor woman. She must be devastated."

"We need to scour the area," O'Malley said. "Are there any

paths through the woods nearby?"

Her face lit up. "I'd nearly forgotten about that. There's an abandoned hunting lodge."

The men shared a look, and O'Malley asked, "How far from here?"

She paused to think. "A quarter of a mile or so. There's an overgrown path on the left. You'll miss it if you aren't looking for it. I don't think anyone has been to the lodge in years. The old duke used to have hunting parties there. Such a commotion and goings-on between Flemington Hall, the gatehouse, and the duke's hunting lodge back then. More than one inebriated lord tramped through my herb gardens."

"I'm sorry to hear that," O'Malley said. "Not all of Society acts like that."

"Aye," Flaherty agreed. "His Grace and his relations are all honorable men."

She slowly smiled. "It sounds as if the duke is a man of high moral fiber."

O'Malley mounted his horse. "The highest. Thank ye for yer suggestion. May we stop back here when we find Miss Langley? We may need yer help."

"Of course," the widow replied. "It's refreshing to hear how positive you are that you will find her. I pray it is so, and promise to have my poultices and herbs set out. Always pays to err on the side of caution."

With the violet-eyed beauty on his mind, and in his heart, O'Malley nodded to her. "Thank ye."

"I forgot to tell you!" the widow called out. "One of the serving maids at the inn told me a dark-haired man about your height was asking if anyone had seen two young women traveling together."

O'Malley's gut iced over. Two women. Emily and Helen. *Coincidence?* O'Malley did not believe in them. He had a feeling deep in his soul that Widow Dawson described the killer he and the rest of the guard had been searching for. "Did the stranger have any distinctive features?"

"The young woman mentioned a straight-ish nose, heavy, dark brows, and that he scowled. Especially when she told the man she hadn't seen two women without escort at the inn. She also told me that one of the stable lads mentioned a dark-haired stranger riding a roan gelding. Not sure if that will help."

"Thank ye, ye've been a great help."

Flaherty picked up his reins. "When I stopped by earlier, the hostler mentioned ye have yer son living with ye. Will he return soon?"

"I believe so. Do you need to speak to him too?"

O'Malley answered, "Nay, we're concerned with ye being alone while the stranger could be lurking about. Don't go anywhere unescorted."

She held his gaze long enough to have him wondering if she'd be disagreeable. Finally she inclined her head. "I am usually cautious around strangers. The two of you would be the exception."

O'Malley was humbled. "Thank ye for yer trust, Widow Dawson. Me ma would have me hide if I disrespected a woman. His Grace would have me drawn and quartered."

Her eyes rounded. "Would he?"

Flaherty shook his head. "O'Malley is known for stretching the truth. His Grace would not. But he may take one of us to task, or dismiss us from his guard."

"Make certain that ye alert yer son to what's happened," O'Malley warned. "We'll be back soon with Miss Langley and the blackguard who kidnapped her. We'll be needing to speak to the constable. The man is dangerous."

"Do you really believe he abducted Miss Langley?" the widow asked.

"Aye."

"I pray that you will find her soon. I overheard talk at the inn about the dowager's latest outrageous plans. No one should be treated that way, and I pray that it was just talk."

O'Malley frowned. "Ye mentioned that before. Just what did ye hear?"

"The dowager was incensed that the person who answered her advert was not what she purported to be and that the lord she worked for did not inherit his title. Apparently, the dowager duchess sent out a half a dozen messages to her closest circle."

"I take it she has done this before."

"She has. I think her heart shriveled up and shrank after her husband, the former duke, passed away. Well, that is neither here nor there. I shall be waiting and praying you find Miss Langley quickly."

Flaherty grumbled, "News travels fast... Gossip, faster."

"We need to find her before dusk falls," O'Malley said. "I pray she doesn't have extensive injuries."

"No matter what she has suffered, I will be ready to tend to her wounds," the widow replied.

"Thank ye." He and Flaherty urged their horses to a fast trot. They didn't have far to go, but that did not stop O'Malley from asking for a bit of divine intervention. For good measure, he rubbed the side of the stallion's neck and urged it, "We've got to find her, laddie."

Flaherty clenched his jaw. "We *will* find her."

They rode in the direction of the inn, keeping an eye out for the path into the woods that would lead them to the duke's abandoned hunting lodge...and Helen.

"There!" Flaherty shouted, pointing to the nearly obscured path.

O'Malley led the way, with a prayer in his heart that she would be there. "Hang on, lass. I'm coming for ye!"

# CHAPTER ELEVEN

HELEN FLOATED NEAR consciousness and struggled to open her eyes. Her mind slowly cleared, and she prayed she would remember what had happened after she tripped, but for a moment her mind was blank. Then she recalled the humiliating conversation with the dowager. She shuddered just thinking of having to walk back toward Flemington Hall, intent on finding the cottage the butler told her about. Why had the dowager duchess dismissed the duke's coachman without telling her? And why in Heaven's name would she make Helen walk when she'd arrived in the Duke of Wyndmere's carriage? Everyone else respected the duke, so why didn't the dowager?

Her eyes opened, and the face staring down at her brought it all back. She was being held by the dark man hovering over her because of Baron Hardwell. His eyebrows connected into one thick line as he frowned at her. How could she have escaped the baron once, only to be tracked down by the man's henchman and held for ransom? Thank goodness Emily was safe. Garahan would not let anything more happen to her.

Mulling over everything that had happened since she and Emily arrived at the duke's estate, she wondered if she had made the wrong decision striking out on her own, when she had had an offer of protection and marriage—from an honorable, strong, handsome Irishman.

She dismissed that thought. O'Malley did not know of her past. A man in his position could never marry someone like her. She concentrated on what she needed to find—the coachman. The cottage.

She barely registered that she'd mumbled the words aloud.

"What cottage?" This time when she heard the deep voice, a sliver of unease slithered through her belly. She acknowledged the emotion, but did not give in to it. She had faced down the devil—Baron Hardwell—and could hold her own against the man who held her captive.

At least her vision was clear, though her chin ached. She shifted on the pallet where she lay and immediately wished she hadn't. Her wrist throbbed. It would make escaping more of a challenge, but she would not be cowed by the man hovering over her. His presence unnerved her, but so far, he had only mentioned coin, not what he would do if there was none forthcoming. Would the duke pay the ransom...for her?

She shivered, realizing the man had been speaking to her. "I'm sorry, what did you ask?"

"Is your traveling companion waiting for you at the cottage?"

The depth and tone of the man's voice now had a hard edge to it. She'd best answer him. "I did not have a traveling companion. I came at the dowager's request...but then she told me to leave."

He clenched his jaw and glared at her. "I'm not talking about the dowager. I want to know about the other woman!"

"There is no other woman." The ache in her chin was spreading along her jawline. She ignored it and fought to hide her fear of the man. "You misunderstood what you heard when I mentioned the cottage. I was told by the dowager's butler that there was one just out of sight, beyond the gates to the estate. Is that where I am?"

"Is she hiding at the cottage?"

Her heart sank to her toes. Had the man been hit on the head one too many times? Why else would he insist on asking about another woman, when Helen had told him that she had traveled alone? From the man's very mien, she did not think he planned to hold his temper for much longer. Nor would he help her. What, then, did he intend to do with her? "Who are you talking about?"

"Bloody hell! Montrose's daughter! Her life was worth that bag of coin he already paid me to end it. But she escaped, and I was not able to fulfill my end of the bargain. The baron will see that I am paid double if I capture her. You are going to be the way I lure her from where she is hiding."

Bile sloshed in her belly. *Emily!* She needed to protect her friend, and the babe she carried, at all costs. She would never agree to help him. "I think you overestimate her loyalty to me."

"We shall see. Until I have Montrose's daughter, I'm keeping you." His gaze dipped below her chin and settled on the swell of her bosom before he looked into her eyes. "I'm certain I can find a way to entertain myself…until the ransom is paid."

Helen prayed her stomach would not rebel at his inference. "How long do you intend to wait?"

He tipped up her chin. Her skin crawled at his touch, and ached when he pressed on the sore spot on her chin. She flinched and jerked to the side to escape his painful hold, fighting against the feeling of dread that filled her. She would fight, if she had to. The realization that she had no idea where she was nauseated her. She was far from those she knew and trusted. She ached in so many places, but what hurt the most was her heart.

*O'Malley.*

Thoughts of the broad-shouldered guard had her wondering if she would have been captured and held for ransom if she'd been caught walking in the village of Windermere. Had this man been lying in wait for Emily or herself for long, or had he just arrived? Had he followed her from the Lake District to the Borderlands?

She knew in that instant that she'd had made a grave error in judgment leaving Wyndmere Hall. The intensity in the brilliant green eyes of the man who'd offered his protection filled her mind.

*Lord, why did I refuse O'Malley's offer?*

Her captor glared at her and took a step closer to where she lay. She braced her weight on one hand, intent on trying to move away from him, but her wrist buckled. A sharp pain sliced through the injured joint as it began to throb in earnest.

Helen willed her tears not to fall. She had not had the chance to look at her wrist yet. A quick glance had her head swimming and her hopes flagging. She could not tell if her wrist was sprained or broken just by looking at it, though it had begun to bruise and swell. She carefully touched her wrist to see if the bones felt out of place, and spots swam before her eyes. *Not a good sign.*

She did not want to let her kidnapper know how frightened she was, but she did need to know if he intended to do anything about her injuries. "If you're keeping me, do you plan to bind my wrist?"

The dark-haired man's grim expression worried her. There was not an ounce of concern in his black-as-night eyes. "I haven't decided yet."

"Would you let someone else bind it for me?"

"The closest physician is an hour away on horseback, longer by carriage."

Would he leave her here alone to fetch the physician? Could she escape then? She had to try—how else would anyone find her? She had no idea where she was, or how much time had passed since she left the dowager's home. It was as dark inside the building as it was outside the window. When she escaped— because staying here with this madman was not an option—she would have to dig deep and use her will to survive to force herself to walk...to run...no matter how much pain she was in. Helen knew she had to try, because she would not give in. If she fell down, she would get up. If he caught up with her, she would scratch at his eyes, kick his shins, or, Heaven help her, knee him where all men had a weakness. Dear Lord, she hoped it would not come to that, but Lord Montrose had instructed her and Emily to use that as a means of defending themselves. She was resourceful, and knew there would be somewhere to hide, but first she had to cause a distraction to prevent him from following her... But what?

"There is, however, a local woman who tends to those in need. I suppose if I want to collect the full ransom, I may have to contemplate bringing her here, once darkness falls." He locked gazes with her, his expression now unreadable. "If you lose the use of your hand because the bones are broken and do not heal properly, you could develop a fever from infection and die. Then I won't get paid."

His words horrified her. Fear sliced clear to her bones. She absorbed the emotion and then tucked it into a box to open up and worry about later. The thought of becoming crippled, losing the use of her hand, terrified her. It was that terror that galvanized Helen's vow to fight to her last ounce of strength, and last drop of her blood, if that was the Lord's plan for her. O'Malley slipped into her mind once again, this time wrenching a heartfelt prayer from her: *Dear Lord, I need Eamon to save me!*

She lifted her hand to her face, and he slapped it away. "Your hands are covered in dirt! I mean to get paid. Like broken bones that don't heal, if your face gets an infection because you rubbed dirt in it..." He leaned close and grabbed hold of her sore wrist again until she cried out in pain. "I won't get paid. And if I don't get paid...you die!"

Her captor reminded her of Baron Hardwell—soulless. Heartless! Completely, totally mad! Drawing in a breath and slowly exhaling helped her regain her composure and control her fear. "Do you have water that I may wash with?"

He looked bored, as if she were a stain on his waistcoat that refused to wash out. "No."

"A clean cloth?"

He glared at her. She took the look, and lack of response, to mean that he had no clean cloths either. At least he had not bound her hands together. Did he plan to now that she was awake? She'd have to be very cautious and move slowly so that she did not startle the man.

The longer he stared at her without speaking, the deeper her fear, but she could not give in to it. Needing to occupy her mind with thoughts—any thoughts—she concentrated on Wyndmere Hall. Her reasons for leaving the position she had enjoyed—watching the duke and duchess's twins, caring for Patrick and Gwendolyn's babe—no longer held validity. Not in the face of her abduction, or the realization that if her kidnapper would not be paid the ransom, he promised that she would die. But how?

Her mind raced. There were so many different ways that she could die. Without food or water, she could die of starvation or thirst. If the cuts on her face, or a broken bone in her wrist, got infected, that could kill her too. The way he had leered at her got under her skin like a sliver of wood until her heart began to pound—she would fight him! Helen knew she would welcome the beating if he chose to take his frustrations out on her...but she would never, ever submit to him.

Those dire thoughts circled around and around in her head until she thought she'd scream. Suddenly, a still, small voice inside of her whispered O'Malley's name. Why hadn't she had the common courtesy to have a conversation with him before leaving Wyndmere Hall? There was a chance that she could have gauged his reaction as she confessed her past, and stopped before confessing all of it. At least she would have known whether the man would have accepted her, despite her childhood thievery.

That voice whispered again, reminding her of the duke's magnanimous offer to welcome her back. She *did* have some-where to go, someone who cared for and about her, but did the duke know of her past? His Grace was a cautious man, who protected his family with every means at his disposal. He would use his connections to Bow Street, and those through Captain Coventry. No doubt he would have had information on all of Lord Montrose's staff before he sent Aiden Garahan and the others to escort Emily to the Lake District. The duke was known for planning down to the minute details. He would have had to know.

Did O'Malley know? If he did, why would he offer for her? In her mind, he could not know. She could not bear it if he rejected her because of her past. A hint of what he must have felt when she rejected *his* offer of marriage nauseated her. Helen needed to apologize! When she saw him again—if she saw him again—she would swallow her pride and apologize for refusing his suit...without giving him the explanation as to why.

She should have done that in the first place. It would have been the decent and correct thing to do. But she had been afraid that he would not accept her, even though she was more than just the woman who had worked as Emily's maid and companion. Not all of it was something she was proud of. She had had a troubled family and lost them, and had a brief stint picking pockets on Bond Street until she bumped into Lord Montrose, and he realized what she was doing. But he had not turned her over to the Watch. He had given her a second chance, had given her a position on his staff that helped her rebuild her pride in a job well done. Something thievery had not engendered.

Even though she knew she did not have to continue to believe she was alone and without a soul who cared for her, one question continued to pound in her brain: would O'Malley have accepted her anyway, or would he have shunned her?

The possibility of the latter had had her skulking away, like the thief that she was. She never said goodbye to him! Her headache trebled in intensity. What if he did not shun her—what if he could accept the reasons she had turned to crime when she had no other way to obtain food?

If she escaped...*when* she escaped, if she did not have the chance to speak with him, she would pen a note to O'Malley and apologize for the angst she'd put him through. He deserved far better than her, but the feelings rioting in her breast right now had everything to do with the handsome guard and not fear of her captor.

Her mind still on O'Malley, she reasoned that if she spoke of her childhood, the loss of her father and then her mother, he would understand the reasons she felt that they would not suit. Her past breaking the law—and her unsuitability as a proper wife for a man of his caliber—were still at the forefront. Still the reason why she could not marry him.

Her mind began to wander, but kept coming back to the same question—*why* had the man abducted her? She had been alone, walking, not riding in the duke's carriage. How would he have known of her connection with someone who had the coin to pay a ransom?

The answer was plain as day—he had followed her from Wyndmere Hall.

While she was turning all of these thoughts over in her mind, her captor had walked toward one of the windows that looked out into the dense woods tucked around the abandoned lodge. She took a moment to study her surroundings. It was small. One room... No loft... One door, and two windows on either side of the cottage. A table with three legs, and one chair, leaned against the wall beneath the other window.

The cold seeping up through the pallet she lay on in front of the stone fireplace had her shivering. Not wanting to attract his attention by shifting to pull the thin linen cover over her exposed shoulder, she lay still. Any sound might call attention to her and have him returning to taunt her, or to spew more of his contempt.

She should not have worried about it—of his own volition, he spun around and strode toward her.

"Sit up."

The thick rope in his hands had her swallowing the bile that rushed up her throat. She would not disgrace herself in front of the man by casting up her accounts! With an eye on the rope, she tried to comply, but her wrist gave out again.

He muttered a curse, bent down on one knee, and yanked her

upright. Grabbing her hands in his much larger one, he wound the rope around her wrists. She flinched. The rope burned as it rubbed the underside of her wrists. Not wanting to watch him tie the knot, she averted her eyes, and a flash of movement in the window behind him caught her eye.

A heartbeat later, both windows exploded! The resounding crash and flying shards of glass distracted her captor, and gave her the courage she needed to escape. A roar that sounded like that of a large, wild animal filled the window and then bounced off the walls, as a broad figure dressed in black dove into the cottage. His auburn hair and fierce expression had her heart leaping to her throat, until she noticed the golden harp and emerald-green *Eire* embroidered on his frockcoat...over his heart. Just like O'Malley's!

She struggled to her feet, braced a hand to the wall, and dug deep to ignore the tearing pain shooting through her wrist. Biting her lip, she put distance between herself and where her captor and the auburn-haired member of the duke's guard fought. Would he set her free? With her back to the wall, she inched her way to the other window, stumbling twice, but catching herself before she fell. Her half boots crunched on the broken glass in counterpoint to the sound of flesh pounding flesh. Finally, she felt the edge of the window frame. Her prayer of thanks was cut off when strong hands wrapped around her waist and pulled her backward through the window!

"Ye're safe now, lass."

The voice she'd never thought to hear again soothed her jagged nerves. She was spun around until she could look into the eyes of her rescuer. "O'Malley! How did you find me?"

He brushed a lock of hair out of her eyes and gently took hold of her hands, swearing when she cried out in pain. "Where are ye hurt, lass?"

"Please, don't leave me here?"

"I did not come all this way just to leave ye behind, lass. Where are ye hurt?"

Helen didn't answer him fast enough. He grabbed hold of her wrists, and she groaned.

"Forgive me, lass, but if ye'd have answered me..." He gentled his hold on her. "Which wrist?"

"The right one."

"Is that yer only injury?" She shook her head and moaned, while he frowned. "Where else?"

"My chin aches, and the side of my face stings."

He gently cupped her face and studied her closely. "Ye've a few cuts and scrapes, nothing deep." Helen started to lift her hand, and O'Malley took hold of it. "Yer hands have a bit of dirt and grit on them—'tis best not to get any of that on yer face. Let's get ye out of here. I've arranged for ye to be tended to."

"How did you know where to find me?"

"There aren't that many roads north to Flemington Gatehouse." His expression darkened. "From the look of yer hands, and the disturbed dirt Flaherty and I found where ye tried to save yerself when ye tripped over that rock in the road, we guessed someone must have come up from behind ye."

"How did you know? Were you there? If you were, why did you let him take me?"

"Ah, lass, did ye hit yer head then?"

"I don't... No, I did not! I was grabbed from behind and a large hand covered my mouth and nose."

O'Malley gritted his teeth, then cleared his throat to speak. "Could be the terror of what happened that has ye rattled, lass. Ye're not thinking straight if ye believe that of me. I was not there, and I never would let any blackguard abduct ye." He reached into his frockcoat pocket and pulled out a black cloth. "Easy now, while I wrap this around your poor wrist."

"Is that a cravat?"

"Aye, the lads and I carry spares—they're handy for binding wounds, or tying a blackguard's hands together." He trailed the tip of his finger along the line of her jaw and tapped her chin. "'Twill only take a moment. If it helps, close yer faery eyes, lass."

She did without hesitation, trusting him, while he immobilized the joint with the cravat. She could not hide her wince of pain as he fastened the knot. "I'm sorry to cause ye discomfort, but we need to ensure that if yer wrist bones are cracked, or broken, that they don't shift out of place." He lifted her in his arms and carried her over to a fallen tree...a distance away from the building. Setting her on it, he warned, "I'll try not to hurt ye, but I need to fashion a sling for ye, and I need both hands to do that."

She was silent as he moved her arm. "Hold it against yer waist for a moment. There's a lass. I've already used me spare, and will have to use the one I'm wearing. I hope ye don't mind." Helen watched as he removed the cloth from around his neck and explained, "I'm going to slide a corner of me cravat under yer arm now." He paused and told her, "I'm not after startling ye, lass, but I cannot fashion a knot behind yer neck without moving the hair that slipped from its pins."

She lost the ability to speak, positively mesmerized by the intensity in his eyes and the sight of his strong neck. She nodded.

"I need to pull ye closer, lass, otherwise I may bump yer wrist, which I do not want to do. May I?"

Her gaze locked on his, and this time she answered, "Yes."

Helen could not look away from the width of his neck and muscles of his throat.

His voice rough, he grumbled, "Ye'd best stop looking at me like that, lass. 'Tis not the time or place to be thinking what ye're thinking."

She licked her dry lips. Even in the waning light, she could see that his eyes had darkened. "How do you know what I am thinking?"

"Ah, sweet Helen, ye're innocent to be sure if ye're asking me that. I'll kiss ye senseless once I tie off this knot. Mayhap it'll satisfy yer curiosity until Flaherty and I deliver ye to Widow Dawson."

Confused, she wondered if the widow was a close friend of

O'Malley's. She had heard that some bachelors preferred forming an attachment with a widow rather than an unmarried woman. The thought of him with another woman had her rubbing the ache in her heart.

"Are ye feeling pain in yer chest?"

The concern and intensity of his gaze had her answering honestly. "I am."

"How long has it been happening?" She didn't answer quickly enough. He took hold of her arms and pulled her closer. "Yer heart may be reacting to yer fear, but it could be something more serious, lass. Answer me question!"

Unable to control the reaction she always had whenever she was worried, she bit her bottom lip.

"God in Heaven, lass. Don't be biting yer lip now!"

It was then that it hit her... O'Malley was not just worried about her. He cared for her...mayhap even deeply! "Which would you have me do first, answer your question or stop biting my lip?"

He scooped her into his arms, stared deeply into her eyes, and lowered his mouth toward hers. His lips hovered over hers for a heartbeat. With a moan, he took her mouth in a possessive, devastating kiss that numbed her body from head to toe. The last thing she remembered was the wondrous thought that O'Malley had indeed kissed her senseless.

⟫⟫⟩⟨⟨⟨

FLAHERTY STUCK HIS head out of the window and swore. "What did ye do to the poor lass? She was standing when I grabbed hold of her captor. 'Twasn't me job to keep an eye on her, while I roughed him up a bit. 'Twas *yers!*"

O'Malley ignored the question. "I pulled her through the window and had to use both me cravats. One to bind her wrist, the other for a sling. I cannot tell if it's sprained or broken. We need to get her to Widow Dawson."

Flaherty stared at the woman in O'Malley's arms. "She looks like she's sleeping peacefully."

"I think it's her injuries, and having the life scared out of her. She'll come round in a moment or two."

Flaherty climbed out of the window, reached back inside, and tugged his prisoner by the arm to pull him through. "Ah, well now, that makes sense. Poor lass."

"Who do you think you are?' the battered man grumbled. "You'll pay for laying a hand on me. I have connections!"

"Well now, as I'm in an accommodating mood, I'll tell ye we're members of the Duke of Wyndmere's private guard," O'Malley replied. When the lass stirred in his arms, he glanced at her face and watched her eyelashes flutter. Ignoring her for a moment, he told their prisoner, "We have connections and the law on our side. Ye'll be answering for the fact that we found ye in this abandoned hunting lodge, about to tie off the knot on the ropes ye placed around Miss Langley's wrists."

Flaherty sent O'Malley a look out of the side of his eye—a sly look that Flaherty was fond of using when he meant to confuse one of their prisoners. "Well now, if ye tell us yer name, we might be letting ye go with a warning."

"Warning? I'll have the both of you arrested!"

O'Malley and Flaherty ignored him. "I don't think we can just let the man go," O'Malley said, keeping up with Flaherty's game of misdirection. "Even if he tells us his name and that he worked for Hardwell. Besides, the poor lass is coming to. I know she will attest to what happened to her and our actions rescuing her."

"Yes," Helen rasped. "I certainly will!"

"What do you know about the baron?" the prisoner asked.

Flaherty and O'Malley glared at the man, who must have realized he'd said too much. He shifted from foot to foot.

"I don't recall saying 'baron'—did ye, Flaherty?"

"Ye didn't, and neither did I. Neither did the lass."

"Well then," O'Malley said, "I'm thinking this bleeding bugger has more than a passing connection with Hardwell. Probably works for the man."

"Just because I took coin—" The man's face grayed.

The bleeding bugger realized he'd just damned himself, confirming what they suspected. He *was* the blackguard Wilson, and had all but confessed to the crime.

O'Malley grabbed the man by his collar with his free hand and shook him hard enough to rattle his brains. This was the man responsible for the death of Lord Montrose! "Did ye follow the lass from the Lake District, Wilson?"

O'Malley had been present more than once to see the face of a condemned man as he faced the gallows. 'Twas the expression he saw on the man's face now. Though Wilson didn't admit to the name, O'Malley knew the only way the man could have found the lass was to have followed her here from the duke's estate.

"Flaherty, take the lass for a moment." He passed her off to his cousin then turned back to the man he still had a hold of. Tightening his grip, O'Malley shook the bastard harder. "Ye'll be joining us on a short trip to the village to speak to the constable, and then on to Summerfield Chase. His lordship will be waiting to speak to ye, and mayhap one of our connections from Bow Street will make the trip up to interrogate ye. Have no fear, arrangements will be made for yer transportation to London." O'Malley leaned close to the prisoner and pitched his voice low so the lass wouldn't hear him. "'Tis where ye'll answer for the charge of murder."

"I did not murder anyone. That's a lie!"

O'Malley wanted to strangle the man for shouting out what he'd wanted to keep from the lass. He glanced over his shoulder at Flaherty, who frowned. Helen quickly looked away. Judging from the tears in her eyes, she had to have heard. Turning back to the man, he ground out, "I never lie."

"'Tis part of our vow to the duke," Flaherty said. "None of us lies. Ye'd best rethink yer plan to plea that 'tis all a mistake, because every one of Captain Coventry's men, Gavin King of the Bow Street Runners, and the duke and his connections know veracity is part of the oath we took when we joined the duke's guard."

"We have two witnesses who saw someone fitting yer description the night ye shoved Lord Montrose into the path of a fast-moving carriage. He died from his injuries." O'Malley turned to Flaherty and said, "I'm thinking our man here didn't know that His Grace, the Duke of Wyndmere, would do anything to protect his ward. He was named guardian to Montrose's daughter." He turned back to Wilson. "His Grace means to see that ye pay for yer crime."

"You'll never be able to prove it."

O'Malley wanted nothing more than to club the blackguard in the gob. "We'll be adding kidnapping to the charges against ye."

Wilson's mouth hung open a moment before he clamped it shut.

O'Malley was satisfied for the moment. They'd gleaned enough information to add weight to the already damning evidence Gavin King had. O'Malley noted the hatred in Wilson's expression and was satisfied the man knew he was well and truly caught. He would pay for his crimes.

"Well now, the trip to Summerfield Chase will be more pleasurable if he doesn't talk."

Flaherty sent a knowing look at O'Malley and passed Helen back to him.

O'Malley nodded and held the lass to his heart, prompting Flaherty to ask, "Why don't ye tell me what really happened back there?"

"If ye must know," O'Malley grumbled, "she swooned after I kissed her." Flaherty's knowing grin irritated him. "Don't say another word!"

"That might work on someone who isn't related to ye, Eamon. I'll be telling ye what I think whether ye like it or not.

We've all heard about the way the two of ye couldn't keep yer eyes off one another the day Garahan arrived with the woman he loved."

O'Malley should not have been shocked to learn that had spread this far north. "Were there rumors in the village?"

Helen gasped. "People near Summerfield Chase are spreading rumors about Eamon and I?"

Flaherty grinned. "No need to listen to or spread rumors. Aiden's wife shared the news in a letter she wrote to her sister-in-law, Darby's wife, who delighted in passing on the news to Ryan's. Ye know not one of the Garahans can keep their gobs shut where our sainted O'Malley cousins are concerned. Neither can their wives."

"Neither Emily nor I have met their wives," Helen whispered.

"Don't start up with that moniker again," O'Malley warned. "O'Ghill never should have said it to Ryan. All the Garahans, and now yerself, have taken to using it."

Flaherty ignored him and continued. "Too many of the men in the duke's guard are falling, too fast for me liking, and for the lasses they're rescuing. And before ye get yer dander up, I'll tell ye I believe 'tis a good thing."

O'Malley stifled the urge to pop Flaherty in the mouth, suppressing it when he saw nothing but sincerity in his cousin's eyes.

"Thank you, Flaherty."

Flaherty stared at Helen for a moment. "Not at all, lass. Kiss her again, O'Malley—I want to see if she swoons."

Helen frowned. "I am sorry I thanked you, Flaherty."

O'Malley looked from Flaherty to the lass and back. "Are ye both out of yer minds?"

"'Twill be like a fairytale. The handsome duke's guard kissing his lady love awake. Go on!" Flaherty urged.

O'Malley did not want to admit that he was tempted, but a glance at the lovely lass in his arms—with the bruise on her chin and scrapes on the side of her face—pulled at him. But it was the glare in her eyes that had him reminding his dull-witted cousin, "She's wide awake and her temper's on the rise."

"Will you please stop talking about me as if I am insensate?"

O'Malley's admiration for the lass grew, as did the feelings rioting inside of him. He stopped fighting against what he felt. She'd already suffered so much already, and had been ridiculed by the dowager and become the subject of rumor and innuendo because of that vile woman.

"Forgive me, Helen."

The poor lass may have a broken bone, and all because of her need to leave in search of a position where she'd be too far away from him to protect her. Why couldn't she have stayed at Wyndmere Hall? The overwhelming need to coddle her, protect her, and love her filled him. He brushed his lips across hers in a featherlight kiss…an angel's kiss.

"Mayhap next time, lass, ye'll not be running away from me. I could have protected ye from this happening."

"He would have followed the trail to Wyndmere Hall—I'd feel even worse if he somehow got inside and threatened Her Grace or her babes, or Gwendolyn and her babe."

"She's got a point there, O'Malley," Flaherty admitted.

O'Malley's heart thundered behind his ribs. Worry for the lass and what could have happened at Wyndmere Hall had him by the bollocks.

"Forget about what could have happened, lass. We need to tend to ye and yer injuries." He'd noticed rope burns when he bandaged her wrist. It must have happened after the blackguard wrapped the rope around them. He had watched Wilson from the window. The man was still holding tight to the rope when Flaherty tugged him away from the lass. *Bloody, fecking bugger* should have let go of his end. If he had, the lass wouldn't be suffering now.

Worry such as he'd never known lanced through him. As gently as possible, he traced the tip of his finger across one arched brow and then the other. "Trust me, lass. I'll protect ye… I need ye." He nearly shouted with relief when she frowned. "That's the way, Helen-lass. Irritated or happy—I'll take either emotion, if ye'd just say ye'll have me."

She met his gaze and whispered, "I've been dreaming of you."

He ignored Flaherty's grunt of satisfaction—he was too busy smiling, and didn't bother to hide it. "Have ye now?"

She licked her lips, and he wished there was a pitcher, or cup even, of water to offer her. But there hadn't been a source of water in the small abode. They were surrounded by dense forest, and there was no water source nearby that they'd noticed on the path leading to the hunting lodge. Water for the lass would have to wait until he could get her to Widow Dawson. Thankfully, they did not have far to go.

"Ye can have a bit of water as soon as we arrive at Widow Dawson's home." He turned to Flaherty. "I'll ride ahead with the lass. I'm thinking the prisoner needs a bit of time to reflect on his sins. Do ye have enough rope to tie around Wilson's waist with a bit of length left over to hold? Ye can let him walk beside ye, while ye ride yer horse to the widow's cottage. 'Tis what I'd do."

"Ah, we think alike, O'Malley. I'm hoping her son has returned. Never hurts to have an extra pair of hands."

"The blackguard is going to pay for thinking he could just take ye," he told Helen.

"I vaguely remember his grabbing my sore wrist and pinching my chin where it hit the ground." Her eyes welled with tears. "Then his huge, gloved hand covered my nose and mouth—I couldn't breathe. I'm sorry that I left without saying goodbye to you, O'Malley."

Tears welled in her eyes again, tying O'Malley's gut into knots. "Don't be crying now, lass. Ye're safe."

"Thank you, Eamon."

He nodded. She was a bonny lass, even with the scrapes and light bruising on her pretty face. Her other injury was worrisome until the widow verified what he feared—that her wrist was broken. Even if it wasn't, he planned to reciprocate, and give the bugger Wilson a few bruises and mayhap a broken bone of his own.

O'Malley tamped down on his building anger—he would be speaking to the prisoner alone later and would leave his mark on the man then.

'Twas time to get moving. The lass's eyes appeared clearer than they had a few moments ago. "Now then, Helen-lass, as far as I can see it, we have two choices here."

"Two?"

Lord, she was adorable the way her nose wrinkled when she frowned. He pressed his lips to the tip of it, and she sighed. "As I was saying, two choices. I can toss ye over me shoulder, or ye can ride in me lap. Which do ye prefer?"

The emotion in her violet eyes captivated him. The yearning...the hesitation...the *trust*. "I would like to ride in your lap. I think I'd be dizzy if I were upside down over your shoulder."

"On me lap, then." When she nodded, he admitted, "That's me preferred way to deliver ye to the Widow Dawson's cottage. She's promised to tend to yer wounds. I'm thinking ye'll want something to eat. From me impression of the woman, she'll want to feed ye, too. Then we'll see if there is a wagon we can borrow—or buy—to transport the prisoner to Summerfield Chase."

Her expression changed to one of worry.

"What has ye worried now, lass?"

"Will you be leaving me behind?"

He gently cupped her chin. "Not on yer life. From this day forward, ye'll go where I go."

"But that would be scandalous!"

He stared into her eyes, waiting for her to realize his intention. She bit her bottom lip, sending a shaft of heat from his heart to his gut.

"Not if we're married. Will ye have me as yer protector, yer husband, the man who'll kiss ye good night, and good morning, every day for the rest of our lives?"

She hesitated, and he struggled not to groan as impatience warred with the knowledge that he should not press the lass. She had to accept him of her own free will. But O'Malley wanted her answer—now! At this moment, he wanted nothing more than to mold his mouth to hers, drink from her lips, and swallow her sighs—but she had to willingly agree to marry him first.

"Will ye, lass?"

She blinked, and sorrow filled her gaze.

His gut felt as if he swallowed the shards of glass that littered the floor of the abandoned cottage...they sliced him from the inside out.

She was going to refuse...again!

Braced for her rejection, he straightened, shutting down the hope that had been vibrating inside of him a moment before. He had his pride and would not beg her to marry him!

"Before I answer, I need to tell you about my past. You have a right to know. When you do"—her voice broke—"you will retract your offer."

*Not in this lifetime.* Then her words hit him and he nearly crowed with victory. She did not say nay!

He kept his expression neutral, because it would not do for his bride-to-be to think he was ignoring the seriousness of her words. O'Malley's world once again made sense. And in that moment, he knew what worried the lass.

Lifting her onto the back of his horse, he leaned close and whispered, "If ye're worried about that wee bit of thievery, and pockets ye picked, I know all about it."

Her gasp of shock had him chuckling. Her frown had him clearing his throat.

"How long have ye known?"

O'Malley told her the truth: "Since we learned of Lord Montrose's will, naming the duke as Emily's ward. Coventry and King wanted to ensure that Emily was safe—even from her staff. His Grace authorized the captain and King to look into their backgrounds. Her safety was paramount to the duke—and to us." Her look of confusion had O'Malley nearly at the end of his patience. "Is that a problem?"

"Why didn't you say anything?"

"I did not realize it would be an impediment to yer accepting me offer. Are ye thinking I should have told ye when I asked ye to marry me the first time?"

"You didn't ask me," she reminded him. "You said, and I quote, 'That would be me.'"

And there was the feisty lass he'd come to love. O'Malley knew then she wouldn't be refusing him a third time. "Aye, in answer to yer question of who would marry someone like you…let me repeat, that would be me."

When she remained silent, he slipped an arm around her waist and pulled her flush against him. He needed her to hear him—nay, to *listen* to him! Her dazed look of hope, and desire, nearly drove him to his knees.

Calling on all of his control, he told her what was in his heart: "I'm proud of what ye've overcome. Impressed by the way ye turned yer life around when given the chance by his lordship. Ye've a work ethic that matches me own, a loving way with babes and little ones, and a heart of gold, lass. I'll never love another like I love ye. Ye're *mo chroí, mo ghrá.*"

She stared up at him with tear-bright eyes. "You're certain that you won't change your mind?"

"Never." He gave in to need and kissed her with a tenderness that had her melting against him. O'Malley would remember this moment till he died. "I promise to cherish ye and any babes the Lord blesses us with, Helen-lass." Deeping the kiss, supping from her lush mouth, he nearly groaned when she placed her hands to his chest and gently pushed. *God in Heaven, what now?*

"Would you answer just one more question?"

His bride-to-be had an irritating habit of asking questions when he needed to be kissing her. But he loved that irritation as well as her spine of steel. O'Malley imagined winning her over without words…but now was not the time… *Later.* He kissed the tip of her nose. "Ask away, lass."

"What do *mo chroi* and *mo ghrá* mean?"

"Ye're me heart, me love." Everything she felt was right there in her violet eyes. "Say yes, Helen-lass."

"Yes."

His heart stumbled to his feet and then jumped back up behind his ribs. "Yes?"

She put her arm around his neck. "Yes, Eamon O'Malley, I would be honored to marry you."

He spun around, shouting, "Did ye hear that, Flaherty?"

"Aye, and so did Lady Phoebe and his lordship all the way back in Summerfield-on-Eden."

O'Malley didn't care that his cousin was ribbing him. Nothing mattered at the moment beyond the fact that the woman who'd had a hold of his heart from the moment he set eyes on her had agreed to marry him.

He mounted his horse, pulled her onto his lap, and wrapped an arm around her. "Ye can close yer eyes and rest. 'Tis but a short trip. We'll see that ye're tended to and send missives off to His Grace, and the others, that ye have been found and that we've apprehended Lord Montrose's murderer. Though I'll ask Flaherty to do that while I offer me two hands to help the widow if she needs them."

Just when he thought she'd remain silent the rest of the ride back to the cottage, she whispered, "Thank you, Eamon."

"Sure and ye'd be welcome, lass."

"Eamon?"

"Aye?"

"I was afraid to tell you how I felt, for fear that you would revile me."

"Never, lass. I couldn't."

"Why?"

"Because I love ye, lass. With the whole of me heart."

She snuggled into the curve of his arm and sighed. "Do you

know what, Eamon?"

"What?"

"I love you too."

He kissed the top of her head, inhaling the faint scent of wild roses and sunshine. A scent that would always remind him of the moment the woman he loved professed her love in return. As they rode, he let the warmth of her words sink into his heart...all the way to his soul.

*Thank ye, Lord, for the gift of her love. I'll protect the lass with me life and surround her with me love...until I breathe me last.*

# CHAPTER TWELVE

WIDOW DAWSON OPENED the door to her cottage as O'Malley swung his leg over his horse and smoothly dismounted with Helen in his arms. The widow paused, blinked, then opened the door wide to admit them. If the woman was surprised that he could dismount with someone in his arms, she'd obviously never met any of the men in the duke's guard. Strength and agility were essential in the performance of their duty.

O'Malley appreciated the way the woman schooled her features after a quick glance at Helen. He didn't want the lass to worry about her injuries before Widow Dawson even unwrapped them. "We found her right where ye said to look. But there was no water nearby. Do ye need me to fetch some from yer well?"

"I already drew water from the well and have a large pot heating on the stovetop, and a pitcher of water for drinking on the table." She nodded at the oak table in the kitchen area. "Why don't you set Miss Langley on the chair by the table and wash up while I fetch her a cup?"

As if she were made of glass, O'Malley set Helen on the chair. He kissed the top of her head, then walked over to the alcove by the back door where the pitcher and bowl sat on a small table. Though he did not want to contribute to the conversation between the women, he felt justified in listening to what they were saying.

Helen's safety was more important than her privacy, given the danger that had been following her from the moment Garahan arrived at Montrose House to protect Emily. Besides, Helen was to be his wife, and they would be privy to one another's conversations once they wed. Well—at least *he* would be privy to hers. A good many of his conversations revolved around the duke and his family, and he would not be sharing those with anyone.

O'Malley walked over to stand beside Helen, who drank the water greedily. When her hands holding the cup trembled, he steadied her, wrapping his hands around hers, mindful of her wrist. His palms tingled from the contact. Waiting for her to finish her drink, he nodded to the widow. "I'm ready if ye need me."

Widow Dawson worked quickly, beginning with the fabric he'd wrapped around the lass's wrist first. Helen flinched when the cravat loosened. It took all of his control to hide his reaction from her—she needed his strength, not his concern as to the severity of her wound. Though a glance at the deep purple of the bruise and swelling were indicative of a break, which would take longer to heal.

"I need that larger bowl of hot water. The first thing I need to do is wash her arms and hands." The older woman was careful to keep any expression out of her gaze. He appreciated that. "I will need your help with that."

O'Malley was on his feet in an instant, returning with the bowl of water. He placed it near the widow's elbow. A glance at Helen had him realizing the poor woman had begun to tremble. It was either the shock of all she had been through...or a reaction he'd seen happen with a broken bone. She would not be able to hold herself still. A delayed reaction from all that she'd suffered since leaving the dowager's had begun to set in.

The widow took a cloth from the stack on the table, dipped it in the hot bowl of water, then added a few slivers of soap. Wringing out the extra water, she began the task of washing

Helen's injured arm. Halfway through she told O'Malley, "To save time, take another cloth off the stack and wash her other arm."

He'd never washed any part of a woman before. The task seemed intimate to him. "I've never done this before, lass, so if I scrub too hard, ye need to let me know. Ma always taught me brothers and I to wash all of the dirt off the first time—or she'd have us washing a second time."

Helen's lovely lips lifted as she smiled at him. "Don't tell me, you and your brothers scrubbed until your skin stung."

He laughed. "Am I that transparent?"

"No, but some of the young men his lordship hired had to be shown how to wash without scraping skin off in the bid to have the first full meal they had eaten in a long time."

"Why was that?" the widow asked while she gently began washing Helen's wrist. "If you do not mind my asking."

"Not at all. Lord Montrose was known for giving those of us without a home a second chance. The first thing we had to do upon arriving was to soak off the dirt in a hot tub of soapy water." She smiled, and it warmed O'Malley's heart. "The second thing was a meal fit for a king. Not one of us were able to eat everything on our plates. It had been some time since we'd gone to sleep with a roof over our heads and our bellies full."

Her tears tugged at O'Malley's heartstrings. "Montrose was a great man. I'm sorry I did not have the opportunity to meet him."

O'Malley and Widow Dawson finished their tasks, and she asked him to fetch more water. He did as told, dumping out the used water into the bucket by the back door. He returned with another bowl full of hot water.

"Thank you. Now then, why don't you wash Helen's face, while I'll set out what I need to immobilize her arm? I'm going to need your help lining up the bones."

Helen gasped, and O'Malley had to control the urge to flinch. "Close yer faery eyes, lass. I don't want to get soap in them." He carefully and thoroughly washed her face, memorizing the curve of her cheek, the length of her lashes, and the sprinkling of freckles across the bridge of her nose that he had not noticed before. "There now. Let me blot yer face dry." A few moments later, he glanced at the widow. "Did I miss any spots?"

She smiled at him. "Not a one. Thank you."

"Ye can open yer eyes now, lass." He watched the flutter of Helen's lashes as they slowly lifted, revealing her violet eyes.

"Now then," the widow said, "all you need to do is sit behind Helen, wrap your arms around her, and hold her arm still."

The lass looked worried.

"And what will ye be doing?" he asked the widow.

"I will be standing in front of you, holding on to Helen's hand and manipulating her wrist until I'm satisfied the bones are where they should be."

Before Helen could ask, or the widow could warn them, O'Malley told her, "This will hurt, lass, but ye need to stay as still as possible. Lean into me as close as ye can get—I'll help absorb yer pain."

Helen couldn't speak. She nodded.

"The only way this will work is if the lass sits on me lap—unless ye have a bench?"

"I'm sorry, I don't."

"Not a problem. Hang on, lass." O'Malley lifted Helen into his arms, sat down, and settled her on his lap. "I'm going to put me arms around ye, and hold yer arm steady. All right?"

He had to lean forward to hear her whispered yes.

"Do ye have wood slats to hold her wrist in place if it's broken?" he asked the widow.

"I do over on the table by the far wall. I think two will do."

"Now that her face is clean, I can see there is more bruising than I thought, and scrapes on her face."

The widow nodded. "I shall take a close look at those after we set the bone. Do not worry, I'll take good care of Miss Langley."

He murmured quietly to the lass while the widow held Helen's arm in her hands, manipulating her wrist. The lass trembled with what O'Malley knew was a combination of pain and fear.

The widow stopped. "Do not move!" She reached for the wooden slats and placed one on either side of Helen's wrist. Holding them in place with one hand, she began to wind a length of linen around the wrist until she was satisfied. "There, that's finished."

O'Malley silently thanked God that Helen's wrist had not fractured with the bone poking through the skin. He'd witnessed that type of a break more than once—had known more than one man who'd lost an arm or leg due to a break of that nature.

"Ye're a brave lass, Helen Langley."

The widow agreed. "You will need to keep your wrist dry and leave the bandage on for at least a sennight unless you are experiencing an unusual amount of pain. Then, of course, seek the advice of your physician, who may wish to unwrap it and see how the break is healing."

"Thank you for taking care of me, Widow Dawson."

"I'm thinking ye're going to be depending on me more than ye bargained for, lass," O'Malley added.

She nodded. "I'm grateful that it's you."

"Is there another man ye've given yer heart to that I need to have a conversation with?"

Helen slowly smiled. "You are the only man I have given my heart to."

He puffed up with pride. "Well now, that's as it should be, as we'll be married tomorrow at Summerfield Chase."

"Before you leave, I have a poultice that you can take with you," the widow interjected. "It's on the table by the stove."

O'Malley got up and carefully set Helen on the chair. "I'll be right back." He lifted the poultice and sniffed it. "Comfrey root. Ma has a section of her garden where she grows it—with the four of us and Da, she needed it more often than not."

The widow was smiling when he rejoined them. "When you remove the splint after a sennight, you can use the poultice to reduce the swelling."

"Shouldn't we have done that before ye wrapped her wrist?"

"If it was just a sprain, yes. But not with a break. Oftentimes bones heal faster than one realizes, and you run the risk of bones healing in the wrong position."

"I cannot thank ye enough for taking care of me intended."

"One more thing." The widow reached for a large linen square, folded it in half, and slid it beneath the lass's arm. "O'Malley, would you hold Helen's hair out of the way? I don't want to get any tangled in the knot. It hurts when it's pulled out."

Her hair was soft as silk, distracting him with thoughts of running his fingers through it. O'Malley set those thoughts aside. Now that the lass had been seen to, his brain immediately focused on the next problem on his list. He needed to get moving as soon as possible. They had a prisoner to deliver before dark.

As her husband-to-be, 'twas his duty to ensure that she received the best of everything from this moment on, but delivering the prisoner had to come before that.

"Why don't you carry Miss Langley over to the settee? She'll be more comfortable there."

He lifted Helen into his arms and nearly groaned—she fit perfectly. Her curves filled the planes and hollows of his body. His mind took a short trip to their wedding night, and he had to call on his ironclad control to keep from salivating, thinking of the thousands of nights ahead where he could undress her, touch her...whenever he wanted. *Wherever* he wanted.

"O'Malley!"

He blinked. "Aye? What? Sorry, me mind was elsewhere."

The widow pursed her lips and had her hands on her hips. "I was just telling Miss Langley that she will rest and keep her arm in a sling. She is not to use that hand, or it will strain her wrist and could cause further injury."

The distress on Helen's face bothered him. "How will I eat or write to Mrs. Minnover and the others?" she asked.

"I'll be helping ye, and if I am on a shift away from

Wyndmere Hall, then we'll enlist Constance or Merry to help ye," O'Malley replied.

"But I cannot expect you or—"

"Did ye forget that ye agreed to marry me? Ye'll need to learn to listen to the man who'll be yer husband."

"Only if he makes sense," she countered.

He laughed. "Isn't she wonderful?"

The widow smiled. "I believe you two will have a long and happy marriage…if you learn to listen to one another and to compromise."

"Listen?" Helen echoed.

"Compromise?" O'Malley asked at the same time.

"Your days will be smoother as you learn one another's likes and dislikes, fears and sorrows."

"What about happiness?" O'Malley asked.

"I wish you a lifetime of it," the widow replied.

"Thank you for taking such good care of me," Helen said.

"It is my calling in life, but you are most welcome."

"Ye have me gratitude as well," O'Malley added. "Did ye happen to notice the sparkle in me intended's faery eyes?"

"I was preoccupied—let me take a look now." The widow stared at Helen. "I do not believe I have ever seen violet eyes before. I do believe I see a bit of sparkle."

"Everyone who sees me bride-to-be will be captivated by her eyes. Ma always told us that violet eyes were a gift from the fae."

"Did she?" Helen's voice wavered, but thankfully she wasn't crying. O'Malley had expected her to when the widow was manipulating the bones in her wrist, but she hadn't.

"That she did. She also told us that the fae would take the babe from yer cradle and leave a dark-haired changeling in its place."

"Do you believe that?"

Pleased that he was able to distract Helen, he chuckled. "Did ye not notice that all of me Garahan cousins have dark hair and eyes?"

He wasn't surprised when Helen did not laugh, instead leaping to one particular Garahan's defense.

"Aiden is not a changeling, and has been wonderful! He protected Emily and I when we were ambushed in the park in London, and then along the route to reach Wyndmere Hall. How can you—"

O'Malley interrupted, "I'm after distracting ye, lass, not arguing with ye. There isn't a Garahan who would not lay down his life for those he protects. The same is true for our Flaherty cousins—and naturally, meself and the rest of the O'Malleys."

"Aye," a deep voice intoned from the doorway, "good to know ye haven't forgotten yer better-looking cousins, O'Malley."

"I'll pack up the poultices for you," the widow said. "If you do have a physician examine her wrist, and he agrees that it is healing well but the swelling has not gone down as much as it should have, use the poultices. Soak them in hot water, then leave it on for at least half an hour."

"Aye. Thank ye," O'Malley said.

Widow Dawson glanced at Flaherty and frowned. "You'll need your knuckles tended to."

He grunted. "A wash will do me fine, but thank ye for the offer. I understand ye have a constable. Is he nearby?"

"We do. You'll find him in the village, which is half a mile past the inn. His name is Saunders, and he's a man you can count on to sort out troubles and get to the heart of the problem."

O'Malley kept his eye on Helen, pleased that she seemed steadier. "Sounds like a man we could use on our side, Flaherty."

His cousin agreed. "I've left our prisoner tied up by the outbuilding. He won't be going anywhere anytime soon. Did ye get the lass a cup of water yet?"

"Do ye think I've bollocks for brains? Of course I did!"

Flaherty snorted. "Bet ye almost forgot, and I'm thinking the lass would not be reminding ye, because she doesn't appear to be one who would think of herself first—even injured."

"I was raised to think of others first," Helen said. "After Lord

Montrose saved me, I continued to put others first—it was essential in my role as maid and companion to Emily."

When Flaherty murmured something, O'Malley was about to blast his cousin, but Helen continued, "If O'Malley had forgotten, I would have eventually asked Widow Dawson for a cup of water...*after* she finished."

Flaherty grinned. "Yer intended is a wise woman, O'Malley. Ye'd best be taking good care of her, or else ye'll answer to me."

O'Malley shook his head. "Ignore me cousin—he's full of blather most of the time."

Instead of taking offense, Flaherty laughed. "O'Malley would know, as he's fuller of it than me."

A muffled sound reached them from the open window. Flaherty strode to the door. "I'd best be checking on the prisoner."

"Want me help?"

Flaherty looked over his shoulder and grunted. O'Malley understood it was an answer...and an insult.

"If you two are through, I'd like to find out what accommodations you've made for Miss Langley," the widow said.

"We aren't staying," O'Malley answered. "We need to reach Summerfield Chase by nightfall."

"I'm here to act as escort," Flaherty said. "After we send a missive off to His Grace and another to his lordship, we'll be on our way. Do ye feel up to riding, Helen?"

She didn't hesitate to answer. "I'll be fine."

When Flaherty closed the door behind him, Helen thanked the kindly healer again. "You did not have to take me in and tend to my wounds, Widow Dawson. But you did, and I thank you for your kindness. You don't even know me, and yet you have gone out of your way to help me. I'm afraid I lost my reticule. What can I do to repay you?"

The woman smiled. "It would be wrong to ask payment for the gift of healing. But there is something you can do for me, while I ask my son to fetch the constable."

"Anything. Just tell me what you need."

O'Malley was proud of the way his bride-to-be quickly agreed without knowing what the widow would ask of her.

Widow Dawson motioned toward a chair by the fire. "I know that O'Malley is in a hurry to be on his way, but given the fact that you were unconscious for more than a moment, I'd like you to stay a bit longer to satisfy me that you are well enough to travel."

When Helen agreed, Widow Dawson told O'Malley, "I shall be right back to straighten up. We'll have tea with some of the bread I baked this morning."

He waited until she closed the door behind her before he saw to the task himself, gently placing Helen in the chair.

When the widow returned a few moments later, she stopped and stared, then slowly smiled. "Thank you, O'Malley. Redmond will be back in a little while. Let me see to our tea."

While she measured out the tea leaves, she asked O'Malley to set out the cups and plates, then nodded at Helen.

"I believe our tea is ready."

O'Malley walked over to where the lass sat, scooped her up, and carried her over to the table. "I can walk, Eamon," she protested.

"I know." He placed her on a chair, then pulled out the healer's chair and waited until she sat before taking a seat himself. Widow Dawson poured their tea and passed around plates of thick-sliced bread.

O'Malley waited until the ladies had helped themselves before he added butter and jam to two pieces of bread. After sliding one onto Helen's plate, he sliced it into manageable pieces for her.

He sniffed his slice before taking a bite. "Heaven, Widow Dawson. Thank ye."

The widow smiled. "Do you think Flaherty will want a cup of tea and jam and bread?"

O'Malley chuckled. "Aye. He's mad for jam, but there's no reason to interrupt his guard duty. If there is any left, we can share it with him."

Helen frowned at him. "But he's your cousin."

"That he is, lass."

"And he jumped through the window and subdued the man who abducted me."

"Aye, and now Flaherty's guarding him to ensure he doesn't escape." O'Malley couldn't hold back his snort of laughter. "Ah, lass, I'm sorry to be teasing ye. Yer sense of fairness does ye credit. Thank ye for thinking of me cousin."

"We'll set aside a plate for him," Widow Dawson remarked.

A short while later, the widow got up to brew a second pot of tea for Flaherty. "My son should be returning soon. Would you like to lie down, Miss Langley?"

"No, but thank you for asking."

"I'm curious to know if you traveled alone, or with a companion, Miss Langley?"

"The Duke of Wyndmere was kind enough to have a footman accompany me as protection..." Helen's voice trailed off, and she was silent for a moment before adding, "I'm afraid I have no idea where he or the coachman ended up."

The widow turned and frowned at O'Malley. "Didn't you tell her what happened?"

"Forgive me, lass, but I was a bit preoccupied earlier and neglected to tell ye that Widow Dawson tended to the duke's coachman earlier at the inn. He's got a nasty bump on the back of his head, but will recover, and may be able to return to Wyndmere Hall in a day or so. No word on the footman's whereabouts."

"I see."

From the expression on her face, he knew Helen sensed what he suspected—that the footman had been injured, potentially by the man in their custody. They would not leave the area until they found him.

"Wouldn't it be more prudent to travel together?" Helen asked. "That way, if the coachman has difficulty on the way back to the duke's estate, we would be on hand to help him."

Instead of readily agreeing, the older woman was still frowning. "I don't believe that would be acceptable at all."

O'Malley could not imagine why. The lass would have protection on the way to Summerfield Chase, and to Wyndmere Hall on their return journey. "And why not?"

"Miss Langley's reputation is at stake if she travels without a female companion."

"I did not think of asking someone to act as chaperone on my journey here," Helen said. "I was so confident that I would be offered the position of companion to the dowager. Companions do not have chaperones—they *are* the chaperones. I am certain that His Grace already considered the ramifications of the poor woman traveling alone back to Wyndmere Hall if I had asked to have one with me. What of *her* reputation?"

"The lass has a point," O'Malley added.

The widow was shaking her head again. "Arrangements could have been made by the dowager, if she were not so stiff-necked."

Helen pressed her lips into a thin, disapproving line. "I do not want anything from her."

O'Malley agreed and crossed his arms over his chest. "I wouldn't trust her."

"Mayhap, if they have decided to linger at the inn..." Her voice trailed off, and O'Malley wondered whom the widow was talking about. She tapped a finger to her chin, obviously deep in thought.

"Who may still be at the inn?" O'Malley asked.

"As I was getting ready to leave the inn, a carriage arrived with two white-haired, amiable-looking women. If they are still there, you could ask for their assistance."

"For reasons I am not at liberty to discuss, time is of the essence," O'Malley grumbled. "We need to return to Wyndmere Hall."

"There would have been another way," the widow mused. "It

would ensure Miss Langley's reputation is not damaged, but you would have needed to have a special license."

O'Malley patted his waistcoat pocket and slid his gaze from Widow Dawson to Helen. "The duke secured one for me before I left. Me brother, Thomas, is stationed at Summerfield Chase. I was hoping to have him stand witness, along with me cousins, when Helen and I wed." He was rewarded with a soft smile from the lass.

By the time he could bring himself to look away from his intended, the older woman's face was wreathed in smiles. "Well then, why wait? The vicarage is only a few doors down from the constable. Word would get back to the dowager that Miss Langley, in the company of her chaperones, was wed to one of the duke's guard at our vicarage."

O'Malley studied the widow's face and was pleased that he did not see a hint of subterfuge, or malice, in the depths of her pale gray eyes. She had been generous with her healing talents, and her worry for the lass warmed his heart. "Ye're truly concerned for Helen's reputation?"

"I am." The look of consternation on her face was explained when she continued, "The dowager has no doubt already begun to weave her web of lies. It is what she has always done." She turned to Helen and assured her, "It is not that our villagers judge others as swiftly and without reason as the dowager. But when circumstances seem to point in one direction, they follow the reasoning and arrive at the conclusion the dowager has painted for them. Though not all of us do."

"Manipulative." O'Malley wished he could think of a reason to wait just a bit longer. Thomas was not just his brother—he was his twin. It never mattered to either of them that they were not identical. The resemblance between the two was still there for all to see.

He walked over to where Helen sat, lifted her hand to his lips, and brushed a kiss to the back. "What do ye think, lass? Ye've already agreed to be me wife. 'Tisn't right for me to make a decision based on what I want without asking what *ye* want."

Helen was silent long enough that he prompted her, "Do ye want to wait until we reach Baron Summerfield's estate, where ye could meet me twin, or would ye prefer to have the vicar marry us before we leave? I must warn ye, though, we'll be stopping at the inn first. I need to see for meself the condition the coachman is in, and we'll need to make arrangements for him to stay. Then we'll be meeting with the constable regarding transporting the prisoner, and lastly, there's the matter of locating the footman and sending missives."

Helen met the intensity of O'Malley's gaze with a hesitant smile. "I do want to marry you, Eamon, and would love to have your brother be there to witness our pledges. If I had a family member still alive, I would ask to wait until he or she could make the journey to Summerfield Chase or Wyndmere Hall…but there aren't any left."

Widow Dawson's eyes were suspiciously damp, but she blinked, and relief filled O'Malley. He did not do well with tears. "There is still an outside chance that the two women I mentioned earlier may be willing to accompany you to Summerfield Chase and then return to the inn," she said. O'Malley was about to speak when the widow added, "After all, it is not every day that one has the chance to meet a member of the *ton*."

He shook his head. What was it about the toffs that had those not at their elevated level of Society clamoring to meet them? Hoping it would convince the widow that their party needed to leave without delay, he said, "Did I fail to mention the baron is married to the duke's sister?"

The widow stood and smoothed her gown, though O'Malley did not see any wrinkles. "I do believe your best course of action would be to stop at the inn and see if the sisters are still there. I am confident they would be willing to make the trip. Summer-field-on-Eden is no more than a few hours from here."

"Thank ye, for tending the lass and for caring enough about her wellbeing to help us find a most expeditious plan that will not have an adverse effect on her reputation…other than the lies the dowager has already begun to spread."

He was about to bid the widow goodbye when he noticed the worry in Helen's violet eyes. "What's troubling ye?"

She lifted one shoulder in reply.

"A shrug isn't an answer, lass. Ye'd best be knowing ahead of time that I'll be expecting ye to tell me what is wrong when I ask."

Helen narrowed her gaze and stared at him long enough to have him wondering why that would irritate her.

"Have ye something to say to me?"

"As a matter of fact, I do."

O'Malley was about to tell her to just get it said, but she flinched as if she were feeling pain. How could he have forgotten so quickly that the lass had been badly injured? Helen had been stoic while the widow tended to her—the least he could do was not rush her to answer his question when something was weighing heavy on her mind.

He brushed the tip of his finger along the curve of her cheek. "I'm listening, lass." She grunted, and O'Malley could not help but stare at his bride-to-be, slack jawed. "Did ye just *grunt?*"

"Oh, good. I was afraid you couldn't hear me."

"Why in God's name would ye grunt instead of speaking to me?"

Her smile tipped O'Malley off to the fact that the lass was enjoying his shock. "You have grunted more than once in answer to questions since I have met you. Prior to meeting Aiden and the others, I was never grunted at in answer to a verbal question. I assumed if you communicated that way, then I would need to learn to do the same."

"But ye're a woman!"

Her musical laughter filled the cottage and surrounded him like a hug, and just like that, he ceded the victory to her.

"Ah, lass, ye'll keep me on me toes, just like me ma keeps Da on his toes."

"Just because I am a woman, does not preclude me from responding to you nonverbally."

"I'm looking forward to our first argument."

Her mouth gaped open for a moment before she asked, "Why would you anticipate such a thing?"

"Making up." O'Malley captured her lips in a searing kiss.

She stared up at him when he took a step back, and he'd be damned if the lass didn't frown—again! "That's not a proper answer."

The fire in her eyes and the sharp edge in her voice pleased him. He slid his arm around Helen's waist, and this time, he gentled his kiss, pleased when she sagged against him. "There's where ye'd be wrong, lass. There's more than one type of kiss—with more than one meaning. Ye'll have to pay close attention until ye figure out what I'm saying without words…with me kisses."

O'Malley let go of her, and had to reach out and steady her when she wavered on her feet. "I'm thinking ye'll be a quick learner." She nodded, and he snorted to cover his laughter. "Well now, a nod is an acceptable nonverbal response. In case ye're wondering. Now then, ye have yet to answer me question about what ye're worrying about."

"Will the dowager's attempts to blacken my reputation among the *ton* have a ripple affect on His Grace and his family?"

"I doubt it. If anything, they'll rally around ye and call on everyone they know to do the same. They've done it before."

"What if the duke changes his mind about…things?"

O'Malley knew what the lass was referring to and silently agreed that no one else need to know about her past. "Trust me, lass. Once the duke makes up his mind, he never changes it."

"I do trust you, Eamon."

"That wasn't so hard, confiding yer worries to me, was it?"

She lifted to her toes and kissed his cheek. "It wasn't. Thank you."

O'Malley brushed the tip of his fingers along the curve of her uninjured cheek and kissed her forehead. "Ye're welcome." He turned to the widow. "Ye've been kind to us, taken care of me bride-to-be, and offered yer best advice. Thank ye. Oh, and if ye're ever in need of assistance, I can be found at Wyndmere Hall in the Lake District, or ye can contact me brother Thomas at Summerfield Chase. No matter the reason."

"Thank you, O'Malley, but there is one last thing I can do for Miss Langley."

"Oh, and what might that be?"

"You haven't taken your eyes off Miss Langley since you carried her inside, and yet you still haven't noticed."

"That she needed yer help?"

The widow shook her head. "Take a close look at her gown."

O'Malley shrugged. "'Tis dark blue, and complements her dark-as-night hair and faery eyes."

"Look closer."

He was horrified to have overlooked the dirt, torn sleeve, and tiny spots of blood from the scrapes on her face. "God in Heaven! Forgive me for thinking to take ye to the inn—or anywhere, for that matter—without seeing that ye had a clean gown to wear."

Helen glanced down and shrugged. "I didn't notice either."

The widow tsked. "Completely understandable. You have been so brave through all you have endured today. Now then, if you wait here for a moment, I have a trunk where I store gowns in a few different sizes." At the questioning look in O'Malley's eyes, she added, "Miss Langley is not the first female I have tended to whose gown was unfit to wear. I like to be prepared for any emergency. I have a supply of men's trousers and shirts, too. I will be right back."

O'Malley marveled at the realization that Widow Dawson had been performing the same tasks, and felt the same duty, as his cousin-in-law Michaela O'Malley had—only the widow helped others on the outskirts of the Borderlands instead of the heart of London's stews.

A few minutes later, she returned with a deep green gown,

shook it out, and held it up to Helen. "I believe this will fit. Come with me."

O'Malley stared at the door to the bedroom and tried not to imagine being the one who undid the buttons before carefully slipping Helen's gown over her head. He ordered his heart not to pick up the pace at the thought that soon *he* would be the one to help the lass dress…and *undress*.

An image of ebony hair spilling over slender shoulders had him clenching his hands into fists. Before he could imagine sliding his hands from her shoulders to her wrists and back, while slipping her chemise over her head, the door opened, and a vision in dark green emerged with a hesitant look on her face.

O'Malley felt the punch to his gut first, to his heart second. She slowly walked toward him, and he extended his hand and captured hers—it felt like ice. When she trembled, he drew her to his side, pleased when she settled against him. "Ye're chilled, lass." Regret filled his voice when he said, "I wish we could hold off transporting the prisoner." He tipped her chin up with his knuckle. The uncertainty in the depths of her eyes tugged at his heart. "I do not want ye worrying, but I do need to tell ye that the man who abducted ye is connected to Hardwell."

"I heard what you said before," she rasped, "that he was a murderer."

O'Malley watched tears well in her eyes, but was immensely proud when she blinked them away. He hated to bring up the blackguard's name, but had no choice. She deserved to know whom the prisoner was connected to. Baron Hardwell was the man who'd attacked Emily—and Helen—at the inn a few weeks ago.

He bent and kissed her lips. "There's a lass. I have the feeling Flaherty and I will need a few men guarding our backs—not that we cannot handle an attack from the rear, with one hand tied behind our backs, but 'tis for caution. Whenever coin and the *ton* are involved, trouble follows."

Helen licked her lips and nearly broke through O'Malley's

control. "I'm not afraid. You and Flaherty will protect me." She brushed the tips of her fingers along the line of his jaw. "I'm safe with you." He grunted, and she smiled. "I believe that is your way of agreeing with me."

O'Malley snorted, and for the second time that afternoon her light laughter echoed through the room, surrounding him like a hug. "Right ye are, lass, on both counts. Ye are safe with me and mine—in this instance Flaherty. I was agreeing with ye."

The widow had disappeared while O'Malley and the lass were speaking. She approached them now with a woolen shawl in her hands. Handing it to Helen, she said, "You'll need this shawl to ward off any chill riding to the inn, as dusk is not far off. O'Malley, see that Miss Langley does not catch a chill."

The nearness of the lass had his body putting out enough heat to start a fire. There would be no problem keeping Helen warm. "As long as the lass agrees to ride on me lap." He paused, staring at Helen until she gave a brief nod, then continued, "She'll be warm and safe in the circle of me arms. Ye have me word. Thank ye again. Don't forget to send word, should ye need me."

"Thank you, O'Malley. I won't forget, and please thank His Grace for watching out for Miss Langley. Oftentimes, when I am called to care for a young woman who has been injured, she has no one."

Helen shifted in his arms, and O'Malley released her. She walked over to the widow and hugged her. "Thank you for taking care of me, and for caring about me. I am so lucky to have His Grace and his guard looking out for me."

"I'll be doing more than that once we're wed, lass." The flush on her face pleased him. When he got her on his lap, he planned to ask if it were embarrassment or anticipation that caused that reaction.

He opened the door and escorted Helen outside. Flaherty was waiting for him, but he wasn't alone. A tall, lanky young man stood beside him.

"Redmond Dawson, meet O'Malley. Redmond just told me

the constable was in a meeting when he arrived."

"I alerted the constable that you and O'Malley would be stopping at his office after you stop at the inn."

Flaherty stared at Helen's sling and shook his head. "Ye should not have to be riding on a horse in yer condition, even if it is essential to yer safety."

"She won't be riding the horse," O'Malley replied as he lifted her on to his horse's back. He waved to the widow and nodded to Redmond and Flaherty. After mounting his horse, he gently settled Helen onto his lap and wrapped an arm around her. "'Tis a short ride, then we'll see that ye have at least half a pot of tea with a warming meal. Me ma always stressed that a warm meal was best when traveling."

Helen waved to the widow and her son and leaned against him. When he didn't feel an ounce of warmth where she was pressed against him, despite the borrowed shawl, he slipped out of his frockcoat, wrapped it around her, and settled her higher up on his lap. O'Malley prayed she didn't notice his body's instant response to the weight of her curves in his lap.

The distance may be short, but the ride would seem an eternity!

✦◆✦

# CHAPTER THIRTEEN

O'MALLEY'S BODY-WARMED FROCKCOAT immediately cut through the chill that had settled in her bones at the thought of Baron Summerfield or the baroness knowing of her past and judging her. To be fair, she had heard of the close familial relationship the duke had with two of his distant cousins—Baron Summerfield and Viscount Chattsworth. He treated them as brothers…though not at first. She had been told it was later, when it counted, and they had proven to be cut from the same cloth. Summerfield married the duke's sister and Chattsworth married a close friend of the duke's wife and sister. *Family* by design…by love.

Even knowing that, the worry got stuck in her brainbox, and Helen could not jar it loose.

"Lass, ye need to relax. Ye're stiff as a board in me arms." She shifted, and he muttered something unintelligible before asking, "Does yer wrist pain ye?"

"Not as much as before."

O'Malley bent his head and brushed his lips to the top of her head. That small but tender caress wormed its way into her heart, beside his declaration earlier that she was his heart…and his love. He must have felt the stiffness beginning to leave her. "Stop thinking of things ye have no control over. Ye'll upset yer stomach."

Helen huffed. "I have never heard that before."

"It must be true—Ma said it to us when Da and Uncle Patrick were in prison."

She gasped. "Prison? What happened? Are they still there?"

"Wrongly accused of theft. They're not still there. Me uncle took ill hours before the false charges were dropped, and they were to be released. He passed away in Da's arms."

She cupped the side of his face. When his eyes met hers, she murmured, "I wish I hadn't hurt my wrist. I'd be able to cup your face with both hands." Feeling bold, she slid her hand around to the back of his neck and watched his emerald eyes deepen to forest green. Her heart nearly stopped when he captured her lips in a devastating kiss.

"I won't be kissing ye again until we arrive at the inn. I need to be on the lookout for trouble, lass, and ye're a distraction."

"I understand. I can wait."

He snorted and muttered, "That makes one of us." A shout from behind them had her clinging to the arm he wrapped around her. "'Tis just Flaherty spouting off because he doesn't have a beautiful woman in his arms to kiss."

As if he could tell she was looking up at him, his gaze dipped and then returned to diligently scanning the area surrounding them as they rode toward the inn.

"Ye don't believe me."

She sighed. "No one except Emily has ever said that to me before."

"Garahan married a wise woman. Believe Emily—ye *are* beautiful, lass. Never doubt it."

Helen felt tears stinging the backs of her eyes, and dug deep to will them away. "You are the one who is beautiful."

His deep, rumbling laugh warmed her heart. "'Tis the curse we O'Malleys have to bear in life, being handsome as sin. Close yer eyes for just a bit longer, and before ye know it, we'll be there."

Helen did as she was told and felt her stiff limbs begin to

relax. The warmth of O'Malley's big body wrapped around hers, and the promise of more drugging kisses in her future, lulled her to sleep.

⟫⟫⟫⟨⟨⟨⟨

O'MALLEY HATED TO wake the lass, but knew the noise from the inn yard up ahead was bound to rouse her. "We're here, lass."

Helen stirred in his arms, and he wondered what it would be like when they shared a bed. O'Malley imagined watching her sleep. He'd slowly wake her with his lips, and tongue, and teeth.

Before his body betrayed his thoughts, he called her name, and had the pleasure of watching her thick black lashes flutter open, revealing the eyes that had captivated him from the start.

"I'm glad ye were able to fall asleep."

"I did not mean to."

"Ye're awake now. We need to find four people."

"Four? I thought we were only looking for the duke's coachman."

"We are, as well as the footman and the two ladies Widow Dawson mentioned seeing." He murmured to his horse and gave a slight tug on the reins, signaling for the animal to stop. "I'll set ye on yer feet as soon as I dismount."

"Thank you, that would be—"

Helen's gasp of shock had him struggling to contain his laughter. He wouldn't want her to think he was laughing at her. He gently set her on her feet and settled his coat more firmly around her when it started to slip off one shoulder. "Can't have ye catching a chill."

Her eyes were round with wonder.

"Something wrong, lass?"

"That's the second time you've done that. How can you possibly swing your leg over a horse like that, dismount, and not drop me?"

He grinned at her. "I've had lots of practice, and before ye start thinking the way a female is bound to, 'twas with me cousins. Though I'm usually carrying one of them over me shoulder."

"Injured?"

O'Malley nodded. "Oftentimes bleeding."

Her face paled, but she didn't waver on her feet. "I did not realize how dangerous it would be to guard the duke until I watched Aiden and the others, although I don't believe they were part of the guard."

"Ye'd be right on both counts. 'Tis dangerous, but that is part of the appeal. Working for a man of His Grace's integrity, honor, and dedication to his family is a privilege. I believe it was Tremayne and Bayfield who were originally tasked to assist Garahan. They are part of Captain Coventry's group of retired military men, who have assisted both the duke and Gavin King on more than one occasion. His Grace has connections."

She placed her hand on his arm. "Thank you, Eamon, for finding me—rescuing me. Marrying me."

Unable to resist, he kissed her forehead. "Ah, lass, we aren't married yet. To be honest, I look forward to after we're wed and ye can *properly* thank me."

Her expression of desire-laced shock was a pleasure to watch, but he'd best leave off. He'd teased the lass enough for the moment.

O'Malley was still smiling when the hostler approached them. The man was staring at him intently, and O'Malley wondered if Flaherty had mentioned him.

"You must be O'Malley."

"Aye, and ye just answered the question I was about to ask. Flaherty will be joining us shortly. Miss Langley and I rode ahead, as we were not encumbered by having the prisoner tethered to us while he walked."

The hostler laughed. "I like the way you and Flaherty think. I'll water your horse while you take Miss Langley inside. The inn isn't full, but there are two women who arrived a short while ago who would no doubt enjoy the company."

"I won't be leaving the lass alone, but would not mind meeting the ladies and introducing her to them. Thank ye for the suggestion. I'll be inside when Flaherty arrives."

"I'll send someone to fetch you."

O'Malley whispered words of encouragement to his horse, patted the animal on the neck, and turned him over to the hostler. "He's a fine stallion and would enjoy a cup of oats along with a bit of hay, if ye have it."

"I do, and promise to treat him like the fine Thoroughbred he is."

O'Malley nodded, smiled at Helen, and placed his hand atop hers where it rested on his forearm. "Yer hand feels warmer than before."

"Thank you for letting me borrow your coat. I think the chill I felt lying on the floor in the cottage must have seeped into the marrow of my bones. I can't recall being that cold in quite some time."

"Well now, we'll have to see that ye have something warm to eat. Maybe a hearty stew, or meat pie. Let's see what they're serving."

They stepped in through the door to the inn and were greeted by the scent of savory spices and freshly baked bread. O'Malley drew in a breath and sighed. "Smells of Heaven in here."

"Thanks to Mrs. Bertrum's culinary talents," a tall, baldheaded man greeted them. "Bertrum, at your service. Welcome to our inn."

"Thank ye, Bertrum. Me name's O'Malley. I'm one of the Duke of Wyndmere's guard. May I present Miss Helen Langley, me intended."

The innkeeper smiled at the couple, then noticed the lass's sling and that she was obviously wearing O'Malley's frockcoat. "Let's get Miss Langley over by the fire. One of my daughters will be out in a minute to take your orders. We're a family-run inn.

Lucky for me, we have three daughters and two strapping sons to help us, as my wife is a very talented cook and we keep her in the kitchen as often as possible."

As if the red-headed lass had heard her father call her, she hurried over to join them. "My name's Meghan. I'll take care of them, Papa. If you'll follow me, I was just about to ask the Misses Hinkle if they wanted more tea. This way, please."

O'Malley scanned the taproom as they passed through it to one of the private rooms on the other side of the inn.

"Here we are. I brought company for you, ladies. Would either of you care for a fresh pot of tea?"

The two women sitting by the fire greatly resembled one another and were garbed in identical outfits, the only difference being the color. One woman was dressed in pale blue, the other in pale pink.

The woman in blue answered, "That would be lovely. My name is Josina Hinkle, and this is my twin sister, Jeannette. And you are?"

"O'Malley. This is me intended, Miss Helen Langley, and by the way, I'm a twin meself."

"How fascinating. Do sit down and join us, won't you?" Josina asked.

"I'm afraid I'm on duty, waiting for me cousin to arrive. When he does, we have business to attend to, though I know Helen won't mind sitting for a bit."

If her frown was any indication, Jeannette—the woman in pink—seemed to notice the scrapes and bruises on Helen's face and her arm in the sling. Her frown intensified. "Would you care to explain how your intended seems to have either had an accident...or has been treated abominably?"

O'Malley admired the older woman's spunk and immediate defense of the lass.

Helen answered, "O'Malley rescued me—and, as a matter of fact, was sent by His Grace the Duke of Wyndmere to find me."

Both women were drawn in by her statement. "Is that so?"

Josina remarked. "Were you set upon by brigands traveling? My sister and I were a bit concerned about the possibility of being set upon as we journeyed closer to the border between England and Scotland."

"Actually—"

Whatever Helen was about to say was interrupted when Meghan returned with the promised tea, additional teacups, and a plate of teacakes. "Here we are. Aren't you joining the ladies, Mr. O'Malley?"

"Just O'Malley, if ye please. I will, after I'm off duty."

The innkeeper's daughter smiled. "Just let me know when you are ready for tea and something sweet, or a meal. Will anyone else be joining you?"

"Me cousin should be arriving any moment." He glanced out the window. "Here he is now."

Jeannette looked out the window. "Is your cousin the one leading a man with a rope tied around his waist?"

Josina gasped. "The man has his hands tied behind his back. Oh dear, just look at the bruises on his face."

O'Malley noted the lass did not turn around to look. She shivered. "Ye have nothing to fear, lass. I will not let him near ye, or harm ye again. Ye have me word."

Helen lifted her head and met his eyes. "Thank you, Eamon."

The sisters turned back and smiled at Helen. From the hint of concern in their eyes, he had a feeling the sisters had reasoned out for themselves that the lass's injuries were caused by the man being led into the inn yard.

"You are more than welcome to keep us company as long as you like, Miss Langley," Jeannette said. "We were in the middle of discussing where we will head next when you arrived. Are you familiar with the area? Do you have any suggestions?"

"Summerfield-on-Eden is a lovely village," O'Malley told them. "As a matter of fact, that's where we're headed. Baron and Baroness Summerfield are related to His Grace. Me twin Thomas and two of me cousins—also members of the duke's guard—are stationed there."

"I believe we have heard of the village. It has marshes and ponds for those that enjoy studying the habitats and lives of birds and other creatures," Jeannette said. "You remember my suggesting we visit, don't you, sister dear?"

"I do, but we decided against it because of something that occurred there recently. Those awful rumors."

Jeannette frowned. "A terrible business involving a family, of all things, who treated one of their daughters—I do apologize. We do not normally stoop so low as to gossip, but when we hear of injustice, well…"

"It lights a fire inside of us," Josina finished for her. "Doesn't it, Jeanette?"

"It does."

Belatedly, the sisters must have realized O'Malley's connection. "Please forgive us if we have inadvertently been discussing your family or someone that you are acquainted with," Josina said. "Do pour a cup of tea for Miss Langley before it goes tepid," she told her sister.

Jeanette did as bidden, then asked O'Malley, "Would you care for a cup before you leave your bride-to-be with us?"

"No, but thank ye. I am grateful that ye'd welcome the lass and keep her company." He smiled at Helen. "I won't be long."

"I promise I not to go anywhere, unless I send word to you first."

O'Malley did not like the sound of that at all. He wouldn't be able to concentrate on his duties without her promise not to leave this room until he came back for her. "Lass, I need yer word that we won't leave this room."

She frowned at him, and once again he could not help but notice how adorable she looked. "I may have no choice."

"There's always a choice, lass. Yer choice will be to stay here. I cannot be in two places at one time and need yer word."

She shook her head. "I'm afraid I cannot accommodate you."

O'Malley folded his arms across his chest. "I cannot protect ye if ye won't listen to me."

"Are you really so single-minded that you do not realize why I would *have* to leave this room?"

"Is that a polite way of saying I'm thickheaded?" The sisters had their hands over their mouths to muffle their laughter. "This is no laughing matter. I will not go into detail, but the lass's life depends on her staying put!"

"I beg your pardon," Jeanette apologized.

"I hate to be rude and bring up a topic that is normally private in nature," Josina said, "but you are not thinking past your worry for Miss Langley. You have our word that both Jeannette and I will accompany Miss Langley to the necessary, if she needs to make use of it."

O'Malley wasn't often caught off guard. "Thank ye kindly." Turning to Helen, he asked, "Why did ye not just tell me?"

"It *is* rather personal, O'Malley."

He squatted beside her chair. With the tip of his finger, he turned her to face him. "We'll be married in two days' time. There's nothing that ye should be too embarrassed to confide in me, lass." When she didn't speak right away, he brushed his lips to hers. "I'll return shortly."

She blew out a breath that sounded irritated, though her voice did not when she answered, "I'll be waiting."

He'd never had trouble walking away from a woman be-fore—not that he made a habit of it, but he'd had more than one lass who captured his interest over the years. Walking away from Helen felt as if he were leaving a part of himself behind…his *heart*.

Lengthening his stride, he walked through the taproom and stepped outside in time to hear Flaherty's warning: "Shut yer gob or I'll shut it for ye."

O'Malley had the feeling that this would take longer than he'd anticipated.

# CHAPTER FOURTEEN

H ELEN SHIFTED ON her seat, staring out the window. As soon as she saw O'Malley striding toward Flaherty, she sighed. "Are all men so singled-minded?"

Josina nodded. "My Herman was. So protective of me."

"As was my Samuel," Jeanette added.

Their faces had twin expressions of sadness, leaving Helen to wonder what had happened to Herman and Samuel. Rather than ask, as it would be rude, she replied, "I am sorry for your loss."

Jeanette sighed. "It was a long time ago, longer still since they purchased their colors. Do you remember how proud we were of them, sister dear?"

"Enormously proud of the Standish men. They were brothers, though not twins like my sister and I," Josina added. "How fine they looked in their regimentals."

Sensing she needed to distract the kindly Hinkle sisters, Helen said, "Lord Montrose received his title for bravery in battle."

"Who is Lord Montrose?" Josina said.

"A relative of yours?" Jeanette asked.

Now that she had mentioned his name, Helen wondered if that had been wise. She was about to change the subject again, but thought of Widow Dawson and her insistence that Helen have a chaperone accompany her to Summerfield Chase. She decided to share a tiny bit of her story. "Lord Montrose literally saved my life when he offered me employment. I was his daughter's maid, but more of a companion, as we were close in age."

Jeanette poured the tea while Helen shared more of her story. "Mum had recently passed away. My father had been gone for years." She paused to sip from her cup. "I was alone with nowhere to go."

"He sounds like Herman," Josina remarked. "It takes a man of courage and fortitude to take up arms in defense of his country."

"The Standish brothers died in battle," Jeanette said. "Many fine young soldiers did. If Lord Montrose received his title for bravery, he must have been an excellent man."

"He was, but his life was cruelly cut short a few months ago…by design."

The Hinkle sisters snapped sharply to attention, setting their teacups down in the same manner, at the same moment.

"Forgive me—I did not mean to disclose so much. I am not at liberty to discuss what happened unless given leave to."

"Then it is no wonder O'Malley wanted you to remain here under our protection," Josina said with a nod.

"Do not discount our ability to defend ourselves, or you," Jeanette added, then glanced at her sister. "Let us show her."

Intrigued, Helen watched the sisters reach into their reticules. To her surprise, but not entirely to her shock, they held folding knives. "O'Malley will be highly impressed and relieved to know you travel with a means to protect yourselves. I think I may need to purchase one for myself."

"You have O'Malley," the sisters reminded her.

"Ah, but I did not when I answered the advert for a companion to the dowager duchess."

"I thought you were O'Malley's fiancée," Jeanette said.

"About to be married," Josina added.

Finding herself compelled to explain, Helen did just that, but again, with the barest of facts. "He has a special license and wants us to be married when we arrive at the baron's home."

The sisters' expressions showed their disapproval. "You traveled with O'Malley without a chaperone?" Josina asked.

"Initially, we were not traveling together. When I received the summons to meet with the dowager, I was led to believe that I would be hired by her. The duke insisted that I travel in one of his carriages, under the protection of one of his coachmen and a footman. At the time, I thought that was sufficient."

"We heard part of what happened after your meeting with that woman," Josina said. "We believed it to be a Banbury tale, didn't we, sister dear?"

Jeanette agreed. "Furthermore, we heard that you arrived in a duke's carriage. Due to a duke's elevated position in life, he is normally a very good judge of character. He would not have been so magnanimous toward you, unless you were someone he admired."

Before Helen could thank them for their belief in her character, Josina added, "But that was before circumstances took a turn for the worse with whatever happened to you. We do not need the details, unless you wish to divulge them."

"Suffice it to say," Jeanette continued, "with O'Malley by your side, you are no longer in physical danger, but your reputation is." She turned to her sister. "Need I ask if you agree with what I am about to propose?"

Helen watched the sisters look into one another's eyes for a few moments before Josina replied, "You do not. I am in wholehearted agreement. We would like to offer ourselves as chaperones on your journey to Summerfield-on-Eden."

Helen's heart warmed at their generous offer. "But what of your traveling plans—won't they be interrupted?"

"We are always up for an adventure," Jeanette told her.

"Now then, being as I am the more practical twin," Josina began, staring at Helen's sling, "do not be embarrassed when I ask if you require assistance tending to *personal* matters."

Helen felt her face flame. "I do not believe so, but thank you for the offer."

Jeanette beamed. "As for when it comes time to wash, we will of course assist you, as we have done for one another for years. Saves on coin and the tedium of traveling with a stranger."

Worry began to slither into Helen's belly. "Oh, but I am a stranger."

Josina stood first, then her sister. "Not after a trip to the necessary, and the washstand afterward. Now then, if you will accept our offer to act as your chaperones in the spirit in which it is offered, then we shall be happy to become better acquainted on our journey to Summerfield Chase."

"After we deliver you, with your reputation intact," Jeanette said, "we shall look for accommodations at the inn in the village. I certainly expect there to be an inn, given that Baron Summerfield's estate is nearby."

Helen rose from her chair and walked over to stand beside them. "I believe there is, but would have to ask Flaherty—O'Malley's cousin is part of the duke's guard stationed there."

Though neither of the Hinkle sisters gave the impression that they would welcome it, Helen reached out a hand to Josina, who gave it a quick squeeze before releasing it, and then to Jeanette, who did the same. "Thank you both from the bottom of my heart. I know that O'Malley and Flaherty do not think it necessary, but I am concerned that the baron and his wife may not be as welcoming to me as O'Malley believes if I arrive without a chaperone."

Josina linked her arm through Helen's while Jeanette stood on the other side of her. "From our brief introduction to O'Malley, and I am certain my sister would agree, we do not think he would speak without knowledge of the facts. Most men do not let emotion cloud their thoughts. They rely on logic and reason."

Helen smiled as the sisters accompanied her from the private room, through the taproom, where Meghan was serving an older couple and happily pointed them in the direction when they asked. "Do you need me to accompany you?"

Surprised that she would ask, Helen thanked her but refused. "I have the Misses Hinkle with me." O'Malley's serious expression when he spoke of her remaining in the private room took form and swept up from her toes to poke her in the forehead. "Oh, and if O'Malley asks, please let him know that I appreciate his diligence in looking out for me and that I did not leave the room alone."

Meghan slowly smiled. "You are a very lucky woman, Miss Langley."

Flanked by two women, who had been strangers an hour before, humbled by their readiness to avail themselves as her chaperones, Helen readily agreed with the innkeeper's daughter. "I truly am. Thank you, Meghan."

⇶✦⇷

O'MALLEY STRODE TOWARD Flaherty. "Trouble?"

His cousin grunted and shoved Wilson toward the empty stall, whipped the cravat out of his waistcoat pocket, and tied it around the man's mouth before he could respond.

"Nice work, Dillon." Flaherty swore, and O'Malley grunted. "While I agree with the sentiment, I cannot say for sure if he is a cock—" He nearly bit his tongue cutting off the rest of the word as Meghan rushed toward him.

"I offered to go with them, and now they're gone!"

"Slow down, lass, and start again. Ye offered to go with who?"

"Miss Langley and the Hinkle sisters—and they disappeared."

"How long ago?"

"Don't you want to know where they were headed?"

O'Malley grumbled, "The outhouse behind the inn."

"How did you know?"

"I have me ways. How long have they been gone?"

"At least a quarter of an hour. I was going to give them longer, considering the three women were headed there at the same time, but remembered that you seemed anxious about Miss Langley leaving the room at all."

"Thank ye, Meghan." He turned to his cousin. "Send for the constable—he should have finished his meeting by now. Ask the hostler for two men to help ye guard Wilson."

Flaherty nodded. "Find the lass and the sisters, Eamon."

O'Malley's heart threatened to jump through his skin, and his hands were drenched with nervous sweat—a sign that he needed to collect his thoughts before his kneejerk reaction to act first and ask questions second took hold of him. He rubbed his hands on his sleeves—shirt sleeves, not coat sleeves. O'Malley had forgotten that he'd wrapped the lass in his frockcoat.

Within minutes, he rounded the building and noticed the door to the small building was askew. Sprinting toward it, he grimaced. It had been ripped off the hinges. The only evidence that anyone had been there recently were two reticules that he recognized immediately as belonging to the Hinkle sisters: one pink, one blue. He tucked them into his pockets. "What did we miss? How did someone slip past us?"

He balked at making the time to search the area between the back of the inn and the outbuilding but forced himself to perform the task. It turned up a surprising clue—one of the buttons from his coat. He'd recognize it anywhere: it was black with the imprint of a Celtic harp. Rubbing his thumb across the harp soothed the edge of his fear as he tucked it in his waistcoat pocket. O'Malley had found the button from his frockcoat, so he would find the lass. And when he did, he would not let go of her until they were safe within the walls of Baron Summerfield's estate.

One of the stable lads called out to him. He looked up from where he knelt by the side of the necessary. "Has someone gone for the constable?"

"Didn't have to," the lad replied. "He just arrived with two men who asked to speak to Flaherty first and then you. Can I send them over?"

"Did they tell ye their names?"

"They did: Hennessey and Jackson."

The familiar names smoothed another edge off O'Malley's concern. Hennessey was one of Coventry's men. Jackson worked as a runner for Gavin King. Either there was a new development regarding the death of Lord Montrose, or they were heading to Summerfield Chase for a different reason. The latter could mean one of two things: the squire and his wife had been found guilty of the crime of attempted murder of a member of the *ton*'s wife— Lady Phoebe, Baroness Summerfield, who was the Duke of Wyndmere's sister. Or Hardwell had escaped. O'Malley prayed it was the former.

"Send them over." O'Malley used the time to search the area once more. He was about to leave when something caught his eye. There—in the grass a few feet behind the building was a miniscule bit of pink fabric. Cautious now, moving slowly, he traced an imaginary line in his head that led to the break in the trees in the distance. He stopped for a second and third time along the way to pick up bits of fabric, putting them in his pocket.

"Thank ye, Jeanette." The woman had left him a clue in the form of a pale pink trail. He'd follow it to the end, because he knew it would lead to the lass. He was nearly to the narrow path leading into the thick forest when he heard a deep voice call his name.

He didn't bother to stop, or turn around, simply shouted, "This way!" O'Malley kept moving forward. The men reached his side a few minutes later.

Hennessey was the first to question him. "Where are you headed?"

O'Malley dug in his pocket and showed Coventry's man the bits of fabric.

"Miss Langley was wearing a pink gown?"

O'Malley shook his head. "One of the Hinkle sisters. She's left a trail for me to follow."

"What about Flaherty?" Jackson asked. "King wanted Hennessey and I to ensure you found her and delivered her to Summerfield Chase."

"Flaherty was to go for the constable if I did not return in the time frame I gave him."

"The constable is with him now," Hennessey remarked. "Why don't we split up, Jackson? I'll go with O'Malley, while you accompany Flaherty to Summerfield Chase."

"There's still the matter of the missing footman."

"Whose footman?" Jackson asked.

"One of the duke's newest hires," O'Malley told them. "His coachman pulled into the inn earlier today in a bad way. He'd been struck on the back of the head, and when he regained consciousness, the young footman was missing. The coachman's at the inn recovering." He moved forward onto the path. "Ye should question him before ye leave. With luck he will have recalled something important before he was struck."

"That changes things," Jackson said. "I'll wait for your return. Go! Find whoever took Miss Langley and the sisters."

As Hennessey jogged to catch up with O'Malley, who had moved a distance ahead of him, O'Malley said, "There are two other women with Helen. The Hinkle sisters, who are twins, and apparently think quickly on their feet."

"So three women to rescue. I would hazard a guess that at least that many men may have abducted them," Hennessey muttered.

O'Malley held out his arm to the side to keep Hennessey from stepping on the bit of pink on the path. He bent and picked it up, then explained what he'd found by the outhouse. "We're on the right path, but need to make up time—they have been gone for a least three-quarters of an hour by now."

"We'll find her," Hennessey assured him.

O'Malley's gut churned, and his heart ached. "We have to." He would find the lass, and he would make whoever had snatched her pay. Every time he or Coventry's man picked up another swatch of fabric, he envisioned plowing his fist into the perpetrator's face, gut, or kidneys. What did not waver was his vow that he would find her.

"There aren't any more pieces," Hennessey reported.

O'Malley fought the urge to bellow with rage, turning it inward and harnessing the rage into cold, clear logic. "We'll turn around and retrace our steps to the bend in the path with the forked tree."

Hennessey nodded. "And we'll take the overgrown path."

"Aye." Making up for lost time, O'Malley strode forward.

Hennessey lagged behind collecting the pink clues. Every time he found another one, he called out, "Keep going!"

A few miles into the woods, O'Malley held up a hand and pointed to the left, where the woods thinned out and a ramshackle abode stood. Finger to his lips, he motioned for Hennessey to slip around the right side of the small cottage. O'Malley took the left.

Working his way around the corner to the side, he noticed a window and heard a commotion coming from inside. He was about to continue around the back to rendezvous with Hennessey when he heard a bloodcurdling scream.

O'Malley launched himself through the broken window with a roar, his arm covering his face to protect his eyes. He landed on his feet at the same time the door to the cottage splintered as Hennessey broke through it.

He blinked, but the sight before him did not change. The lass was clinging to the back of a huge man with her fists full of his long and greasy hair, yanking on it with all her might, while the man shouted obscenities at her.

Before the behemoth could reach around to pull her off him, O'Malley grabbed hold of Helen with one hand and kicked the man in the side of his knee. He went down with a howl.

"I'll tie him up," Hennessey said. "You can check the ladies for injuries."

O'Malley held on to his temper by a thread. The terror of

what could have happened, if the man managed to toss Helen off his back and into the far wall, had him by the bollocks.

"What in the bloody hell do ye think ye're doing?" He knew the lass was trying to protect the sister in pink, who stood with her back to the wall. Jeanette looked fragile enough to be in danger of keeling over at any minute. Her face was devoid of color, and her hand trembled where she held it to her cheek. But her eyes blazed with anger, not fear. The woman may appear frail, but she was livid.

"Has it escaped your notice that Miss Langley was trying to keep that excuse for a man from hitting my sister again?" Josina's voice wavered as she walked toward her sister and wrapped an arm around her. Chin tipped up, mouth in a stern line, she glared at O'Malley. Side by side, he noticed that the twins were in a sorry shape—their hair was in disarray, half up in pins, half down. Both had bruises on their cheeks, but by all that was holy, the women looked ready to do battle!

"Forgive me, ladies. Me temper—and concern for yerselves and me bride-to-be—overwhelmed me. Never happened before," he admitted, loosening his hold on the lass. He carefully straightened her sling and slipped her injured wrist through it. He noticed the way Helen was trembling and was not certain if it was from anger or fear for the Hinkle sisters. The lass had already proven she had the heart of a lion, trying to protect Emily when they had been attacked by Hardwell. He brushed a lock of ebony out of her eyes and warned her, "'Tis a good thing the widow splinted yer wrist, or ye may have damaged her wrist further when ye grabbed hold of him."

A deep grunt from behind him had him turning around in time to see Hennessey elbow their prisoner in the ribs, fighting not to smile.

"Trouble?"

Coventry's man shook his head. "Proving a point."

The man tried to shift away from Hennessey, who noticed O'Malley striding toward him, and let go as O'Malley grabbed the man by the throat. "Who paid ye?"

The man glared at him.

"Wrong answer." O'Malley delivered a right cross followed by an uppercut that lifted the man off his feet and into the wall. "Now then, ladies, we need to ask a few questions. It may not be safe for us to leave without answers." They all seemed to be paying attention to him, so he asked, "How did he get the jump on you? Was he alone?"

Helen sighed. "He was hiding inside the outhouse, waiting for me."

O'Malley clenched his teeth, and Hennessey asked, "How did he convince the three of you to go with him?"

Without missing a beat, Helen replied, "It was the way he asked me. I couldn't say no."

O'Malley narrowed his eyes and frowned at the lass. "Ye said no to me easily enough."

Her smile was a bit ragged around the edges when she added, "Mayhap it was the blade he held to my throat."

O'Malley couldn't feel the top of his head, and his vision narrowed before clearing. He tried to speak, but couldn't push the words past the knot in his throat. Hennessey nudged him in the shoulder, and O'Malley snapped out of it. "Let me see."

She tilted her head to the side, and his stomach turned over. Controlling the urge to heave, he stared at the thin red line on the side of her throat. It was shallow, or it would have been bleeding profusely. "Let me take care of that before we leave." He slipped the handkerchief from his pocket and folded it lengthwise, then carefully placed it against the cut. "Hold it for me while I tie me cravat around yer throat."

Hennessey was quietly speaking to the sisters when O'Malley completed the task. A good thing, or else the man would have noticed that O'Malley's hands weren't steady and never let him forget it.

Jeanette spoke up. "We had best head back to the inn. Sister and I need to be on our way."

"Ye're leaving without having yer injuries tended to?"

"Of course," Josina replied. "I am quite sure you will want to leave at once."

"While I do, we have yet to locate the duke's footman, and we'll need to have the cut on Helen's neck cleansed properly first." The way the two women were staring at him had him wondering if he had missed a vital part of the conversation. "Have ye decided where ye'll be visiting next?"

"We have," Jeanette said.

Josina nodded. "We're going with you to Summerfield Chase as chaperones to Miss Langley."

Unsure if it would be a help or a hindrance, O'Malley said, "Thank ye for staying with Helen, even though ye were injured in the process. Ye kept yer word, and I'm grateful."

The Hinkles graciously accepted his thanks. He'd thought he had his anger at what happened to the lass under control. But the sight of his cravat tied around her throat gutted him.

O'Malley schooled his features and turned to his intended, wondering if the lass would always attract trouble. 'Twas best to save that question for another time. Now was not the time.

"Thank *ye* for holding to yer promise not to leave without Miss Josina and Miss Jeanette."

Helen did not hold his gaze for long. Something was on the lass's mind, but that question would have to wait as well. As soon as they located the footman, they needed to leave.

"I'll need to speak with Flaherty, Jackson, and the constable to organize a search party for the duke's footman." When no one contradicted him, he asked, "Is everyone able to walk back without assistance?"

The Hinkle sisters narrowed their eyes and lifted their chins again—a sign that they were displeased with him. But he didn't mind—that meant that they were definitely ready to walk. A glance at the lass, and he knew she would not need assistance either, though he planned to have her walk between the sisters.

"Hennessey, lead the way with the prisoner."

Coventry's man nodded, grabbed hold of the blackguard, and tossed him over his shoulder.

Ignoring the murmured comments from the women, O'Malley said, "Miss Josina, I need ye to steady the lass on one side. Miss Jeanette, if ye could walk on her other side, I'll bring up the rear."

Though grudgingly accepted, he knew his orders would be followed.

*About* fecking *time.*

✦ ✦ ✦ ✦ ✦

# CHAPTER FIFTEEN

O'MALLEY DIDN'T HAVE the sense of satisfaction he normally felt before a bare-knuckle bout, especially if he was about to go a few rounds with one of his brothers or cousins. The wary look on the prisoner's face wasn't unexpected. He was leading him to the back of the stable. O'Malley nearly smiled because he knew what the man was thinking—no witnesses…and that horses wouldn't talk.

He swallowed the laugh at the expression on the man's face, and stripped out of his shirt. But fair was fair, and he needed to explain. "'Tisn't what ye think." He tossed his shirt on the stall door. "'Tis me last clean shirt. Turn around so I can untie ye."

"Why?"

"I'm giving ye the chance to tell me what ye know in exchange for having the chance to go a few rounds of bare-knuckle with me. I need to diffuse some of me anger. Fighting always works for me."

The man was silent as O'Malley untied the rope binding his hands behind his back. Freed, he stood and stared at O'Malley.

"Normally I prefer to interrogate me prisoners…and do enjoy beating the *shite* out of them when they don't answer me questions. Would ye prefer that method, or a chance to test yer skill against me own?" He appreciated the speculative look on the other man's face, cracked his knuckles, and nodded at the man's coat. "I prefer to fight unencumbered. Are ye wanting to take yer coat off?" When the man still didn't respond, but started searching the pockets of his coat, O'Malley snickered. "Are ye daft enough to think I'd leave yer pistol in yer pocket?"

"I didn't see you take it."

"Ye were seeing double at the time. Now then, the rules are simple: if I land a punch, ye answer a question."

"If I land a punch?"

O'Malley laughed. "Ye won't."

"Sure of yourself, aren't you?"

O'Malley waited for the man to toss his coat over the top of the empty stall next to them. When his opponent turned around, O'Malley hit him with a jab followed by a right cross. "Now then, that's two blows landed, two questions. What is yer name, and who sent ye?" The man staggered and blinked. Impatient to have the answers, O'Malley said, "If ye don't want to end up bound and gagged and back in that cottage we found ye and the ladies in, ye'd best start talking."

"Bailey."

"Well now, Bailey, who do ye work for?"

Bailey frowned. "That's not the question you asked."

"Amounts to the same thing, though I see yer point…who sent ye as opposed to who do ye work for."

Bailey shook his head, turned and spat blood—and a molar—on the straw.

Out of time and desperate for answers, O'Malley lunged toward him, but Bailey raised his hands to guard his face. "The baron."

Satisfaction warred with the need for another detail. "Which one? There are quite a few of them."

"Hardwell."

Without warning, O'Malley jabbed Bailey in the nose. The sound of it breaking was almost as satisfying as the blood. "Baron Hardwell is behind bars—who sent ye?"

When the man didn't answer fast enough, O'Malley lunged

forward again.

"Wait!"

O'Malley stopped with his fist a hairsbreadth from the man's bleeding nose.

Bailey swiped at the blood with his sleeve. "Wilson."

"When did he give the order?"

"Why should I tell you anything else?"

O'Malley snorted. "'Tis Flaherty's turn, and he and I were bare-knuckle champions back home. Then it'll be Hennessy's turn, and finally Jackson's."

As the man was not a complete *eedjit*, he answered, "A fortnight ago, before Wilson traveled to the Lake District. A few days ago he sent word that I was to come here and wait at the cottage in the woods near the inn until he sent word that he had the Langley woman."

"What was the rest of the plan? If ye tell me, we may ask Gavin King of the Bow Street Runners to consider the help ye're giving me answering me questions before he interrogates ye and sends ye off to Newgate."

Bailey seemed to realize that he had no other choice but to tell O'Malley what he knew. "That's the odd part," he replied. "Wilson told me I could do whatever I wanted with her."

"What about payment?"

"He paid me in advance, and I knew from past experience not to cross him."

O'Malley's heart ached for the lass. "We heard her scream when we were outside the building."

Bailey shrugged. "It was right after I slapped both the old ladies. I guess the Langley woman didn't want me to hit either one of them again."

"Was that before or after ye held a knife to me intended's throat?"

Every ounce of color drained from Bailey's face. "Your who?"

"Intended—me bride-to-be."

"Bloody hell."

"Aye, that's what ye'll be paying for holding a knife to the lass's neck. But I'm a man of me word, and I promised Flaherty I would not use up his time. 'Tis his turn next."

"But I thought you agreed to stop."

"Did ye now? I don't recall saying as much. Though I do remember saying that Flaherty would go next, then Hennessy and Jackson. Is there something wrong with yer hearing?"

Bailey wavered on his feet, but caught himself. "I just thought—"

"Ye *thought?*" O'Malley repeated, pleased that the man was turning a ghastly shade of gray.

"—that since I answered your questions, you would be satisfied."

O'Malley shook his head. "Have ye a wife or special woman in yer life, Bailey?"

The man stiffened then nodded. "I do."

"Put yerself in me place, and tell me how would ye feel if you found out that someone not only abducted her, but held a knife to her throat, threatening her life?"

Color suffused Bailey's face as he narrowed his eyes and fisted his hands. "I'd make the man pay. Everything he did to my sweet Eileen, I'd do to him. There wouldn't be anywhere he could hide." He locked gazes with O'Malley and growled, "I'd find him…and when I did, I'd hold my knife to his throat, but my hands have a tendency to slip when I'm angry."

O'Malley nodded, pleased with the man's answer. "And of course ye'd warn him of that ahead of time."

"It would only be fair," Bailey admitted.

O'Malley studied him for a moment before deciding that the man's answer had just saved his life. Though he wouldn't be telling Bailey that just yet. "That changes things a bit. I have one last question for ye. Is Eileen employed, or does she still live at home with her family?"

Anger vanished, and Bailey sank to his knees and begged O'Malley, "I will do whatever you ask, for the rest of my life, if you promise you'll not harm Eileen. She has no idea what I do to earn coin on the side. Would never understand that it is the only way I'll ever earn enough blunt to rent a place for us to live. She deserves the best, and I mean to give it to her."

Touched by Bailey's declaration of what he sensed was the truth, O'Malley sighed and put his shirt on. "Ye've given me something to mull over."

"I know I don't deserve Eileen, but if you promise not to harm her or her family, I'll tell you without your asking that there is one other man working for the baron. One you wouldn't suspect." Bailey looked around them. "I know I could face time in the gaol"—he swallowed audibly—"or swing from a rope. But I'll gladly pay for my crimes as long as Eileen is safe. Her life is worth far more than mine."

O'Malley felt the same about Helen. "Tell me the name of the other man, and ye have me word that ye won't hang."

Bailey rubbed his neck as if he could feel the rope tightening around it. "Hardwell never told me the man's name, but I do know he was recently hired by the Duke of Wyndmere to work as a footman at his estate in the Lake District. In fact, he was supposed to insinuate himself among the staff and wait until Miss Langley left the duke's home—for whatever reason. He was to accompany her, if and when she left the duke's home."

O'Malley saw red, and seethed with anger, but controlled it. "Did ye ever see the man? Can ye describe him?"

"I'm ready to go a few rounds with the prisoner," Flaherty announced, walking toward them. Staring at O'Malley, he frowned. "Ye never fight with yer shirt on, though from the looks of his nose, yer punches connected a few times. Do ye have all of the answers already?"

"All but one." O'Malley nodded to their prisoner and said, "Bailey here is about to describe the other man who was in on Hardwell's plan—a footman recently hired by His Grace."

"Bloody hell!"

"Aye," O'Malley agreed. "Tell us what he looks like."

"Wait," Flaherty said. "Do ye know his name?"

"Do ye think I haven't asked him?" O'Malley demanded.

His cousin shrugged and motioned for Bailey to continue.

"If I knew, I'd tell O'Malley. I have seen him, though—he has light brown hair, pale gray eyes, a weak chin, hawkish nose, is rail thin, and stands about five feet, nine inches tall."

"'Tis detailed enough that I know we'll find him soon," O'Malley replied.

"All you have to do is wait until dusk," Bailey told them.

"Oh?" Flaherty said. "Why?"

"He was to wait until dusk, then go to the cottage and collect Miss Langley."

"And?" Flaherty asked.

"That's it, and before you worry if the young man would seek to harm Miss Langley, there is no fear of that. I, er…overheard that the footman has a preference for boys. He won't touch Miss Langley. It was part of the reason Hardwell hired him."

O'Malley didn't question the validity of Bailey's words, and needed to verify what he'd hinted about the baron and his henchman. "What of Wilson? Does he share the same preference as the footman?"

Bailey shook his head. "Nay. Believe it or not, Miss Langley would have been safer with me—I'd never tarnish what I have with Eileen like that."

Flaherty looked at Bailey then O'Malley. "Eileen?"

"The woman he loves," O'Malley said.

Bailey nodded. "As I was saying, Miss Langley would be safe with me, but not with Wilson or Hardwell's latest pet hire."

"Pet hire, ye say?" Flaherty asked.

Bailey shrugged. "Everyone who works for Hardwell knows to follow his orders to the letter, or they'll end up spending time in his secret room."

O'Malley held up a hand. "Ye don't need to go into further detail."

"We've heard enough," Flaherty said. "Hennessey and Jackson are with Miss Langley and the Hinkle sisters, ready to leave, but from what we've just heard, we won't be leaving until after dusk."

O'Malley nodded. "There's time now to send word to King. We'll see to it the lass and the Hinkle sisters have been taken care of to me satisfaction before dusk. We'll apprehend the footman using Bailey's technique at the outhouse—we'll be waiting for him inside the cottage. Oh, and Flaherty?"

"Aye?"

"I have promised Bailey that he will not hang for his part in any of this in exchange for information. I'll explain more later."

Flaherty eyed the prisoner and nodded. "Good enough. Bring him with ye. We'll need to put our plan together with Hennessey and Jackson. We'll either be on our way to Summerfield Chase late tonight, or early in the morning."

"I'm thinking we should leave in the morning. I'll reserve a room for the lass and her chaperones."

Flaherty swore beneath his breath, then declared, "I'm never going to lose me heart to a woman. Because the head's the next thing that follows once the heart falls."

O'Malley wanted to contradict his cousin, but in truth couldn't. The better part of valor was to remain silent. For the second time in a sennight, Eamon O'Malley clamped his mouth shut.

# CHAPTER SIXTEEN

ELEN SAT WHILE Mrs. Bertrum, the innkeeper's wife, tended to the Hinkles, grateful that they had not suffered more than a bruising blow to the face. She knew from experience that it ached until a soothing poultice was applied to it, but would heal.

"Now then, Miss Langley, your turn. Though I do not know why you did not allow me to tend to the cut on your neck first."

"It isn't deep, and I am still very concerned about Miss Josina and Miss Jeanette. Are their eyes clear?"

"We're fine, dear," Josina replied.

"No sign of concussion to worry about," Jeanette added. "Let Mrs. Bertrum cleanse and dress your wound before your handsome husband-to-be returns demanding to know why you have not already been taken care of."

Dutifully chastised, Helen tried not to wince as the soap stung the shallow cut.

"I know it stings, Miss Langley, but my special healing salve soothes as well as heals." The innkeeper's wife applied the ointment, then the folded bit of linen over the cut, and wrapped a length of linen around Helen's throat to hold it in place. "There, all finished. You are not to get the bandage wet, but should ask someone"—she glanced at the Hinkle sisters, who nodded—"to cleanse it and bandage it for you."

"Oh, but am quite certain—"

Jeanette interrupted, "That you will allow us to do so."

Her sister added, "Though I am sure O'Malley is more than capable, you cannot ask him to perform such an intimate task before you are wed."

Mrs. Bertrum nodded. "I'll send a jar of my ointment and extra bandages with you, in case your plans change and you are delayed reaching your destination." She brushed her hands over her apron. "The stew I have had simmering for the last few hours is ready. Anyone hungry? I have a round of bread, freshly churned butter, and my mother's currant cake for dessert."

"I'm not really hungry, though I wouldn't turn down tea with bread and butter," Helen said.

The older woman's sympathetic smile had tears welling in Helen's eyes. Chilled, she pulled O'Malley's coat closer until it was snug around her. She hated to appear weak. Before she could blink her tears away, a large handkerchief appeared in front of her face.

"Does it pain ye, lass?"

Helen stared at the large hand with the split knuckles and knew what had kept O'Malley. His hands told the story of the present and his past: a strong and honorable man who would use whatever weapon necessary to extract the truth from those who would prey on the weak, and to see justice served.

Her voice was unsteady when she replied, "Not really."

While she struggled to regain her composure to show that she was worthy of his regard, he gently dried her tears and caressed her face with the tip of his finger. In that deep, rumbling voice that spoke to her in dreams, he asked, "Why the tears, then?"

She rasped, "The kindness of strangers."

"Surely Miss Josina and Miss Jeanette are no longer strangers," O'Malley said. "And neither should Mrs. Bertram be."

"I could not have said it better," the innkeeper's wife remarked while gathering her healing supplies and placing them on her tray. "There are those who pass this way but once, and will leave knowing they are always welcome to return. You are all included among those special guests." She lifted the tray. "I shall return with your meal in a few moments." To O'Malley, she said, "Mayhap you can change Miss Langley's mind. She only wants tea and bread."

"With butter," Helen reminded her.

"Well now," O'Malley replied, "I'll do me best."

Mrs. Bertrum sent a silent message to Helen, which she received as if it had been said loud and clear. The innkeeper's wife would be bringing her a bowl of stew along with the bread, butter, and tea—and Helen had best be prepared to eat it.

"Did Mrs. Bertrum warn ye about infection?" O'Malley asked.

"The cut was not that deep," Helen protested.

"How clean was the blade? Did it have any rust on it?"

She shivered at the implication. That thought had never occurred to her. Her only exposure to a blade for protection had been via Lord Montrose, who was very particular in keeping his blades honed and free of dirt and rust.

"Knowing yer kind heart, lass, ye had Mrs. Bertrum tend to Miss Josina and Miss Jeanette before ye let her look at yer wound."

"You know your bride-to-be well," Josina remarked.

"That will make the adjustment easier," Jeanette added. "Though ours was not to married life as we had hoped."

Josina placed her hand on her sister's arm. "It was to bury the brave soldiers we gave our hearts to and promised to wait for."

"Ye waited faithfully," O'Malley said as if he knew it was fact, "and made certain they were buried with honors. They would have been proud to have ye for wives, as we're proud to have ye accompany us as chaperones. Thank ye, ladies."

Helen's heart broke for the sisters and all they had endured. What she had suffered could not compare.

She reached out and brushed O'Malley's hand. He entwined his fingers with hers. "I've sent word to King apprising him of the situation. There's one more duty I have to see to this evening, and while I do, I'm leaving ye in the company of these two fine women and the Bertrums."

She wondered if he would be using his fists on the prisoner again. "Where are you going?"

He paused as if deciding whether or not to answer her. "All I can tell ye is that it's a meeting. Know that I shall return shortly and explain what I can. I'll need ye to trust me until then." He brought their joined hands to his lips and kissed the back of hers. "Can ye do that, lass?"

Trust in O'Malley released a sense of peace that flowed through her. "Yes, Eamon. I can do that. We shall be waiting for your return."

He brushed another kiss to her hand before releasing it. As he turned to go, she called his name. O'Malley paused and looked over his shoulder. "Aye?"

"Be safe, *mo ghrá*."

His emerald eyes gleamed. "Aye, *mo chroí*. I'll return shortly to collect a kiss from ye."

Helen felt her face flame and her heart race. She could not wait to feel his lips possessing hers as she lost herself in another of his devastating kisses. Though her head told her it was unwise to say what popped into it, watching his lips caress her hand, her heart overruled her head. "I may need two kisses."

O'Malley's rumbling laughter warmed her from her nose to her toes and had the Hinkle sisters sighing. Helen could not wait for his return.

⟫⟫⟫⟪⟪⟪

O'MALLEY AND FLAHERTY were inside the cottage waiting for dusk to fall and the traitorous footman to arrive.

"Bailey?" a voice called as the door slowly opened. "Do you have the woman?" The man slipped inside and froze.

O'Malley and Flaherty stood side by side, arms crossed, glaring at him. O'Malley should not have been surprised, given Bailey's description of the footman. "Foldroy!"

The footman's eyes rolled up in his head a second before he passed out.

"That was unexpected," Flaherty said. "So ye know him, but how did ye not know that he was the footman who accompanied Helen?"

"I was on an errand for the duke when the man was hired, and arrogant enough to think that anyone wanting to join the duke's staff had already been vetted by Coventry—as well as the duke." O'Malley nudged the unconscious man with the toe of his boot. "When I met Foldroy, I noticed that he rarely spoke to the women on the staff, though he was open enough to speak to the men. Given his age, I thought it odd, but then thought he did not want to lose his position working for the duke by flirting with the women. I should have questioned it."

Flaherty grunted. "Unless ye've figured out how to be in two places at one time, I'm thinking ye need to forgive yerself for not questioning it. Besides, given what I've heard from Garahan's wife—and yer brother's wife—when would ye have had the time? Wyndmere Hall has been in a state of semi-upheaval since Emily and Helen arrived."

"True, but—"

"But nothing. Let it go and concentrate on what's in front of us. His Grace is going to want answers, and will want to avoid issues such as these in the future."

O'Malley knew his cousin was right.

"I'll be honest and tell ye, I'm happy I'll be here in the Borderlands when the duke hears of it," Flaherty finished.

"I should have—"

"Should have what? Read this bugger's mind? Time to face that fact that ye aren't perfect," Flaherty said, "even if ye think ye should be, as ye're one of the *sainted* O'Malleys."

O'Malley shoved Flaherty. "*Feck* off!"

Flaherty snorted with laughter as he bent and hauled Foldroy over his shoulder. "We'd best get moving. I'll take care of the prisoner, while ye go and soothe Helen's worry that ye aren't dead."

O'Malley followed his cousin out of the door. "How can she worry about something like that, given me reputation as a bare-knuckle champion back home, and the number of blackguards I've dispatched since joining the duke's guard?"

"Has she had time to hear of yer exploits and feats of strength yet?"

O'Malley grumbled, "Faith if I know. The sooner we get Foldroy back to the inn, and restrain him, the sooner we can settle the women down for the night, and prepare them to leave just after dawn." He slanted a look at his cousin as they walked side by side on the path. "From what I've heard from our cousins' wives at Wyndmere Hall, that may take some doing. A woman doesn't just roll out of bed, already half dressed, to toss on trousers and boots."

Flaherty snorted. "I won't be arguing with ye on that point."

"If ye were one of our Garahan cousins, ye might." When Flaherty laughed, O'Malley suggested, "Mayhap we'll tell them we're leaving at dawn, and when they start in with the reasons why we should not, we give in, and ask them to be ready after we break our fast."

"Aye," Flaherty agreed. "Then they'll be ready to leave when we are—though not at dawn."

"Ah, but you're the thinking man, Flaherty."

"Ye finally realized it?"

O'Malley laughed in his face. "Nay, but I wouldn't want ye to think I'd hurt yer tender feelings on purpose."

"Bloody bugger."

They approached the back of the inn, and O'Malley asked, "Do ye want me to help ye unload yer burden?"

"*Feck* no. I'll see ye inside, after I've spoken to Jackson and the constable's men."

"I'll be speaking to Hennessey before I speak to the women."

"Good luck," Flaherty called out. "Ye'll need it."

O'Malley did not bother to answer his cousin—he would have to raise his voice to be heard over the cacophony of sound in the inn yard. Besides, he wouldn't want to be overheard swearing, and having His Grace find out that he'd been crude with women in the vicinity. Another rule he tried hard not to break.

He was smiling when he opened the rear door to the inn. "Time to collect me kiss."

# CHAPTER SEVENTEEN

O'MALLEY ENTERED THE inn and walked along the hallway, nodding to the innkeeper's wife as he opened the door to the private dining room. He braced in time to catch the lass as she threw her arm around him. "I was so worried!"

He gathered her to his heart, breathed in her scent—sun-warmed roses—and sensed all would be right with his world as soon as they were wed. While her trembling ebbed, he thought of the different ways he'd soothe her—if they were already married. He held in his sigh, knowing he'd have to wait before letting his thoughts continue along that path.

"Ye never need to worry about me, lass. I can handle meself."

She lifted her head back and tilted it to one side. "You're awfully sure of yourself."

"Why wouldn't I be? I've skills ye'd probably rather not know about. Shall I tell ye?"

The irritation on her face had him chuckling. Helen did not seem pleased. He swallowed his laughter.

"I'm meaning me skill with *weaponry*, especially with a lance."

"I thought that was a weapon Medieval knights used to joust with."

"Aye, but any iron bar or blade long enough—even a small tree—can be used as a lance with the same results: unseating or overpowering your opponent."

Helen's expression softened. "And have you done that more than once?"

"Aye, lass. Mayhap ye require a demonstration. I'd be happy to accommodate ye, once we arrive at Summerfield Chase. Me brother is always willing to cross swords with me. He feels he has the edge as the duke's rapier."

"We wouldn't mind attending a demonstration," Josina said. "How many of the duke's men are stationed there?"

O'Malley smiled. "Three. Me twin Thomas, who is in charge of the duke's men at the baron's estate. Then there's Flaherty, who is taking care of the prisoner at the moment, and Garahan."

While the sisters were discussing the possibility of seeing some of the duke's men showing off their skills, he glanced down at Helen. Her lovely face held the expression of fascination-wrapped desire that slammed into his gut. Digging deep to control it, he reminded her, "Ye owe me a kiss, lass." Her hesitant smile brought out the devil in him. "Pay up."

O'Malley claimed her lips in a kiss that held the promise of a thousand nights of passion, a houseful of babes, and a lifetime of love. She sagged against him, and he softened his kiss to one of reverence. "I'll love ye forever, lass, and promise to be a good and caring husband to ye, and patient father to the dozen babes I've asked the Lord to grace us with."

When he heard the delighted laughter from across the room, he realized that he had well and truly compromised the lass in front of witnesses. "Well, now there's no getting out of it, nor changing yer mind, lass. Ye have to marry me, or else the rumors will abound that ye've made promises to me that ye don't intend to keep."

Helen rested her head over his heart and sighed. "You may live to regret your decision if we have daughters."

"Nay, lass, I've cousins enough, and brothers as well, who will gladly lend a hand watching out for them. Besides, between me married cousins and brother, there are bound to be a few sons born into the mix, as the lot of them have wives who, if they are not already pregnant, will be soon. Ye've met the first of the new generation of O'Malleys to be born—Patrick and Gwendolyn's daughter Deidre. Me brother Sean and his wife Mignonette have a son, Iain, and me other brother Michael and his wife have Harry—"

"Harry?"

O'Malley laughed at the confusion on Helen's face. "Aye, 'tis short for Harriet, a widow with a son who is four and ten."

O'Malley noticed the wistful tone of her voice and faraway look on the lass's face when she asked, "Are there any more babes?"

"Aye, me cousin Patrick's brother, Finn. He and his wife Mollie have a new babe—Boadicea."

"They named her for an ancient warrior queen?"

O'Malley snorted with laughter. "'Tis a long tale that usually requires a bit of the Irish to tell. Ye'll not be hearing it until we're wed good and proper, as it's a bit scandalous."

Her eyes widened and her cheeks flushed, endearing her to him as she burrowed further into his chest.

"So ye see, ye've nothing to worry about, as me brother's stepson is old enough to watch out for any daughters we have, and will no doubt have a hand in teaching any sons the rest of me family have, as they'll be a wee bit older than our daughters."

Helen's frown was yet another telling sign of the lass's innocence. He leaned close and pitched his voice so the Hinkle sisters would not hear when he asked, "Ye do know how long it takes from conception to birth, don't ye?" When she frowned at him, he couldn't resist kissing the tip of her nose. "'Twas an honest question, lass." She grunted, and he laughed. "If not that, then what's got ye frowning at me again?"

"We shouldn't expect your family to watch out for our daughters. You will need to teach them how to defend themselves, as I am certain your brothers and cousins will do the same with their babes. If it wasn't for what Lord Montrose taught Emily and me about a man's weak spot—"

O'Malley would later swear his bollocks shrank at the thought of what Montrose had taught his daughter and Helen. "Ye have me word that I will teach our daughters to protect themselves. Now then, lass, 'tis yer turn to kiss me."

The lass shocked him when she slipped her arm around his neck, lifted to her toes, and pressed her plump lips to his. God, the taste of her went to his head like a shot of *poitín*.

The sound of more than one throat clearing had him realizing they still had an audience. Breaking the kiss, he smiled at the dazed expression on her face. "Ye've a potent kiss, lass. I'm thinking I might need another." He lowered his mouth to hers.

"Kiss yer intended later, O'Malley—we're hungry."

He ignored Flaherty, held Helen against his side, turned, and glanced at the two men standing behind the Hinkle sisters. Instead of embarrassment, he felt pride. The lass's kiss hadn't just affected her—it had his head feeling light and his heart full. "Helen-lass, I'm sure ye remember meeting Hennessey and Jackson."

"I do. Thank you for coming to our aid."

"You're more than welcome," Hennessey replied.

"A pleasure," Jackson said.

"Ye'll be meeting Constable Saunders and his men, Ames and Grant, later. They're guarding the prisoners at the moment and will be accompanying us to Summerfield Chase. On another matter, Flaherty and I have spoken with the duke's coachman— although he has rallied and is recovering as expected, we feel he needs another few days to rest. By the time we are ready to return, he'll be ready to drive the duke's carriage to Wyndmere Hall.

"We'll stop here at the inn, and either see Miss Josina and Miss Jeanette safely on their way, or they will continue the journey with us. I've already sent word to Their Graces explaining the situation, and anticipate they will welcome ye as their guests at Wyndmere Hall for courageously protecting Helen in her hour of need."

"It sounds delightful," Josina remarked.

"We would be honored," Jeanette added.

"Now that that's settled, who's hungry? I caught the savory scent of stew simmering when I walked in the rear door."

As if on cue, Mrs. Bertram and Meghan entered, each bearing a huge tray. One carried bowls of stew and a sliced round of bread and butter. The other had two teapots, cups and saucers, plates, napkins, and utensils.

O'Malley kept his arm around Helen as he led her over to the empty chair between the Hinkles. Though he would not have minded helping her eat, he realized that it would be something he could do as her husband without the worry of her reputation being besmirched. *Soon,* he told himself. Tomorrow at the latest—prisoners and the weather cooperating—they would arrive at Summerfield Chase in plenty of time to marry. And from that day forward he would fall asleep every night with the lass tucked in his arms after a satisfying lesson in lovemaking...and wake her every morning with more of the same.

He could not wait to marry her.

# CHAPTER EIGHTEEN

To ensure the absolute safety of the women, O'Malley and Flaherty took turns on the overnight shifts—half the men kept watch over the women, and the other half the prisoners. As expected, the night was quiet, but there was a niggling feeling in the back of O'Malley's mind that something was about to happen. He'd never claimed to have the sight, like his brother Michael, who had been plagued with visions all his life.

Now that dawn had arrived, and Hennessey and Jackson took over their shifts, O'Malley and Flaherty were eager to get on with their plans for leaving.

"I'll speak to the hostler and his men." Flaherty stared at the activity in the inn yard. "No one skulking about, or paying undue attention to any of the guests or those working for the Bertrums."

O'Malley had just scanned the area and come to the same conclusion. "I can't help but feel something's wrong."

"'Tis normal for a man on the verge of taking vows."

He should have known his cousin would be ribbing him until he actually wed the lass. The hard shove from behind was a none-too-gentle reminder from Flaherty. "Bloody hell! Pay attention, or ye'll end up dead, not wed, like Emmett."

The thought of dying like his cousin arrowed through O'Malley's heart. "After hearing what happened to Emmett, I'm apt to believe he died, but it wasn't his time, so the good Lord sent him back."

Flaherty scowled. "I'm not sure I believe that, though Darby witnessed it and was there when it happened. Both he and Michaela swear that Emmett stopped breathing. As skilled a healer as Emmett, Michaela was trying techniques none of us have ever heard of to shock his heart into beating."

"I've heard part of the tale—ye must have heard the rest from Ryan Garahan's wife."

"Enough of such talk. The hostler just noticed us, and I'm for checking the carriage wheels, the team, and our horses. Then I'll meet ye in the taproom—me gut's empty."

O'Malley gave his cousin a shove toward the hostler before retracing his steps, returning to the inn. The first person he saw was Hennessey. "Everything under control?"

"Aye, Miss Langley and the Hinkle sisters should be downstairs momentarily." Hennessy frowned. "Is there something I need to know?"

O'Malley didn't know how to put what he felt into words, other than to say, "Be on yer guard and watch yer back."

Hennessey had been a lieutenant in the Royal Marines too long not to immediately take O'Malley's gut feeling to heart. "Understood. I'll warn Jackson."

O'Malley nodded and, when hailed by the innkeeper, walked over to speak with him. "Morning, Bertrum. Something on yer mind?"

"It was unusually quiet last night. I had the girls warm the sheets for the ladies. Climbing into a warm bed after a long day that included the ladies being abducted—and from our outhouse, no less—I'm thinking they fell asleep within minutes of climbing into bed."

Bertrum's words went right to the part of O'Malley that kept him wide awake when he should have been sleeping—centered around thoughts of the black-haired, violet-eyed lass he planned to wed tonight! He called on every bit of his control and said, "I know the lass and the sisters appreciated yer kindness—and the warm linens. Thank ye."

"O'Malley, there you are." Mrs. Bertrum bustled toward him, her eyes as bright as her smile. "I hope you and the others are hungry. I have cooked enough to feed a small army, but need to know how you want to handle feeding everyone. In shifts, or shall I send meals out to the men guarding the prisoners? I did prepare enough for the prisoners—do they get to eat, too?"

"I'd appreciate it if ye'd send the meals out to the men…and the prisoners, thank ye. According to Hennessey, Jackson should be escorting the women downstairs at any moment."

She nodded and asked her husband, "Would you mind taking the food outside? I do not want our daughters to get too close to the men being held in our stables."

"Of course. I was going to offer, if and when you brought up feeding the men outside."

O'Malley observed the exchange between the couple and prayed that one day, after being married more than a decade, he and Helen would have the same thoughts at the same time. "How long have ye been wed? If ye don't mind me asking."

Bertrum answered, "Sixteen years next month. Do you mind a bit of advice?"

"I'd welcome it."

"Never go to bed with harsh words or a disagreement between you."

"Is that it?" O'Malley would have thought the innkeeper would have more to say.

Mrs. Bertrum smiled. "Trust one another completely, especially when you are afraid you cannot speak your mind. Holding in your worries could lead to misunderstandings aplenty."

O'Malley smiled back. Now *that* was more along the lines of what he was expecting, and sounded like advice his ma would have given him. "Thank ye both. I'll be sharing yer advice with me bride-to-be."

He heard footsteps on the stairs and turned to watch the woman he loved walk toward him. Studying her face, he looked for signs that she was suffering from more than her injuries, but did not notice any. She was pale, but not flushed from a fever—a good sign. Her sling was in place, and when she saw him, her eyes lit up as if she had swallowed a shooting star.

"There ye are." He held out his hand and placed hers over his arm. "I trust ye had a good night's rest."

Her smile set off a volatile reaction inside of him…one he'd best get under control before things got out of hand. The Hinkle sisters seemed to be in good spirits and greeted him effusively. It was going to be interesting adding them to their small party traveling to Summerfield-on-Eden.

"Before we sit down to eat, ladies, do ye have yer things packed and ready to go?" As soon as the words left his lips, he could have kicked himself. He had forgotten to ask the duke's coachman if he still had the lass's portmanteau.

"We do," Jeanette replied.

"Thank you for agreeing to let us act as chaperones," Josina added.

HELEN STIFFENED FOR a moment, then relaxed. She did not hold out any hope of finding her bag—whoever had hit the coachman on the head probably took her portmanteau with them. She wished she had her reticule, but that had not turned up either.

As if an angel whispered in her ear, she had the thought that whoever had taken her things must have needed them far more than she did. She sent up a prayer that the person's life had improved with the taking of her things.

O'Malley slid his hand so it was cupping her uninjured elbow. "Lass, I am so sorry not to have thought to ask the coachman if he still has your bag stored on the carriage. I can ask him now and join ye in a few moments, or if ye'd rather, we can wait until after we eat and you can accompany me when I speak to the coachman."

"We will order for the both of you," Jeanette said.

Her sister added, "Your breakfast will be waiting for you by the time you return."

Helen smiled at him. "I'd like to go with you now, and see for myself that the coachman is on the mend. It is all my fault that he was injured."

The sisters immediately protested. O'Malley held up a hand, and the three of them fell silent.

"Ye'd best listen to the Hinkle sisters and meself when I tell ye to get that thought out of yer head, right now! 'Twasn't yer fault that Hardwell had a vendetta against Lord Montrose." He told the sisters, "Thank ye for ordering a meal for us. Helen and I will be right back."

He escorted her from the room and lowered his voice so only she could hear him. "I have more to say, but it'll wait until we're alone in the hallway."

A few moments later, he said, "I'll repeat what I said just now—ye are not to blame. The what and the why of it, we have yet to discover. The one thing King and Coventry have helped uncover is that the man had three contingency plans regarding Lord Montrose—and made sure that no one would have been able to connect him with what happened to his lordship, his daughter…or yerself."

"What if the reason for his vendetta had to do with nearly starving, without a way to earn coin to buy food?" When O'Malley shook his head, she quickly confided, "I understand about the basic need to survive—find food. You said you know about my past—a decade ago. I did steal from those I thought could spare the coin. I never took more than I needed to buy enough food to survive. My only other choice would have been the workhouse. Boys and girls my age died there."

O'Malley paused in the hallway and pulled her into his arms. "The thought of ye slaving with the others, doing tasks until yer fingers bled, will haunt me, lass. Far better that ye used yer cunning and skill to pick the pockets of those who would have spent their coin on fripperies…something they didn't want, nor need, but desired."

Her wrist ached where he'd crushed her against the wall of muscle that defined his broad chest, but she couldn't move, did not want to break the connection that tied them together. The comfort of his words, and the warmth of his body, wrapped around her, cocooning her. Eamon's strength, his faith in her, was a balm to the deep wound in her soul that she had all but forgotten existed until that moment when it throbbed to life.

She gasped from the pain of having it exposed and open until his lips found hers and he poured every ounce of what she sensed he held in his heart for her. His mouth caressed hers while invisible strands of hope closed the wound. Her need to open her heart to him was met with his need for the same. Their hope added the healing salve that would prevent her soul from being scarred.

O'Malley kissed away her tears, sliding his hand low on her waist, pressing her intimately against him. They would fit their bodies together after they said their vows. She was not quite certain how that would work, but she knew in her heart that once they were completely one, not even death could part them. They would love each other long after their hearts stopped beating.

Time would pass. Worlds would collapse. But their souls would be entwined forever.

He groaned. "Lass, ye should not encourage me when me will to leave ye untouched is stretched to the breaking point. Ye have me word that I'll not make ye mine until we've our vows have been said before the vicar …and God himself."

She sighed and tucked her head beneath his chin. "How long will it take to arrive at Summerfield Chase?"

His strangled laughter had her smiling. A lightness settled around her as the love between them grew and solidified with each moment they shared.

"Ye'll be the death of me, lass."

Fear that he would be taken from her before they reached their destination swept up from her toes. She pushed away from him, bumping her wrist in the process. Her sharply indrawn breath had him easing his hold on her to cup her elbow.

"Here now, I did not mean to cause ye more pain than ye're already feeling." While she fought to control the ache, he brushed away her tears, trailed his fingertips along the line of her jaw, and brushed a strand of hair from her eyes. "Try to slow yer breathing, lass—controlling it with yer mind is the first step."

When she was finally able to draw in a deep breath and slowly exhale, he said, "That's it, lass. Two more deep breaths."

She did as he asked and met his worried gaze. "When you kiss me, Eamon, I get swept away to the point where I can ignore my wrist and what happened since I left Wyndmere Hall."

"Me mind goes places best left unsaid, if I'm to leave ye untouched until after we're wed."

His brilliant green eyes glittered with emotions she had yet to name, and could not wait to experience with him. "Your honor is just one of the things I have come to love and depend upon."

He scrubbed a hand over his face and raked it through his hair, making it stand on end. The sight of this giant of a man fighting the need he confessed to her, as if it were a battle, only made her love him more. Eamon O'Malley—this handsome-as-sin man—was temptation in the flesh. She would have to be strong to help him step back from the precipice of the heat and want that flared between them.

"You started to tell me that you thought the baron had plans for Lord Montrose." Helen felt her cheeks heat with embarrassment at the intimate way he'd held her against him. She cleared her throat. "What were they?"

Though his eyes still swirled with desire and passion for her, he drew in a deep breath and slowly exhaled. He blinked, and his face once more held the neutral expression she was accustomed to.

"Thank ye, lass. Ye've more strength that meself."

She smiled. "Mayhap because I have yet to experience even a smidgeon of what I think I saw reflected in your beautiful eyes."

He cocked his head to one side. "Ye think me eyes beautiful?"

"Oh yes. And your strong jaw, sculpted lips, and handsome face."

"Handsome, is it?" He dipped his head toward hers and froze. "Lass, I need ye to give me a moment." His groan seemed to come from deep inside of him. "Ye're wreaking havoc on me senses when I need to be concentrating on protecting yerself and the others."

She did as he asked, and he nodded. "Hardwell's plans didn't just involve ending Lord Montrose's life. That was just the first part. The second was to steal his daughter's virtue, her dowry, and her inheritance. The third was to destroy yer reputation and add more coin to sweeten the pot and pay for someone to steal yer virtue, too."

His words did not reassure her, but they did ease some of the self-inflicted guilt she'd accepted when she and Emily heard that Lord Montrose was dead. "Did he actually confess his plans?"

"Nay, lass. He *bragged* of them. Hardwell underestimated the power Gavin King has within the Bow Street Runners. 'Twas a misstep by the baron. He may have connections high up within the *ton*, but between King, Captain Coventry, and His Grace, he won't be wiggling out before he is exposed as the one who planned the murder, and paid others to execute his plans." His eyes met hers, and his conviction washed over her. "Aiden and Masterson—one of Coventry's men—stopped Hardwell from carrying out the rest of his plans for Emily and yerself."

She shivered, and he reached for her, but at the last moment dropped his hand. "Remember that he failed. Now then, if we're going to reach Summerfield Chase before teatime, I'd best be checking on the duke's coachman before I forget meself, toss me control to the winds, and ravish your mouth as yer eyes are begging me to."

Helen couldn't seem to form the words in her mind, let alone speak them. She inclined her head and followed O'Malley to the bedchamber at the end of the hallway.

# CHAPTER NINETEEN

Flaherty stalked into the taproom and demanded, "Where in the bloody hell is O'Malley?"

Hennessey didn't move from his spot guarding the door to the private dining room where the Hinkle sisters waited. "Miss Langley accompanied him to speak with His Grace's coachman. Something to do with her missing bag."

"She didn't have one with her when we found her. Has anyone searched the carriage to see if it was still on board?"

"Aye, it wasn't there." Hennessey smiled. "Here's O'Malley and Miss Helen now."

"What kept ye?" Flaherty demanded.

"A private matter," O'Malley replied. "Ye'll be pleased to know that the coachman's eyes were clear and his mind not muddled just now when we questioned him about what happened after he delivered Helen to the dowager's estate. He advised that when he came to, the lass's bag was missing."

Flaherty's eyes narrowed as he studied O'Malley's face, then looked away to do the same with the lass.

"Leave off, Flaherty. *Private* means I'll not be disclosing it to ye."

Flaherty smirked. "Care to place a wager on that?"

O'Malley snorted. "Ye'd be losing if I did. We have a schedule to keep, and—" His words were drowned out by the unladylike growl from the lass's stomach and the adorable look of embarrassment on her flushed face.

Hand to her belly, she said, "Do forgive me. I did not have an appetite last night."

"Well now, it seems as if it returned with a vengeance, lass. Ye'd best be feeding her, O'Malley," Flaherty said.

O'Malley's urge to knock his cousin off his feet was strong, but Helen's belly growled again. "This way, lass."

Hennessey stepped aside and waited for O'Malley and Helen to enter the room. At the inquisitive look on O'Malley's face, Flaherty grumbled, "The rest of us have already eaten…while ye were having a *private* discussion."

Instead of responding to his cousin's taunt, O'Malley closed the door in his face.

Three-quarters of an hour later, they departed from the inn with the promise to return in a few days to collect the coachman. Their plan was to ride without changing horses. The hostler had agreed that the team would handle the extra push without a problem.

Flaherty led their party. The constable and two of his men, who formed a circle around the prisoners, were directly behind him. Next in line was O'Malley, who had insisted on driving the coach, his rifle within reach on the seat beside him. Hennessey and Jackson followed the duke's carriage.

Pleased that the road ahead held no obstacles, O'Malley kept an eye on the team of horses pulling the coach. Scanning both sides of the road ahead of them, he was aware that until they arrived at their destination, the lass and the sisters were not completely safe. Thankfully, the uneasy feeling he and the others had experienced earlier that morning must have kept trouble at bay.

A short while later, Flaherty hailed Thomas O'Malley as he led their caravan toward the stables.

Thomas grinned at his brother. "I knew it! Ye've finally found yer calling driving His Grace's carriage."

"Bugger yerself." O'Malley set the brake and jumped down from his perch.

"Who else besides the lass did ye bring?"

"Miss Langley's chaperones, the Hinkle sisters." O'Malley opened the door to the coach to help the ladies disembark. Hand extended, he held tight to Josina as she steadied herself and stepped down from the carriage. "Miss Josina, allow me to introduce me brother, Thomas."

He inclined his head. "Pleasure to meet ye, Miss Josina."

She moved out of the way, waiting while O'Malley helped her sister from the coach. "Miss Jeanette, me brother, Thomas."

"They're twins, like us," his brother remarked.

"That they are." O'Malley turned as Helen disembarked. "Careful now, yer balance is still a bit off." When she was standing beside him, he grinned, unable to contain his joy. "Helen-lass, meet me brother, Thomas. Thomas, meet the other half of me heart."

The Hinkle sisters sighed, and the lass gazed up at him with an expression of profound love. His brother inclined his head. "Well now, I can relax and know that me twin has found what I have with me wife Caro." He nodded to the constable. "Thank ye for yer assistance with the prisoners."

"Happy to be of assistance," the constable replied.

"Hennessey and Jackson were sent to act as additional guards, as we'll be keeping to the plan of escorting the prisoners to His Grace," O'Malley added.

His brother shook his head. "At first it seemed unnecessary for ye to come here first, then head to Wyndmere Hall." He smiled at the ladies and said, "With the bevy of beauties ye've delivered, I understand the need. Welcome to Summerfield Chase, ladies. I'll let me brother escort ye inside. Her ladyship has rooms waiting for ye."

"Once ye have the prisoners secured, we can meet and discuss our plans." O'Malley looked at Hennessey, Jackson, and the constable. "Thank ye for yer aid in me protection detail, men. I'll join ye as soon as I deliver the ladies into the care of his lordship's housekeeper, Mrs. Chauncey."

He held out his arm to Helen, who slipped her arm through his. "Thank you, Eamon. I know Miss Josina and Miss Jeanette are as relieved as I am to have arrived."

The butler was waiting alongside Mrs. Chauncey to greet the women. "Welcome back, O'Malley." He bowed to the ladies. "I'm Timmons, his lordship's butler, and this is Mrs. Chauncey, the housekeeper."

"'Tis nice to see ye again," O'Malley replied. "Timmons, Mrs. Chauncey, may I introduce the Hinkle sisters, Miss Josina and Miss Jeanette, chaperones to me intended."

Timmons dipped his head. "It is a pleasure to meet you ladies."

"Welcome, ladies," the housekeeper echoed.

O'Malley eased the lass closer to his side. "And this is me intended, Miss Helen Langley. Lass, meet Timmons and Mrs. Chauncey."

"Thank you for welcoming us," she added.

Timmons said, "If you'll follow Mrs. Chauncey, she'll show you to your rooms."

O'Malley held on to Helen's hand while the Hinkles followed in Mrs. Chauncey's wake down the hallway toward the kitchen, where he detected the scent of fresh-baked scones. "I'll be leaving ye, lass."

"Alone?"

"Nay. Ye'll be with the Hinkle sisters, and ye've met the housekeeper and butler. No doubt ye'll be meeting me brother's wife, and Garahan's as well."

She clung to his arm. "But what if I meet the baron or baroness and they openly disapprove of my being here?"

"Lass." He tipped up her chin with a knuckle. "Do ye trust me?"

"You know I do, but—"

"I'd be stopping at the word 'do.'"

Mrs. Chauncey turned and looked over her shoulder. "Miss Langley, forgive me. I thought you were walking with us. Her ladyship has ordered a hot bath drawn for each one of you. When Mrs. Garahan and Mrs. O'Malley arrive, we'll bring tea up to her ladyship's upstairs sitting room."

He heard the lass sigh, and her relief fueled his. "Go on, now." He pressed a kiss to her forehead and gave her a tiny push to get her feet moving.

Damned if the lass didn't square her slender shoulders, lift her chin, and slant a smile at him. He could not resist sending her off with just a bit more.

"Lass?"

She spun around and wobbled, but steadied herself. "Yes?"

"Remember that I love ye."

She rushed back to his arms, lifted to her toes, and kissed his cheek. "I love you too, Eamon. Thank you."

When he looked up, he saw three faces wreathed in smiles. He'd done the right thing escorting the lass here, instead of staying a few nights more at the inn until the coachman was well enough to drive her to Wyndmere Hall. "Enjoy a good, long soak, but don't be getting yer wrist wet, or bumping it on the edge of the tub." He watched in fascination as she blushed. "Ask Mrs. Green to save a scone or two for meself and the others. We'd be grateful."

She whirled around too fast, and he held his breath as he stepped forward to catch her when she fell. But the lass surprised him, catching herself in time, before rushing toward the ladies waiting for her.

When they disappeared into the confines of the kitchen, he rasped, "Thank ye, God, for sending the lass me way, and thank ye for protecting her until I was able to rescue her." He paused, frowned, and added, "Though I'm not certain what yer reasoning was when she was abducted again, I'll be thanking ye anyway, for allowing me to find and rescue her a second time." He had his hand on the back doorknob when he paused again. "I forgot to say amen. Amen!"

O'Malley stepped outside, saw movement out of the corner of his eye, and turned a heartbeat too late to deflect the plank of wood aimed at his head. He raised his guard and felt the blow to the bone in his forearm.

Twin gasps of horror had him glancing down. He should have known. "Why, ye little heathens!" He gave chase, but the twin scamps—wards of Baron and Baroness Summerfield—were much lower to the ground and faster than him. "Come back here!" O'Malley ignored the laughter off to the left as he closed the distance between himself and the little boys. He caught one, and then the other. With a grip on the back of the coats, he lifted them off their feet until they were at eye level.

Their faces never showed an ounce of fear, and he wondered why in the hell they weren't afraid. He'd caught them in the act, fair and square, and held them a few feet off the ground. "Fearless little *gobshites*, aren't ye?"

Their laughter had O'Malley shaking his head and lowering them to the ground. He placed his hands on his hips and asked, "Well now, Percy and Phineas, what have ye been up to since last I was here?"

They looked over their shoulders and waved at Garahan— who was cheering them on.

"So, me cousins are in on yer well-planned attack?"

"Garahan, Flaherty, and your brother have been teaching us," Percy told him.

Phineas nodded. "And since we got a blow in before you did, we get to have Mrs. Green's frosted teacakes twice today!"

The little boys reminded O'Malley of him, his brothers, and his cousins, and their rough-and-tumble play growing up. "Well now, I'll have to agree with ye, lad. Ye did get the jump on me."

Percy frowned. "How did you know we were there? We hid real good."

Phineas's face mirrored his brother's. "You shouldn't have seen us."

O'Malley ignored the ache in his forearm and leaned close to answer him, "I've invisible eyes in the sides of me head, and the back of me head as well. Ma told me when I was but two and ten that it would save me life one day. Faith, if she wasn't right about that. It saved me from an aching head this day!"

Garahan was the first to approach them. He lifted Percy and Percival high over his head while they let out the O'Malley battle cry. "Well done, lads! Prudence will be so proud of ye."

As Garahan set them back on their feet, Phineas asked, "Is Cousin Pru well enough to walk to the swamp with us later and collect samples?"

O'Malley's gaze swung to his cousin. "What's wrong with yer wife?"

Garahan's grin relieved the worry gripping O'Malley's heart. "She's expecting."

Percy rolled his eyes at his brother. "Why can't they just say she's got a babe in her belly and Garahan put it there?"

O'Malley roared with laughter. "God, if ye aren't just as smart-arsed as Garahan!"

Garahan wasn't laughing. "We've talked of this before, lads. 'Tisn't enough to hear me—ye have to listen to me when I tell ye that 'tisn't something ye speak of when others are around to hear ye. Yer cousin would be mortified if she heard what ye said."

"But ye told us that's how the babe got there when we asked," Phineas reminded him.

Percy made a face. "We told you how the baron just got this funny look on his face when we asked him."

"Right before he sighed and told us to ask you," Phineas added.

While O'Malley thought the lads' response was brilliant, and correct, it would not be something to speak of in front of a lady—especially the one carrying the babe, crying one moment, gushing with happiness the next. He'd witnessed the duchess, and then his cousin Patrick's wife, showing a frightening range of emotions, and wondered how long the poor women—and their husbands—

would be plagued with the upheaval. Nine months would be a long time to have to put up with volatile emotions.

He cleared his throat. "Now then, lads, are ye after making yer cousin cry?" The horrified expressions on the twins' faces were what he'd hoped to see. "Prudence cannot help that she's happy one minute and sad the next. From what I've been told, 'tis the babe's doing and out of the mother-to-be's control."

"Aye," Garahan agreed. "Don't ye remember how Prudence cried when ye brought her the pair of purple and white spotted rocks to add to her collection?"

Percy nodded. "We thought she'd be happy."

Garahan shrugged. "She was."

"But she cried," Phineas reminded him.

"Aye," O'Malley agreed. "Remember, she cannot help it."

"That's right, lads, and ye know she still loves ye to pieces," Garahan added.

A dark expression settled on Percy's face. "That's what she has always told us."

Phineas's face held the same dark look, and O'Malley knew it had to do with their father—mayhap their mother—striking Lady Phoebe, Baroness Summerfield, on the back of the head. The blow had rendered her unconscious, nearly killing the duke's sister...and the babe she carried. He'd ask Garahan later if the boys parents' were still waiting to stand trial.

"I'm wondering if the two of ye would stand with me cousins and brother later tonight when the vicar arrives to marry me and the lass."

Percy wrinkled his nose. "Why do you and Garahan call ladies 'lasses'?"

"Flaherty and your brother do it, too," Phineas added.

O'Malley grinned. "Well now, if ye're as privileged as me brother and me cousins to have been born on the Emerald Isle— home of the *Tuatha De Danann* and other faery folk—ye'd understand."

"Garahan's told us about the gentry—the little people."

"Ah, 'tis well he should," O'Malley replied. "Always watch out for wisps and swirls of wind—'tis themselves walking about invisible during the daylight."

The lads nodded in unison, and Phineas said, "We're not to toss the buckets of swamp water we bring home with our finds— tadpoles, frogs, fish, and such—without looking around us and warning that we're going to be dumping the water in the herb garden."

"The herbs like swamp water best," Percy added.

"Garahan's been teaching ye well, and I know ye've been minding yer cousin. Just remember to have a care for her reputation and not slur it by speaking of the babe she's carrying."

Garahan's face grew solemn. "'Tis up to us men to protect the reputations of the women we love—and the ones we've sworn to guard with our lives."

"Don't be forgetting now," O'Malley said.

"We won't, we promise," Percy said.

Phineas looked from Garahan to O'Malley and back. "Can we have frosted teacakes three times today?"

O'Malley's heart lightened at the innocence of the lads—and their love of sweets. Thank God they weren't old enough to know the truth behind their parents' motive for striking out at the baroness—or their ill treatment of their niece Prudence before she was locked in one of the attic rooms. They'd all but sold Prudence—with the aid of her mother—to a member of the *ton* who accepted coin to abduct her...and a bonus amount to violate her. There were some truths he hoped neither Garahan nor Prudence would ever tell the lads.

Flaherty made his way over to join them, reminding O'Malley, "The baron wants to speak to the constable before he questions the prisoners. You'll want to be there."

"Aye. Thank ye for testing me reflexes, lads. It appears I need more practice."

"We had a good night's sleep," Phineas said.

"Garahan told us we'd have a better chance of a surprise

attack if we did," Percy added.

O'Malley chuckled. "I don't say it often, lads, but Garahan's right."

"Someone make note of this day and write it down," Garahan said.

O'Malley shoved him out of the way with his shoulder. "Bugger off!"

"We aren't supposed to say that," Phineas said.

"Make sure that ye don't."

"But you just did," Percy said.

"I'm not a lad anymore, and can say whatever I want," O'Malley told them.

"As long as it is not within hearing distance of my wife, or any of the other women under my roof."

O'Malley looked over his shoulder. "Yer lordship. We didn't see ye there."

"Do I need to remind you to watch what you say in front of these two fine, but impressionable lads? Phoebe and I have taken them under our wing and protection."

"Ye do not, and I beg yer pardon."

He saw the baron's lips twitch a moment before he cleared his throat to say, "Vicar Chessy is expected after the evening meal. I hope that is acceptable to you and Miss Langley."

O'Malley's heart soared. "More than, yer lordship. Thank ye."

"Garahan, see that the footmen trained to step in as guards are at their posts. O'Malley, Flaherty, and I are going to speak with the constable, and then question the men. I'm depending on you and Thomas to see to the perimeter. You can resume the patrols to the village and back after we finish questioning the prisoners."

"Aye, yer lordship," Garahan replied. "Run along, lads, and see if ye can convince Prudence to put her feet up while ye tell her the tale of how ye caught O'Malley here unaware."

The baron's expression was telling. He was pleased for the lads. It warmed O'Malley's heart that the boys seemed to have become a part of the Summerfields' home. Wanting to ensure they knew he was not too proud to admit he'd been bested by two lads, he said, "Don't be forgetting to tell her ye remembered the O'Malley battle cry. Brought tears to me eyes thinking of me da teaching me brothers and me the cry when we were just about yer age. He'd be almost as proud of ye as I am."

Percy grinned. "Thanks, O'Malley!"

"We won't forget to tell Prudence," Phineas promised.

"I'll introduce ye to me intended when I return. Ye'll like Miss Helen—she has faery eyes."

The boys were entranced by the thought. "Faery eyes?" Percy asked.

"With her black-as-night hair and violet eyes, I'm thinking she has the blood of the fae running in her veins."

"We can't wait to meet her. Maybe we'll share one of our teacakes with her. The fae love teacakes."

They raced toward the house, and the baron's smile faltered. "Phoebe sent a letter asking that Prudence's aunt, uncle, and mother not stand trial. Apparently my wife has decided that it would be detrimental to the boys to find out that their parents were found guilty of attempted murder. Phoebe has been wrestling with the decision for a while now and hasn't been sleeping. Since she came to the decision, she is sleeping through the night."

"What happens if the court agrees?" O'Malley asked. "Will the squire and his wife be free to collect their sons and return to their home?"

"I am waiting to hear from our solicitors on that matter."

"Yer wife is a generous and loving woman, yer lordship. I do not believe I would be as forgiving. Ye're a lucky man."

"Thank you for recognizing those traits. There are days when I only see the hardheaded, feisty temptress."

"Ye're a lucky man, yer lordship," Garahan said. "A hardheaded, feisty wife will stand by yer side when it seems like yer life is unraveling and every hand is against ye."

O'Malley agreed, "Aye, her ladyship is a rare and wonderful woman. She's got the Lippincott temper. Ye've been blessed."

"I know it. Thank you, men. I'm torn. I know that my wife doesn't want to be the one responsible for the squire and his wife paying for their crime with their lives, but Phoebe could have died."

Garahan and O'Malley shared a pointed look, but did not speak, waiting for the baron to.

He sighed and continued, "Prudence needs to forgive them, too, so that Percy and Phineas understand the power of forgiving others, and will not have to live with the knowledge that their parents were sentenced to hang."

"And I plan to teach them that while ye can forgive what's done to ye—even by yer family—that does not mean ye have to forget it," Garahan rasped.

"Ye're a better man than me," O'Malley mumbled.

Garahan snorted with laughter as he rushed off to man his post. "Faith, haven't I been telling ye that for years?"

"That ye have," O'Malley agreed as he watched his cousin stride off to do the baron's bidding. "I'd want to watch the squire and his wife hang for their crimes."

The baron and Flaherty did not disagree with him.

# CHAPTER TWENTY

HELEN SANK INTO the copper slipper tub and felt warm for the first time in twenty-four hours. The scent of lavender drifted up as she swirled her hand through the dried lavender buds floating in the bathwater.

"Thank you for helping me into the tub, Miss Josina. I thought I could do it on my own, but didn't realize that I normally brace both hands on the edge before getting in."

The older woman smiled indulgently. "I'm happy to help. Jeanette and I understand the need to be self-sufficient. But we also need to remind you to exercise caution while you are recovering from your injury and to not get that bandage wet. You can rest it on this folded drying cloth on the edge of the tub."

"I promise to keep it out of the water."

"That's fine. Now, let me unwrap the bandage around your neck. We'll need to gently cleanse it and use some of the ointment the innkeeper's wife sent along with bandages."

Helen submitted to Miss Josina's ministrations. When the older woman folded the bandages and set them aside, Helen glanced about her, marveling at the opulence surrounding them in the alcove of the dressing room where the slipper tub sat. "I shall be finished in a few minutes, then I can attend you and your sister with your baths."

"Take your time and soak, Helen. I shall return in ten

minutes to help you wash your hair. You'll likely drop the bucket with the rinse water if you attempt it without me."

"I promise I won't. O'Malley would be vexed with me."

"He is a good man, cut from the same cloth as my Herman and Jeanette's Samuel. They would have approved of him, and I believe they guided us to the inn where we met you and O'Malley."

"Do you believe in fate?"

Josina smiled. "I do. Now finish up, and I shall be back to help with your hair."

Alone, Helen washed, though it was awkward with the use of one hand. Add that to the fact that she had never spent time *luxuriating* in a hot bath, and the bath was anything but relaxing. A short time later, the knock on the dressing room door surprised her.

"Miss Langley, it's Mary. Her ladyship asked me to attend you. Miss Josina and Miss Jeanette are neck deep in hot, scented water and loath to come out."

Helen smiled at the idea, and then realized it was probably the first time the sisters had been pampered in a very long time, if ever. "They deserve to soak as long as they wish."

"May I come in?"

"Yes, of course. Miss Josina was going to help me wash my hair, but I can forgo that for now."

Mary was holding a small tray containing bandages, linen strips, and the small jar Mrs. Bertrum had given them. "The baroness wanted to ensure that you took your time and enjoyed a good, long soak. I'm to make sure you keep your wrist dry. When you're ready to get out, let me know."

"Thank you, Mary. It is difficult doing things one-handed. The Hinkle sisters were kind enough to help me again this morning."

"I am adept with a number of hairstyles, if you would like me to do something special with your hair—after you're dried, dressed, and I bandage your throat."

"I'd best get out now—that is a really long list."

Mary set the tray down. "Oh, and her ladyship wanted me to tell you that Vicar Chessy will be arriving after the evening meal to officiate."

A thrill skittered up Helen's spine. "I was not certain O'Malley would remember, though he did tell me that was his intention."

The maid smiled. "When an O'Malley speaks…we all listen. For that matter, Flaherty and Garahan, too."

"Even the baron and baroness?"

Mary nodded. "They are frighteningly good at their job protecting and deterring those who seek to attack the duke or his family."

Helen knew for a fact that O'Malley and Flaherty were warriors at heart. But O'Malley had a gentle side, which she'd seen with the Hinkle sisters, and his kisses—Lord, they rattled her senses until her legs turned to jelly!

Mary seemed nervous, and Helen wondered if it had to do with the prospect of bandaging the shallow cut on her neck. "I don't mind if you stare, Mary. I would if I were in your place. I've never actually seen a cut that could have ended someone's life—if it had been deeper. From O'Malley's reaction, you would have thought it had been the latter. I have never seen such quiet, controlled anger before. He was beyond incensed."

Mary's mouth hung open for a moment. "I beg your pardon, Miss Langley. The image of O'Malley being incensed isn't quite what I would have pictured. Angry, boiling mad, foaming at the mouth like a rabid dog, yes…but not merely *incensed*."

"Have you ever seen him lose his temper?"

"Not once, although with the breadth of his chest and powerful frame, I have imagined it is how he appears to those who try to thwart him."

The maid sighed, and Helen wondered what the young woman was thinking now. She was caught off guard when Mary said, "He and his brother are so handsome with their light hair, emerald eyes, and those shoulders…"

Helen could barely keep up with the conversation. At least Mary seemed to lose her hesitation and worry staring at her neck. Needing to set the maid's mind at ease, she asked, "What of Flaherty with his auburn hair and blue eyes? Then there is Garahan, with his dark hair and brown eyes."

The maid forgot all about the cut and began to help Helen wash her hair. "They are handsome too, but there is just something about a man with blond hair and broad shoulders—" She bit her lip and ducked her head before getting up to retrieve the bucket of water to rinse Helen's tresses. "I do not want you to think that I would ogle your husband-to-be…or Miss Caro's husband. Although I have sneaked more than one peak at Flaherty when his broad back is turned."

Helen could not recall ever having a conversation like this one. Actually, Mary was doing most of the conversing. She rather enjoyed the maid's happy rambling, and smiled when Mary continued, "There are not many men hereabouts half as handsome as the duke's guard—even in the village. There is one exception, the blacksmith, Mr. Coleman. He has an intimidating stature and physique. Most men are not as tall, strong, or dedicated as the men protecting the baron and baroness. Did you know that each one of the men in the duke's guard have taken a lead ball, or been stabbed, protecting them?"

Helen shivered. "I did not, though I do know Garahan's brother Aiden has—and have seen him bleeding. He was sent to protect my former mistress. I was Miss Emily Montrose's maid and then companion for half my life. I confess, it feels odd to be the one in the tub, being waited on."

"I can only imagine," Mary replied. "But her ladyship was adamant that the bride-to-be was to be waited on. She even set out a lovely gown for you to wear. I'm quite talented with a needle and thread, and can make any alterations to fit the gown to you, if need be."

Helen was by turns horrified and humbled by the generosity

of the baroness. "Oh, but I couldn't possibly accept a gown from the baroness. I'm nobody."

"Not true. Just because we are not highborn, like the baroness—she is the Duke of Wyndmere's sister, you know—that does not mean that we do not have worth. Her ladyship has told us that more than once. Besides, you are going to be wed to one of the Duke of Wyndmere's private guard. As O'Malley's wife, you will be treated with the same respect he receives. All of the women who have married members of the duke's guard are treated well…even though they come from all different walks of life. No one is ever reviled. You'll get used to it."

Helen was silent while Mary continued to monopolize the conversation. The maid filled her in on some of the attacks that had occurred at Summerfield Chase within the last few months. When Mary paused for a moment, Helen said, "It sounds like what Emily and I went through on our journey to Wyndmere Hall."

"And more recently, from what we have been told. You are so lucky O'Malley was sent to find you." Mary shuddered. "Now then, wait just a moment while I fetch the drying cloth."

The kind maid returned with the cloth, then helped Helen to stand and lean on her as she helped her out of the copper tub. "Do not worry about getting me wet. I can change."

With little fuss, Helen found herself dried off and helped into a soft, cream-colored chemise and a deep rose gown.

Mary stood back and stared. "Her ladyship will be so pleased. You look radiant, Miss Langley."

"Please, call me Helen."

"Wait until she sees you, Miss Helen." The maid's eyes gleamed. "Wait until *O'Malley* sees you. Now then, I could make a tuck here on both sides, if you like."

"No, I think it's perfect the way it fits."

A few minutes later, again with Mary's expert help, Helen had donned stockings and satin slippers that only needed a bit of fabric stuffed into the toes to bring them down to her size.

"Come sit by the fire in the bedchamber and let your hair dry. We cannot risk you catching a chill by putting your hair up while it's damp. While you sit, I will take care of the wound on your neck. I know from experience that if a cut gets dirt in it, infection is a possibility."

The maid kept up her chatter while she applied the healing salve from the jar. Gently, carefully, Mary folded one of the linen squares lengthwise and held it against the wound. "Hold it there just for a moment, please." Efficiently, she wound a thin length of linen around Helen's neck, snug enough to hold the bandage in place, but not too tight.

"Thank you for helping me, Mary. I truly appreciate it."

"My pleasure, Miss Helen." Mary smiled conspiratorially as she held up what looked like O'Malley's cravat. "Before you ask, O'Malley sent you a clean one—you're to use it as a sling."

Helen's heart trembled in her breast as she inhaled and caught a hint of O'Malley's scent—rain-washed air with a hint of leather—as Mary competently fashioned the sling and tied it around her neck.

"There now, you are all set. After I do your hair for you, I will need to check with Margaret and Elizabeth—they should be nearly finished assisting the Hinkle sisters. Her ladyship will be expecting the three of you shortly. She'll be serving tea in her sitting room. Mrs. Green has made a few batches of her frosted teacakes. Those two scamps Percy and Phineas gobble them up whenever they get the chance."

"I knew the baroness was expecting—how old are their other sons?"

"They are Mrs. Garahan's young cousins...twins." Mary frowned. "Those poor little boys were recently made wards of the baron and baroness. It is not my tale to tell, though I am at liberty to say that Baron and Baroness Summerfield are the kindest of souls to have done so."

Helen did wonder what the story was, but would not press Mary to confide in her. She could always ask O'Malley. There wasn't any information the men in the duke's guard were not privy to.

Surprised at her train of thought, she realized that she was anticipating being able to discuss things that affected their life with him. She hoped that they would grow close, and not just because of what she knew happened in the marriage bed, but because they looked forward to sharing every aspect of their lives together. At least, she hoped O'Malley would share some of his worry and burden from the job he performed for the duke. Time would tell.

$$\text{CHAPTER TWENTY-ONE}$$

# CHAPTER TWENTY-ONE

HELEN WAS HESITANT when Mary handed her a silver-backed looking glass. Digging deep for her wavering composure—no one had done her hair for her, except on one or two occasions when working for Lord Montrose—she managed not to cry.

"Take a look and let me know if you like what I've done. We have plenty of time for me to change the style."

Helen glanced at her reflection and stared. "I don't look like me." She could not help worrying that O'Malley would not recognize her. And what if he preferred this primped and powdered version of herself? She could never be able to replicate what Mary had accomplished.

A knock had Mary hurrying over to open the door. "Oh, I was going to fetch you, but here you are. Come in, ladies—Miss Helen was just going to let me know what she thinks of her hair. I pinned it up higher than normal, and her hair is so silky soft, it just naturally loosened on its own. Not as severe a look, and I think it suits her." She gestured for Miss Josina and Miss Jeanette to enter, followed by Margaret and Elizabeth, the maids assigned to them. "What do you think?"

Though the maids glanced at Helen's sling and bandaged neck, neither one mentioned her injuries or commented on them. Nor did the sisters, though they had been there when it happened and knew what lay beneath the bandages. The thin and shallow cut may leave a scar, but there was not a thing Helen could do to change that fact. She hoped O'Malley would not be put off by it.

The sisters took their time inspecting her hair from all angles. Finally Josina stepped back, clapped her hands together, and declared, "Magnificent!"

"O'Malley will not be able to take his eyes off you," Jeanette predicted. "The gown accentuates your coloring and adds a hint of rose to your cheeks." Turning toward her sister, she asked, "Does she look a bit pale to you?"

"A bit, but with all that has occurred, lack of a good night's sleep will take a toll on a body. Tea and something sweet will add the roses back to her cheeks," Josina replied.

"Or a smile from O'Malley." Mary covered her mouth with both hands, her eyes wide in shock.

Margaret giggled. "Oh, Miss Langley, you are so lucky. Eamon O'Malley is just as handsome as his brother Thomas."

Elizabeth's head bobbed up and down, and a hairpin was dislodged and pinged when it landed on the polished wooden floor at the maid's feet. She picked it up and put it in her apron pocket. "Ryan Garahan is so dreamy with his dark hair and eyes… Not that we spend our time staring at the married men protecting the baron and baroness. As Mrs. Green has told us, there is no harm in admiring God's handiwork."

"You remind me of Emily Montrose…erm Garahan, Aiden's wife," Helen said. "I was hired as her personal maid nearly ten years ago, but then became more of a companion to her. She was adept at describing and pointing out which attributes were more important when considering a husband, and which should be ignored, and in the next breath would laugh and say she never intended to marry." She smiled. "But then she met Garahan, and sparks flew whenever they were in the room together." Having now met O'Malley, she wondered if others noticed what *she* felt.

Josina smiled. "Jeanette and I had that, too. It's lovely to watch and remember."

Helen wished the two lovely sisters had not had to say goodbye to the men as they left to join their regiment, only to have to bury them.

She noticed everyone had gone quiet. Uncomfortable in the silence, she shifted and felt a twinge of pain in her wrist. Given that it had been immobilized, it surprised her. She resolved to become accustomed to being more cautious, expecting her wrist to hurt.

Mary saved Helen from trying to make conversation when she was becoming anxious. "Her ladyship is bound to wonder where we are. We'd best hurry. Oh, Miss Helen, just a moment."

Helen stood waiting, surprised when Mary added one more hairpin to her loose topknot. Then she pulled a few tendrils loose to frame her face, and one that brushed against the nape of her neck. "There. O'Malley won't be able to resist winding the curl at the back of your neck around his fingertip."

"Mary!" Shock at the very idea that O'Malley would want to play with her hair sent a tingle of awareness from Helen's heart to her belly.

Jeanette stared a her for a moment. "I'm happy to see that you did not forget your sling. Thank you, Mary, for tending to Miss Helen. She has been through so much in just a short period of time."

"I'm happy to see that O'Malley thought to send another cravat for you to use as a sling," Josina added. "I do wonder if he wanted everyone to ask why you are not using a linen square, and wearing a bit of black fabric that matches what the men in the guard wear."

That had Helen thinking of the man she would be bound to for the rest of her life. She wondered if he would insist on his husbandly right to bed her tonight. Mayhap he would want to wait until they reached Wyndmere Hall.

"Was there any redness around the injury on Helen's neck?" Josina asked Mary. "She may need to see a physician." Her matter-of-fact tone eased a bit of Helen's worry.

"I did not," Mary assured her.

"I have been enough of a bother to Mary—and yourselves, for that matter," Helen said. "I am beholden to you and Jeanette for your company and chaperonage." She felt her eyes welling up and, for the second time in the last half an hour, sensed her composure slipping. "I could not have managed to get in the tub without your assistance, Miss Josina, or washed my hair without Mary's help. I am grateful to the both of you. It is not something I have ever needed, and I must confess it is a trial to wash my hair even with both hands. Thank you, thank you all. I do hate to be a bother."

"You are not a bother at all, Miss Helen," Mary said. "Your neck did not appear to pain you when I bandaged it."

"Compared to what it could have been, I did not expect it to. It only stung a little when I washed it with the soap."

"That is a good sign," Elizabeth—the shiest of the trio of maids—remarked. "Mum says if it stings when you are washing a cut, the soap is working, getting rid of any dirt and such that could lead to infection."

Josina smiled. "Right you are, Elizabeth."

Mary led the women from the room, down the hallway toward the baroness's sitting room.

Helen wondered if the baroness would first stare at the bandage on her neck or her wrist resting in the sling. Either one might make for an uncomfortable encounter over tea and cake. She wished it were already after supper, and time for the vicar to arrive. How would she be able to wait without fidgeting? Thinking of the man she was to marry in a few hours, Helen envisioned his reaching out to take her hand, and wondered if the heat from his callused hands would send tingles from her palm to her heart as it had before.

It was a struggle, but she managed to push thoughts of O'Malley from her mind as they entered the sitting room. It was empty, although the door had been open and a fire burned cheerily in the fireplace, taking the chill from the room.

"Please have a seat, and get comfortable. Her ladyship will be here in a few minutes," Mary informed them. "We shall ring for tea when she arrives."

⇒⟫⟪⇐

O'MALLEY SHOOK HIS head. "His Grace will be speaking to Coventry and King regarding new staff to be hired. He'll not risk something like this happening again."

The footman in question did not raise his head, or comment, from his position huddled in the back corner of the stall where the three prisoners were being held.

Flaherty grumbled, "He gave up without a fight. Can ye ever imagine a man doing that?"

O'Malley shrugged. "Not a man worth his salt, no."

Baron Summerfield had his hands behind his back as he stared at the footman. "What is his name?"

"Foldroy," O'Malley answered. "He apparently was not on good terms with the rest of the staff, although he preferred being in the company of the other footmen to any of the women. Never interacted with them."

Summerfield's mouth flattened into a thin line and his eyes darkened to a dark and dangerous blue. "I want double the guards on this man."

The footman glanced up and slowly smiled. "I heard you have two young boys living with you."

Flaherty was in the stall a second before O'Malley. Lifting Foldroy by the throat, he shook the man. "Ye'll never get within spitting distance of the lads." With a flick of his wrist, he tossed the man against the wall, watching with a grim, satisfied expression on his face when Foldroy's head banged against the wall. Twice.

O'Malley shoved in front of his cousin and knelt before Foldroy. "Ye think ye're smarter than us because ye weaseled yer way into His Grace's staff. But ye underestimate us if ye think ye'll be convincing someone to set ye free."

Foldroy narrowed his eyes, as if gauging whether O'Malley was bluffing.

"Know this—no one will be able to stop me from breaking yer jaw, and both of yer hands, if ye so much as whisper the lads' names."

Flaherty snickered. "Ye always were soft, O'Malley." He glared at the footman. "I'll be hobbling ye so that ye'll never walk again."

"Hobbling?" Foldroy muttered.

"'Tis a fine and ancient art," O'Malley replied. "All ye need is a sharp blade—preferably one with weight to it." He stared at the footman for a few moments, pleased when the younger man visibly shuddered. "Makes for a deeper cut, though ye don't want yer adversary to bleed out—just sever the tendons and muscles at the back of his knees to keep him from ever walking again."

Foldroy's eyes rolled up in his head, and Flaherty snorted with laughter. "Ye always did have a way with words, Eamon."

Summerfield chuckled. "Impressive, but I have to say that Thomas's description rivals yours."

O'Malley sighed and shook his head. "Me brother is always trying to best me."

Flaherty patted him on the shoulder. "Ye can't let that bring ye down—ye did a fine job convincing Bailey to talk. I'm ready to take a crack at Wilson."

Constable Saunders had been quiet up until then. "Do you know when you will be leaving for the Lake District, and if you'll need my assistance?"

Summerfield replied, "O'Malley will be otherwise engaged as of this evening—"

Flaherty's crack of laughter interrupted the baron.

"Shut yer gob!" O'Malley warned.

"Just having a laugh, not at ye, mind. *With* ye."

O'Malley glared at Flaherty. "I'm not laughing."

"Well, why would ye, when ye're the one getting leg-shackled later tonight?"

"Ye won't think it's funny when ye meet the woman destined to be *yer* wife."

Summerfield raised a hand, and the cousins fell silent. "As Flaherty has so eloquently put it, O'Malley will be getting married tonight, and I doubt he will be leaving in the morning—"

"Actually, that is me plan, yer lordship. The sooner we remove the prisoners from yer home, the better I'll feel. I'm sorry that we had to resort to bringing them here, but we had little choice with what Helen suffered. I'm looking forward to returning to Wyndmere Hall."

"How will you transport the prisoners?" the constable asked.

"They'll be riding in a special wooden carriage, one with a roof and bars."

"I take it Hennessey and Jackson will be leaving with you, guarding the prisoners," Summerfield said.

"Aye, yer lordship. Bailey and I had an enlightening conversation. 'Tis just Wilson that has refused to talk, so far…" O'Malley stared at Wilson, who was still unrepentant and refused to speak. "I'm thinking 'tis time I had a turn convincing him to talk. Flaherty had his turn—I had me hands full pulling the lass to safety at the time. After I have a go at him, we'll let Garahan have a turn. He has a stake in this as well, being as how Wilson murdered Aiden's father-in-law…before Aiden had a chance to meet the man."

Summerfield moved to stand beside O'Malley. "Do you have anything to say in your defense, Wilson? Any reason—though I cannot think of one that would be acceptable—for doing Hardwell's bidding? The charges carry a heavy penalty. Are you ready to face the gallows?"

Wilson's expression changed from bored to hate-filled.

The baron inclined his head. "So be it. I shall be in the library. Have at him, O'Malley."

Anger fought against O'Malley's steely control, but he would not let it get out of hand. He was about to be married, and it would not be wise to beat the prisoner senseless, as word of what was about to happen would surely reach the baroness and the ladies.

"Flaherty, help Wilson to his feet."

His cousin yanked the man up off the straw spread on the bottom of the stall.

O'Malley cracked his knuckles and walked toward Wilson. "I'm hoping this hurts ye more than meself." He punched Wilson in the gut, satisfied that he met more flab than muscle. When the man doubled over, O'Malley grabbed a fistful of his hair, lifted his face, and growled, "That was for the abducting me intended." He delivered a solid jab to Wilson's face, followed by a knee to the groin. "That is for attacking Emily with the intention of violating her."

O'Malley shoved the man away from him, inordinately pleased when Wilson collapsed on the floor, puking up his guts. He nodded to Flaherty and the constable. "Wilson may need a few minutes to compose himself. I'll relieve Garahan so he can have his turn *questioning* the prisoner." He had his hand on the door to the stables when he thought it wise to remind the men, "I've already thoroughly questioned Bailey."

"Bugger it, O'Malley, ye went a few rounds with him."

He slowly smiled at Flaherty. "'Twas me prerogative, now wasn't it?" Flaherty mumbled a curse while O'Malley ignored him and looked to Bailey. "Did ye remember to retrieve yer tooth after I knocked it out?" Bailey shook his head, and O'Malley shrugged. "Ah well, 'tisn't like ye could have shoved it back in yer jaw. Any man who values his wife, or family, above his own life, and tells the truth, is worthy of rehabilitating in me book."

O'Malley told the constable, "I'm thinking that, depending on what the final charges levied against Bailey are, His Grace may be willing to hire him as one of his London contacts on the docks, seeing as how King recently hired O'Shaughnessy as one of his runners."

Flaherty agreed, "We should fill O'Shaughnessy's position on the docks as soon as possible."

"I'll send Garahan in. Oh, and Flaherty?" O'Malley said.

"Aye?"

"See that our cousin doesn't land a killing blow. 'Twould displease His Grace…and Garahan's wife."

"What of his lordship?"

O'Malley chuckled. "I'm thinking he'd be more reasonable than either the duke or Garahan's wife, but ye can add him to the list, too."

He was in a much better frame of mind as he walked out of the stables and whistled. The short, sharp sound was used to warn of an emergency or impending attack.

Garahan sprinted toward him from the other side of the building. "Are we under attack again?"

"Nay. 'Tis yer turn questioning Wilson."

Garahan's eyes turned black with anger. "The man who pushed Aiden's father-in-law in front of that carriage?"

"Aye. Thought ye'd like to have a go at him." Garahan nodded, and O'Malley added, "Ye can let Aiden know that ye've struck a few blows on his behalf."

"Ye've questioned him already?"

O'Malley grinned. "Did me soul good to plant me fist in his face and knee in his bollocks—I told him that was for Emily."

Garahan clapped a hand to O'Malley's shoulder. "Ye're me favorite cousin, Eamon."

"I thought Killian O'Ghill was."

"Ah, but O'Ghill isn't here, and ye've given me a chance to avenge me sister-in-law."

"Happy to oblige." O'Malley watched his cousin stalk toward the door to the stables and yank it open. Garahans fought dirty, and O'Malley was sorry not to be able to watch Ryan take Wilson apart. But a bargain was a bargain—he'd guard the perimeter until Garahan returned. Then he'd see if Mrs. Green needed a hand delivering a tea tray to Lady Phoebe and her guests.

He couldn't wait until after the evening meal to see his bride-to-be, or kiss her senseless. If Mrs. Green did not need his assistance, he'd simply tell his brother that he needed to check on the lass's injuries. Thomas would understand and back him up if anyone questioned his reason for interrupting the baroness when she was enjoying tea with the other ladies.

Satisfied with his plan of action, O'Malley strode off to his post.

# CHAPTER TWENTY-TWO

H ELEN SMILED AT her soon-to-be sister-in-law, Caro—short
for Caroline. She'd noticed the scar on the woman's face,
but did not remark on it, nor did she stare. Though she did touch
her fingertips to the bandage around her neck. Somehow it felt as
if their bond would be stronger because they'd been scarred, and
rescued, by the O'Malley brothers... Not just brothers, Helen
remembered—*twins*.

Caro was such a strong woman, as was Prudence, Garahan's
wife, and the baroness—Lady Phoebe—for that matter.

"You're awfully quiet, Miss Helen," the baroness remarked.
"Would you rather lie down for a few hours and rest? No one
would blame you if you did."

"Just a bit overwhelmed by your kindness and acceptance."
Helen smoothed her hand on the fabric of her borrowed gown
and felt tears well in her eyes. "Your generosity knows no
bounds. I would not have minded wearing my other
dress...though that gown was borrowed, too, from another kind
soul, the Widow Dawson. She was the one who suggested the
abandoned hunting lodge to O'Malley, where he found me. The
widow took extra care cleaning my wound..."

When she fell silent, Caro said, "We are not afraid to hear
whatever you wish to share with us. We have all been there...not
victims, because we chose not to be. We have all been lucky

enough to have been rescued or protected by the duke's guard—even Lady Phoebe. Isn't that right?"

The baroness set her teacup on her saucer and smiled. "Caro would know, as I am quite sure she has heard how her husband tried to protect me when I was staying with my sister-in-law's mother."

Helen was trying to remember if she had heard a connection and couldn't.

Lady Phoebe added, "Lady Persephone is married to my brother Jared—the duke. Her mother is Lady Farnsworth, who was kind enough to chaperone me for a part of my first Season. My brother assigned Thomas O'Malley as my guard when we traveled to London…although things did not quite go according to plan." She smiled. "That is a story for another time."

"You were speaking about Thomas?" Caro said.

The baroness laughed. "I promised Thomas that I would stay put. When I received the ransom note for Marcus, how could I not follow my heart and the man I loved?"

"Marcus?" Helen asked.

"Baron Summerfield, my husband, though he wasn't at the time."

"I would have done the same," Helen told her.

Lady Phoebe's expression was one of determination. "Nothing and no one—not even Jared or my other brother Edward—would stop me!"

Intrigued, Helen had to ask, "What happened?"

"I did not have the coin, but was determined to rescue Marcus."

"Were you now, my darling?"

The deep voice had all heads turning, and the women gathered in the sitting room sighing. "You know I was," Lady Phoebe replied. Before she could rise to her feet, the baron strode across the room and took her hand in his. Ignoring his audience, the baron kissed her hand lavishly, and Helen noticed that the color of his eyes—so similar to Phoebe's—turned a deep, dark blue.

Her heart raced at the thought that O'Malley pulled a similar reaction from her when his lips touched her hand, her face, or her mouth. In that moment she truly believed there was indeed one special person that was destined to find you, no matter what trials and tribulations they had to endure.

When he found you—as Eamon O'Malley had found her—nothing and no one, not even her own foolish self, could keep you apart. Not even circumstances you felt beyond your control.

Helen sighed and reached for her teacup, and nearly bobbled it. The sound broke the tension in the room.

Lady Phoebe laughed delightedly. "You are a rogue, Marcus."

The baron bowed and released her hand. "But you would not have me any other way, would you?" He smiled. "Enjoy your tea, ladies. Mrs. Green's frosted teacakes are coveted by more than the twin rogues-in-training who have found a place in our hearts."

The baroness agreed. "They have brought such joy to us at a time when we did not think anything possibly could. Despite causing more than one uproar in the kitchens over those teacakes in the last few months."

Before Helen could ask, the baron nodded to them and strode from the room. She turned back and noticed the baroness studying her.

"I've seen the way Eamon looks at you, Helen. What warms my heart is that you watch him as if you cannot believe he would care for you. Trust him," she advised. "Trust and follow your heart."

Lady Phoebe reached for her teacup, sipped and asked, "Shall I order another pot of tea, or something stronger? Mrs. Green keeps a medicinal supply of Irish whiskey—mostly for the duke's men. I have been known to sip whiskey or brandy when the occasion calls for something to fortify one's nerves."

Helen did not know what to say, so she remained silent.

The baroness asked, "Is there something weighing heavy on your mind about tonight that you'd like to ask, Helen? I am quite sure Caro, Prudence, and I would be happy to answer any of your questions."

Helen felt as if the baroness had hugged her. "Both Emily and I lost our mothers when we were young. Lord Montrose's housekeeper and cook took Emily aside when his lordship first made rumblings about finding her a husband. They were quite insistent that I be a part of the conversation that they had with her, and went into great detail...explaining things." She was embarrassed to even think of what the women who had been married for a number of years had spoken of. "Things they felt we should know before marrying. They are such kind women, both married for some time before losing their husbands."

"I lost my mother when I was young, too," Lady Phoebe said. "I was fortunate that my sisters-in-law, Persephone and Aurelia—who for some reason fell head over heels for my irritating older brothers—felt the same, and explained far more than I thought was possible about the marriage bed."

Josina patted Jeanette's hand. "If you do not mind, your ladyship, my sister and I would like to rest our eyes for a bit. Thank you in advance for having a heart-to-heart with Helen."

"Of course," the baroness replied. "Beth, would you mind escorting the ladies to their rooms?"

"Yes, your ladyship," her maid replied.

Helen's heart ached for the sisters as she watched them rise and bid the other ladies goodbye. "They were both engaged to be married," she said after they had gone. "Herman Standish was Miss Josina's intended, and Samuel Standish was Miss Jeanette's... They were brothers."

"What happened?" Lady Phoebe asked.

"They bought their colors and fought bravely in their regiment." Helen's voice broke, and she had to pause to compose herself. "They bravely fought for king and country, and died with honor on the battlefield—on the same day."

"And they have never married?" Caro asked.

"I haven't asked them," Helen admitted. "But from the way

they speak of them, I would say not."

"You are so fortunate to have made the acquaintance of the Hinkle sisters, even more so that they offered to stand in as chaperones. It is what Lady Farnsworth did for me. I will always be grateful, though I am quite sure there were times when Persephone's mother questioned her decision."

Helen smiled, thinking of how the Hinkle sisters' offering to chaperone her came about. "O'Malley can be very persuasive."

Caro laughed. "Sounds like Thomas. I have yet to meet their other brothers, Sean and Michael. But I have corresponded with their wives—Mignonette was working as a seamstress for the famed modiste Madame Beaudoine when Sean rescued her, and Harry, or Harriet, was rescued by Michael when she was defending her tenant farm from attack."

"One would wonder what this world was coming to," Lady Phoebe remarked, "when women are still used as bargaining chips, wagers, or a possession. Thankfully, there are men of strength and honor who have fought to free us from those with ill intent."

Helen was not surprised when Caro and Prudence heartily agreed.

Lady Phoebe continued, "Now that it is just the four of us, is there anything you would like to know? I can see that you are worrying about something. I promise we will be frank and truthful in our answers. There are things I wished *I* had known to ask."

Helen dug deep for the required courage and found it. "I know to expect pain, and cannot help but be concerned that I will not be able to bring myself to do what is expected of me. What if I faint, or worse, stare at his...manly parts in horror?" The delighted laughter of the three women was not what she'd expected. "You find my fears amusing?"

"Not at all," Lady Phoebe assured her. "I was remembering how patient Marcus was with me, and the questions I asked that had him tongue-tied. Particularly the part when I asked him how in the *bloody hell* did he expect me not to panic when I saw him naked for the first time. His manly parts, as you referred to them, were huge and intimidating, and seemed to lead the way as he walked toward me."

"I had a similar experience," Caro admitted. "Beyond intimidating."

Prudence flushed, and added, "Mesmerizing."

That caused another round of laughter from the married ladies, prompting Helen to ask, "So it was not painful?"

"It was," Lady Phoebe replied. "But there was also pleasure. The right man—and I do believe Eamon O'Malley *is* the right man for you—will be patient and understanding, and bring you pleasure such as you cannot begin to imagine." The baroness flushed, smiled, and rasped, "With just his hands, his lips, and his tongue."

Helen picked up her napkin and fanned her face, while Caro and Prudence murmured their agreement. "It would seem there is a good deal that Emily's housekeeper and cook left out of their telling."

"Quite understandable," Lady Phoebe said. "Given the age difference, and the fact that not all men are as instinctively sensual as the others."

Helen picked up her teacup and drained it in one swallow. Thank goodness it was tepid and had a cooling effect.

Lady Phoebe got up, walked to the corner of the room, and tugged on the bellpull. "I believe it is time for a sip of something medicinal to calm your nerves." A few moments later, there was a knock on the door. "Come in."

A footman stood in the doorway. "You rang, your ladyship?"

"Would you please remove our tea things and ask Mrs. Green for her bottle of medicinal Irish whiskey?"

The footman did not bat an eyelash at the request. "Of course, your ladyship. Anything else?"

"Yes, the decanter of brandy from the library."

"At once." The footman gathered the remnants of their tea,

placed it on the tray, and picked it up, promising to return momentarily.

"Now then," Lady Phoebe began, "whatever you do, trust me when I advise you to ask your husband if you are worried or confused about…well, anything."

"He may sound gruff," Caro added, "but if Eamon is anything like his brother, he will be struggling to control his need to make love with you."

Prudence nodded. "But he will be patient, and may even ask you to tell him when something feels good, and something doesn't. We all have the same lady parts, though not everyone reacts the same way when touched intimately."

Helen realized her mouth had gaped open. She snapped it shut and wondered if the lush carpet in the room would oblige her and swallow her whole to avoid further embarrassment. Her next thought was that she was addlepated and should be thanking these women for their honesty and advice.

By the time she had her thoughts in order, the footman returned with the requested decanters. He appeared to be embarrassed, and Helen wondered if he had been outside the door when Prudence had been giving her advice. He set the tray on the table, bowed, and retreated. Rather than worry about it, she accepted a glass of brandy when Lady Phoebe offered it.

The baroness raised her glass in a toast. "To Helen and Eamon's happiness." When everyone had sipped from their glasses, she said, "Just one more thing, Helen."

"Yes?"

"Nothing that happens between you and your husband is wrong. No matter what you hear—and people will talk as they are wont to do—what is between the two of you remains between the two of you, unless you are asked to share your experiences in confidence, as we have here today with you."

Helen was moved by Lady Phoebe's care and concern for her feelings and worries. That she, Caro, and Prudence would take the time to ease her fears endeared the women to her. "If there is ever anything I can do for any of you, please, just let me know. I can never repay your kindness, nor thank you enough."

Lady Phoebe glanced at Caro and Prudence, and slowly smiled. "Be happy."

# CHAPTER TWENTY-THREE

THOMAS SNORTED, AND Eamon growled. "'Tisn't funny. What the bloody hell was I thinking? I have no idea what to do with a wife. What *do* I do with a wife?" Thomas glanced at Ryan, who grinned. Eamon threw his hands in the air. "Aside from making love to her whenever I can for as long as I can."

Flaherty scowled at them. "Ye're all a bunch of bleeding *eedjits*. Ye'll not see me leg-shackled like the lot of ye. I can go where I want, when I want. Make love to scores of women, if I want."

"Given the time we spend protecting the baron and his wife," Thomas said, "I'm guessing your time is spent changing up patrols from the rooftop to the perimeter, to the patrol to and from the village."

"Don't forget the interior patrol," Garahan added. "That raises the question, do ye need help making the list of that score of women ye plan to bed...once ye find the time to devote to the task?"

Flaherty's eyes flashed a warning. O'Malley saw it and stepped in front of Garahan, his arms crossed, level with his chin. Flaherty had not been expecting the defensive move, and grunted when his Adam's apple rammed into O'Malley's forearm.

"Get the *feck* over yerself, Flaherty," O'Malley warned. "I'm needing ye to stand with me brother and Garahan when the vicar arrives. Ye're family and are just as important to me as the others."

"So quit being an arse," Thomas grumbled.

"I'm thinking he's more like a wilted pair of bollocks," Garahan said.

"Ah, just what I expected," Summerfield said, entering the fray. "Another tender family discussion." Shaking his head, he turned to O'Malley and said, "Vicar Chessy just arrived. Have you decided who will give yer bride away?"

That brought O'Malley up short. "I have not. 'Tis important, isn't it?"

"I'd like to offer to escort Helen," Summerfield said, "with your permission."

"Would ye?"

"I'd be happy to—on one condition."

"Of course," O'Malley agreed. "What is it?"

"That whoever started this latest round of familial disagreement apologizes, so we can get on to more important matters. Like seeing you wed Helen."

Flaherty grudgingly apologized, and the others accepted.

"Oh, and by the by, Phoebe and I have had the guest room at the opposite end of the hallway from the nursery made ready for you."

O'Malley stared at the baron and slowly shook his head. "I wasn't thinking about where we'd be staying tonight as much as I was thinking..." He raked a hand through his hair. "I'd best not be confiding what I was thinking."

"I would wonder what was wrong with you if you *weren't* thinking of the pleasures the night will hold."

A sudden thought plagued O'Malley. What if she was afraid of him? What if she asked him to stop at a crucial moment?

Thomas put an arm around his brother's shoulders. "Be patient with yer bride. Take yer time, because ye'll reap the rewards if ye do."

"I heartily agree with that," the baron said. "Now then, I shall go present myself to your intended and offer to escort her downstairs. Oh, one more thing."

O'Malley turned toward the baron. "Yer lordship?"

"My darling Phoebe had all of the ladies in her upstairs sitting room for tea earlier."

"That was kind of her."

The baron chuckled. "After the teapot was empty, she had one of the footmen deliver Mrs. Green's bottle of whiskey and a decanter of brandy from our library."

O'Malley frowned. "What in the world would they need that for, if they'd already had tea?"

"Knowing Phoebe, she was having a heart-to-heart discussion with Helen to ensure that there would be no surprises in the marriage bed." Summerfield shook his head. "There were plenty the night I married Phoebe—apparently her knowledge was more limited than I would have thought—but we managed."

"Please send me thanks to her ladyship."

"Caro and Prudence would have added their experiences as well," the baron said. "I'll see you downstairs."

O'Malley turned to his brother and cousin. "Thank yer wives for me."

"Enough stalling, Eamon," Thomas said. "We'd best get ye downstairs to the sitting room. Vicar Chessy is liable to think ye've changed yer mind."

"Not in this lifetime!"

⟫⟩⟩⟩⟨⟨⟨⟪

HELEN ANSWERED THE knock on her door and was instantly concerned. "Your lordship? Is something wrong?"

His warm smile eased the edge off her worry. "Not at all. I was hoping you would not mind if I escorted you downstairs. The vicar has arrived, and O'Malley and the others are on their way to the sitting room."

"I would be honored, but are you certain Lady Phoebe won't mind if you do?"

"I'm positive." He held out his arm, and she slipped hers through it. "You look lovely, Helen."

"Thank you, your lordship."

It was the last thing she remembered saying to him, though they carried on a conversation all the way down the stairs and to the sitting room.

They stopped in the doorway, and the baron cleared his throat. The room fell silent and all eyes turned toward them as they walked toward where the vicar and O'Malley stood waiting.

Helen could not catch her breath until her eyes met O'Malley's, and she watched his expression change from one of worry to wonder. Her nerves smoothed out and joy filled her heart as he strode toward her, meeting them halfway.

O'Malley nodded to the baron and held out his arm. "Thank ye, yer lordship. I promise to treasure Helen always."

"I never doubted that you would, O'Malley." The baron moved off to the side to stand beside his wife. Josina and Jeanette were gathered with Caro and Prudence, who stood with Percy and Phineas, as their husbands were standing beside O'Malley and Flaherty.

Helen could not stop staring at her groom, and wasn't paying attention to half of what the vicar was saying. Then O'Malley grinned, leaned close, and said, "I'm thinking this is where ye agree."

"Agree?"

"Aye, lass, to obey me every word, no matter if ye agree with it or not."

She glanced at the vicar, who looked like he was choking on his laughter. "I do apologize, Vicar Chessy—you see, I am a bit nervous. Could you please repeat what you just said?"

"Of course. Miss Helen Langley, do you take this man to be your husband from this day forward, to have and hold, love and cherish, till death do you part?"

She slid a glance at O'Malley. "I do."

"Eamon O'Malley, do you take this woman to be your wife from this day forward, to have and to hold, love and cherish, till death do you part?"

"I do."

"You may—" The vicar chuckled as O'Malley pulled Helen close and kissed her with gusto. "I believe he was waiting for that part."

O'Malley didn't stop kissing her, even when he swept her into his arms. He ended the kiss only to stare down into her eyes and mold his mouth to hers again. When they were halfway to the staircase, he kissed her again. "I don't want to miss a step and cause ye harm, lass. The taste of ye goes to me head like three fingers of the Irish."

Heart pounding, head spinning, Helen managed to ask, "Where are we going?"

"If ye need to ask, lass, I'm thinking her ladyship did not explain quite enough about what to expect tonight."

Helen did not know what to say to that, because what the baroness and the others had imparted had *seemed* more than enough, though unreal to her. But what did she know? You could fit her experience with what was about to happen in a thimble, or on the head of a pin, and still have room left over.

He reached the top of the staircase and did not even sound winded when he asked, "Didn't the ladies have a private word with ye?"

She lifted one shoulder but couldn't bring herself to admit that they had. What if he wanted her to tell him what they told her? She knew she would die of acute embarrassment.

"A shrug isn't a proper answer."

"Are you going to lecture me about that again?" He grunted, and she laughed. "I thought we agreed a grunt was not a proper response."

"A lot has happened since we had that conversation."

"Are you saying that you don't remember?"

"We may have agreed." O'Malley stopped in front of the last door at the end of the hallway. "Open the door, lass."

She hesitated at the gruff tone of his voice, then remembered Caro's mentioning that O'Malley may sound angry, but he wasn't. It would be his reaction while fighting to keep his steely control in place. She opened the door, surprised when he kicked it closed with his heel.

"I'll set ye down on yer feet, and I'm going to stand over there by the washstand."

"Because?"

"I cannot be responsible for me actions when we are standing so close to that bed."

While she stared at him, his eyes grew darker with each beat of her heart. Was he thinking about undressing her? Kissing her? Touching her?

"Whatever ye're thinking, lass. I promise to do all of that and more." His voice roughened when he added, "If ye'll let me." Yet he still did not move from where he stood, as far away from the bed as he could be while still in the same room.

"Eamon, if I tell you something, do you promise not to be angry with me?"

"Aye, lass, ye have me word."

His immediate agreement soothed her, but still her pulse began to race to the point where her head felt as if it were no longer where it was supposed to be. "You'll tell me if I've upset you, won't you?"

"If that is what ye wish, I will."

It was so hard to get the words out that when she finally did, her voice was barely audible above the pounding of her heart. "I'm afraid."

"Sweet lass. I know ye are."

"I always feel safe when you are holding me, Eamon."

He closed his eyes and stared up at the ceiling. "God in Heaven, but ye're killing me, lass."

"How? I'm only talking to you."

"'Tis the look in yer eyes. As if ye want me to strip ye bare and use me lips, teeth, and tongue to explore every inch of ye."

She blinked, and her vision wavered—Eamon had two heads. She blinked again, and he had but one. "I... I absolutely am not thinking that. Where would I get such an idea?"

Eamon scrubbed his face with his hands and slowly walked over to where she stood by the end of the bed. "Ah, lass, mayhap 'twas in me dreams that ye asked me to do just that night after night."

"Oh." What else could she say, when she would have no idea if she wanted his lips everywhere? Well, in truth, she wouldn't *mind* having his lips trailing a line of kisses from her lips to the hollow at the base of her throat.

He reached out to cup her face in his large, callused hand. She loved the raspy feel of it and wondered what it would feel like if he ran that hand along her spine to her waist and back again. Her heart beat faster, and she felt her control slipping just out of reach.

"Eamon... I feel faint."

He pulled her close, anchoring her to him with his wide-palmed hand at the base of her spine, perilously close to the curve of her backside. His other hand was at the nape of her neck, and he slowly speared it into her hair, tugging gently until the pins began to loosen and fall to the floor and her hair fell about her shoulders.

"I've got ye, lass. Don't be afraid of me. I'll not hurt ye more than is necessary the first time I make love to ye."

His touch helped ground her to where she could once again feel the top of her head. His words sank in. "Necessary? Why would it be necessary to hurt me?"

"I thought her ladyship spoke to ye about the marriage bed."

Helen frowned. "She mentioned many things—in fact, some that you just mentioned—but I do not recall her using the words 'marriage' and 'bed' together."

His rumbling laugh surprised her. "Are ye certain about

that?"

She shook her head. "It's all a blur—and it's all your fault. You are too…"

"Too…?" he echoed.

"Tall. Broad. Handsome. Kind."

"Ah." He brushed a lock of hair behind her ear. "Ye must remember some of what she said."

Images accompanied by the advice she'd received came back in a flash, and Helen decided to share the parts she could tell him without disgracing herself by swooning at his feet. "I was to trust you."

"And?"

"Not be afraid of you."

"And?"

"To tell you if I didn't like the way—or where—you were touching me."

"Anything else, lass?"

She licked her lips before answering. "She said that you wouldn't rush me and would be as gentle as you could be… Or mayhap that was something I had *hoped* she would say. I cannot think straight when you are standing so close."

"Well now, we both seem to be suffering from the same problem. Why don't I help ye out of yer gown and ye can help me take off me frockcoat?"

"But I only have the use of one hand."

"That'll do, lass. Hold still while I remove your sling and then undo yer buttons and lift this over yer head."

She stood perfectly still, though she shivered every time the tips of his fingers brushed against the bare skin below her nape.

"Grab on to the edge of me cuff now, lass, and hold on to it. Ye don't have to do anything else. I'll do it all, though ye'll have helped to undress me, which is what I hoped ye'd be doing tonight."

He slipped out of his waistcoat next, watching her the entire time.

She felt her face warm under the intensity of his gaze as he slipped the coat off his broad frame, revealing the close fit of his cambric shirt. He drew in a breath, and she watched his chest expand and his sculpted muscles push against the fabric until the only thing left to her imagination was if his skin was the same shade as hers. His face and hands were darker, but that could be because of exposure to the sun, or he could have the same healthy glow all over.

Her heart picked up again as she imagined what Lady Phoebe had spoken of…then put her hand over her eyes.

"Lass?" She felt his arms circling her again. "What's wrong?"

She would never be able to go through with this. O'Malley deserved a woman far braver than her. "I'm a coward."

Warm lips pressed kisses along the curve of her cheek and the line of her jaw. "Ye're the bravest woman I know."

"I was terrified when the baron tossed Emily onto the bed and straddled her, spewing such hateful things."

"Ah, lass, look at me. Come on now." He nudged her hand until she lowered it to her side. "That's better. Now take a long look into me eyes."

"They're darker than they were, but there is no edge of meanness in them. Hardwell's eyes looked *mean*."

"'Tis best that ye know straight off—all of us O'Malleys have changeable eyes."

"Changeable?"

"Aye, the color darkens when we are aroused."

"Are you aroused now?"

"Aye, lass." He bent to capture her lips in a kiss that promised more. "They turn piss yellow when we're angry, though sometimes they're so dark green, they appear black."

"I see."

"I hope ye do. I would never willingly hurt ye, but ye must understand that even when I kiss and caress ye in places ye've yet to dream of…even when I stretch ye, so ye can take all of me inside of ye, and are begging me to relieve the bone-deep ache, there will still be pain."

She stared into his eyes and saw the truth of his words. "Mayhap we could start by me helping you remove your shirt."

He cupped her chin and plundered her mouth until she sagged against him. "Ye'll need to open yer eyes."

Helen felt the flush sweep up from her neck to her forehead as she held on to one of his sleeves. He slipped one arm free, then the other, and tossed the garment on the floor behind them. She had not been prepared for the sight of Eamon's heavily muscled chest. He looked like one of the statues she'd seen in one of Lord Montrose's books…one Emily had snuck out of his library when her father was out of the house.

"See something ye like?"

She could not trust her voice to work, so she nodded.

"Well then, lass, why don't ye come closer and touch me? I'll die if ye don't. Anywhere at all."

Helen's hand shook, but she bravely reached out and pressed her hand right to his chest. The heat of his skin, and heavy beat beneath her hand, had her lifting her gaze to his. "Your heart is racing."

He reached out and held his hand above her heart. "May I touch ye?"

"Please."

His large hand was hot where it settled over her heart. The tips of his fingers rested against the fullness of her breast. She drew in a breath and watched his eyes darken and his nostrils flare. But she wasn't afraid, because he had not moved his hand, nor had he squeezed her hard—like the evil baron had threatened to do to Emily.

O'Malley slid his hand around to her back and pulled her close until her cheek was resting over his heart. The beat was slower now. "Will ye tell me what happened just now? Ye didn't seem to be afraid of me, then all at once, ye had this terror-stricken look in yer eyes."

It was easier to tell him when she couldn't see his expression.

She would still know what he was thinking by how his body stiffened beneath her cheek. "I remembered one of the threats."

His breathing slowed. "What threats?"

"At the inn when Hardwell was waiting in our bedchamber. I tried to yank him off Emily, but he struck me and tossed me aside as if I were a pesky fly. Then he threatened to squeeze her...her breasts until she cried out in pain."

"No wonder it took me nearly pulling out Aiden's teeth to get him to tell me what happened after he and Masterson broke down the door." He eased his hold on her. "Will ye lie down with me? I'm thinking ye need to be held while ye tell me everything ye fear. Then I'll talk ye through how I can replace those memories with ones that will make yer heart fly."

She didn't want to cower from the man she'd married. She wanted what Lady Phoebe had. What Caro and Prudence had.

"I do have an important question for you, Eamon."

"I'll do me best to answer."

She glanced at the floor and back to him. "Are you going to throw every article of clothing onto the floor?"

He raised an eyebrow. "I did not toss yer gown on the floor, now did I?"

She looked at the chair where he'd placed her gown, and then the floor where his frockcoat, shirt, and cravat were strewn. "You did not."

"Well then, ye have no worries about yer clothing—'tis just me own that I'll be throwing to the floor."

She was laughing when he picked her up in his arms and gently laid her on the mattress—and moaning when he leaned over her and kissed every last thought from her head.

$$\diamond$$

# CHAPTER TWENTY-FOUR

O'MALLEY REVELED IN his wife's reaction to his kiss. Lord, she was a delight—but she had darkness trapped inside of her from what that bloody bugger had done to her and Emily. In his heart, he whispered a prayer of thanks that Aiden and Masterson had arrived in time to save the women from a lifetime of nightmares.

He ran the tip of his finger along the curve of her eyebrow. "While ye think of something else he threatened, will ye let me show ye the way a man who is aching to make love to his wife on their wedding night would caress yer bountiful breasts?"

Her eyes widened, but she did not refuse. She nodded.

"Ye're so brave, lass." He moved onto his side so he could watch her reaction to his touch. "Remember now, if something doesn't please ye, just tell me. I've many, many ways to touch—and taste—ye, lass."

Her mouth opened, but when nothing but a squeak came out, Helen closed her eyes.

"I take it that was yer surprised sound. Not yer frightened sound."

She opened one eye and glared at him. *Talented lass.*

He swallowed his laughter. "Now then, where was I—ah, yes. I'll start here, so you get accustomed to the weight of me hand upon yer shoulder. Ye've strong shoulders that have carried too many burdens. I aim to share them with ye from this moment forward."

Her faery eyes had a dreamy expression in them.

"I'm going to use the palm of me hand to memorize the curve of yer shoulder and shape of yer arm." When she nodded, he gently matched his touch to his words. "Now then, I'm needing to touch the line of yer collarbone, but me hand is too large—I'm thinking two fingertips will do." She nodded, and he began to follow the outline of the bone until he reached the hollow of her throat. "I'm thinking I'll expire if I don't use the tip of me tongue to taste yer flavor right there, where I see yer pulse starting to beat like mad. Will ye let me?"

"Yes."

He dipped his head and skillfully swept the tip of his tongue into the hollow and onto the bones on either side of that dip. "Ye taste of lavender, lass…not roses."

"I brought dried rose petals with me in my baggage, but whoever has my portmanteau and all it contained is welcome to it. I hope its contents ease their burden."

He lowered his lips to a breath above hers. "Ye have a brave and giving heart. Kiss me, lass. I do not want ye to be thinking of luggage and rose petals when I have me beautiful wife lying beside me, letting me accustom meself to the flavor and texture of her silken skin."

Helen slid her hand to the back of his neck and added a bit of pressure, telling him without words that she wanted to kiss him. He was soon lost in the revelation that the lass remembered how to kiss him back. When the strap of her chemise slid off her shoulder, he pressed his lips there, then eased back. "Forgive me for not asking yer permission first."

"That felt wonderful."

"Will he let me taste ye from yer collarbone down to the tops of yer beautiful breasts?"

She shivered, but nodded.

He eased back and frowned. "I'm sorry, but I can't reach ye

there unless we remove yer chemise. Will ye let me?"

Helen bit her lip and drove him so close to the edge of reason that he felt himself pulsing against her belly. Her eyes shot to his.

"There are some things I cannot control. What I can control is not taking what ye have yet to offer me, *mo ghrá*. Until ye do, I'll be keeping me trousers on."

The tension left her. "Could you help me take my chemise off?"

He kissed the tip of her nose. "That I can, after we strike a bargain, lass."

"Depends on the bargain."

He laughed and kissed her full on the lips. "What I'm thinking is that unless ye have a sharp weapon in yer hands, I can kiss yer face, yer mouth, yer head, and yer hands."

She seemed to be thinking about it, then said, "If you add my throat, the nape of my neck, my collarbone, and my shoulders, I will agree to that."

"I'll be careful and kiss above the bandage around yer throat, and below it." He did that and more, kissing every single part of her that he'd listed—and those parts she'd added. She moaned his name the second time he nibbled beneath her chin, before trailing his lips to the edge of her bandage and back again, kissing her lavishly.

"You nibbled me."

"Ye're delicious."

"Are you?"

"'Tis a fair question—rather bold, but we'll let that pass. Why don't ye pick the part ye wish to sample and go for it."

"Anywhere?"

His gut clenched, and his shaft throbbed.

She stared at the placket of his trousers and gasped. "How do you do that?"

"'Tis the same answer as before—some things I can control, some I cannot."

She slowly nodded. "Do I need to ask you before I kiss you?"

"Nay, lass. I already have knots of anticipation in me gut from waiting for ye to decide where to kiss. God in Heaven, kiss me, lick me, bite me. Any or all will do—just please put me out of me misery."

"I'm so sorry, Eamon. I'm not trying to hurt you."

"The only way you'll hurt me is if you do not touch me, or if ye turn away from me."

She leaned down and trailed the tip of her tongue along his collarbone, and nibbled on his neck before fusing her mouth to his.

When she ended the kiss, his head was spinning, and his heart beat double time. "Ye're going to kill me, lass."

"Don't you want to know what you taste like?"

He closed his eyes and groaned. "If ye're needing to tell me, I'll listen."

"Your taste matches your scent—rain-washed air with a hint of leather."

O'Malley chuckled. "Have ye been in the stables licking saddles again?" Her laughter warmed his heart. "Is there anywhere else you'd care to sample?"

"After you help me take this off."

"Ah, yes. Ye distracted me. Watch that ye don't use that arm." He happily divested her of the chemise and indulged himself in the bounty that lay before him. He could not wait to sample, with his lips and tongue, but it was still her turn. "Now then, would ye like me to roll over so ye can sample me back?"

"I'm still considering it, but if you could turn over, that may help me decide."

"Don't take too long—I've yet to prepare ye for me loving, lass. That takes time and patience, so I'll be certain ye experience as little pain as possible." He rolled over and was shocked when the lass trailed her tongue from the nape of his neck to the waistband of his trousers. Then she licked a path parallel to his waistband. He moaned again, his passion flaring bright and strong. He ordered himself to relax, but his muscles twitched, and he had to bite back what he wanted to ask the lass. She wasn't ready for him, but he was going to explode if he didn't bury himself deep inside of her now!

Helen ran her palms from his shoulders to his wrists and back again, then from the nape of his neck to his waistband, lingering there.

"Lass, I won't beg ye, but if ye're thinking ye've had enough for the night, I need to cover ye up, tuck ye in, and go soak me head in the horse trough."

"Without making love to me?"

"If I must. Me control has been tested to the limit."

He'd started to rise from the bed when Helen reached out and grabbed hold of his waistband. "I am sorry if I have disappointed you."

"God, lass, ye damn near killed me with yer innocent touches, sampling me flesh. And yer flavor is one I will dream of until ye let me taste ye again. We'll be leaving in the morning, so there won't be time for us to lie abed as we have tonight until we arrive at Wyndmere Hall."

She frowned. "When was this decided?"

"Earlier today. I did not have the chance to discuss it with ye. 'Tisn't safe for the baron and baroness for us to remain here with the prisoners, but I did not want ye to marry me with only strangers in attendance, when me brother and more of me cousins were a few hours away."

"I understand, Eamon."

He sat up and swung his legs over the side of the bed, and the lass giggled. "What has ye laughing?"

"Look at our feet."

He ran his hand along the length of her stocking-clad leg. "I'm sorry I didn't get to familiarize meself with yer lovely legs." He stopped abruptly at her ankle, and he chuckled. "Left yer slippers on, did we?"

"And your boots, too."

He moved to the edge of the bed and removed his boots and

socks. "May I help ye with yer slippers?"

"Yes, please. Do you still plan to head to the stables to soak your head in your bare feet?"

He laughed.

"I do understand if you do not want to help me remove my stockings."

"Well now, I'm thinking I like the look of ye wearing only yer stockings." He removed her slippers and set them on the floor by the chair where he'd placed her gown. "If we were going to make love, the feel of them wrapped around me waist would drive me right over the edge."

"Edge of what?"

"Reason."

She stared up at him and tilted her head, considering his words. "Why would I wrap my legs around you?"

"To take me in as deep as I can go from the first position I'll be teaching ye."

"Is there more than one?"

"Aye. Ye'll be a delight to tutor, lass, but for tonight, I've taken all I can without begging ye."

She sat up, and her ebony hair rained down her back, tempting him to touch. He gave in and ran his hands through the silken strands.

Kneeling on the bed, she held out her hand. "Make love to me, Eamon. You've been so careful and patient with me. Seal our vows tonight, please?"

He undid the placket to his trousers and shed them. Moving to the bed, he took her hand in his, pulling her closer. He straddled her and rasped, "Wrap yer legs around me, lass." She did as he asked. He pressed against her core and paused, marveling at the pulsing heat of her. "Do ye feel that?"

Helen gasped. "You are so hard."

"I ache for ye, lass, but I'm not going to make love to ye until ye're writhing in me arms, ready to welcome me into yer hot, wet passage." He slid his hands to her backside and gently kneaded her curves. "Everywhere I touch ye is like a gift." He laid her back on the bed and asked, "Are you certain ye do not want to wait?"

"Kiss me, Eamon."

He was like a man possessed—a man on a mission. That mission being to drive his wife to the brink of sanity until she cried out, begging him to end the madness.

He caressed her where he knew she ached for his touch. She was soon mindless to everything except his touch, and his words of encouragement, as he drove her closer to the edge. She was so close to finding her release.

He whispered words of encouragement as he told her how he would manipulate her, stretch her, so she would be able to accept the length and breadth of him. Words melted into moans, moans into groans.

"Open yer eyes, *mo chroí.*"

Her lashes fluttered, and her violet eyes locked on to his.

"I'll love ye for the rest of me life, will ye love me back?"

"Yes! I will love you for the rest of my life, *mo ghrá.*"

He entered her slowly, kissing her neck, her mouth, and her breasts while her body pulsed around him, accepted him.

They moved together as if they'd been lovers for years. He felt her getting ready to soar, and suckled her breasts until she tightened around him and screamed his name. He drove into her again and again until he could not hold out any longer. With one last thrust, he shouted her name. Filling her to the hilt, he released his life-giving seed. Her hand slid from where she'd clenched his backside, and her breathing slowed. He could not have ever imagined that making love to her would rob him of his strength like this.

He settled her against his heart and rolled on his side, ensuring that her injured wrist was not pinned between them. He would have to see that she continued to use the sling and rest that arm.

O'Malley had started to list the things he would do with the sunrise when she shifted and her mouth brushed his chest, relaxing him to the point where he dozed.

He blinked, glad he had not fallen asleep. He had one more task to attend to.

When he untangled their legs, he had to smile at the way the lass wrinkled her nose. He rose from the bed. The pitcher of water was no longer hot, but room temperature. Better than ice cold. He poured some in the bowl, dipped the soft cotton cloth beside it into the water, wrung it out, and carried it over to the bed where his wife lay.

He bent over her and kissed her until she opened her eyes and smiled at him. "Is it morning already?" she asked.

"Nay, lass, but I have a husbandly duty to perform, and ye'll not argue with me."

"It must be something that I am not going to like, isn't it?"

"Ye'll likely be tender, and it may sting, but I need to wash ye, lass."

Her frown was fierce. "Are you suggesting I let you wash me *intimately?*"

"Aye—as I'm the one who took yer innocence, I'm the one who will tend to ye."

Helen blew out a breath, "Do I have a choice?"

"Aye, ye can close yer eyes, or leave them open."

Her eyes locked on his, and she hissed when he gently washed her.

"I don't mean to hurt ye, lass, but I don't want to cause ye harm by not washing ye and making sure that I haven't done any serious damage to ye."

"Wouldn't I have felt it if you had?"

"That depends—sometimes, when one is in the throes of passion, ye don't always notice an ache until after the euphoria passes."

"I see."

"All finished, love." He got up, rinsed the cloth, and hung it over the rim of the bowl to dry, then walked back over to her.

"Are ye wanting to sleep in yer chemise?"

She smiled and reached for his hand. "I'd rather have you wrapped around me."

He slipped into bed and settled her back against his chest, biting the inside of his mouth to keep from moaning when she wiggled to find just the right spot. When he was about to tell her to stop tormenting him, he heard her breathing slow and knew she'd fallen asleep.

Wrapped around his wife, protecting her, O'Malley finally let himself drift off.

## CHAPTER TWENTY-FIVE

O'MALLEY WOKE SLOWLY, appreciating the warmth and curves that were still snuggled against him. "I'd be happy to wake up the rest of my life, just like this, Lord. Thank ye."

"Eamon?"

His wife's sleepy voice had him nuzzling her ear. "Good morning, Mrs. O'Malley."

"Good morning, Mr. O'Malley. Is it really morning already, or are you planning to bathe my sore parts again?"

He rolled until she was tucked beneath him. "Ah, lass, I hoped that ye wouldn't be too sore this morning. We've a long ride ahead of us."

"It was worth every moment, Eamon. You made it beautiful for me."

"Ye deserve to be treasured, lass. And ye have no regrets?"

"None. How long before we have to leave?"

He looked over his shoulder. "The curtain is in the way. I can't see outside. Though I hate to even suggest it, I need to get up."

"Will you kiss me first?"

"With pleasure, lass." He kissed her gently, tenderly, cherishing her.

"You kissed me differently last night."

"If I kissed ye like that again, I'd be hard as a rock, needing to find release, when I'd best be waiting until ye aren't as sore."

She sighed and brushed the tips of her fingers along the width of his shoulders. "Will we be stopping at the inn to see the coachman?"

"We will."

"Have you spoken to the Hinkle sisters about returning to Wyndmere Hall with us?"

"Weren't you there when I let them know I sent word to Their Graces?"

"I may have been distracted at the time." She snuggled closer and sighed. "You are so warm—it's going to be cold when I get out of bed."

"I'll get out first. That way, the sheets will cool to the point where they aren't comfortable and ye'll want to get out of bed."

She laughed. "I never would have thought of that."

He slipped out of bed and tucked the covers around her. Knowing she was watching him from behind, he swaggered over to the washstand and washed his face and hands. "Are ye as hungry as I am?"

"Maybe more. I was too nervous to eat before the vicar arrived." She shivered and reluctantly got out of bed.

"I'm going to make a suggestion that you may find odd. I can dump the water from the bowl into the chamber pot, and ye can have fresh water to wash in."

"I'm accustomed to making do, Eamon, and rarely have been the first one to use the bathwater." She smiled. "After what we shared last night, I think it would be a pleasure to use the same water that you used."

He slipped the chemise over her head and helped her into her gown. "Wife of mine, will ye always be surprising me?"

"I guess we have the rest of our lives to find out."

She watched him don his trousers and held his shirt for him. Next came his socks and boots. He laughed when he reached for her foot to put her satin slippers on. "Ye're still wearing yer stockings."

"It's scandalous, isn't it?"

"Aye, but only the two of us will know." O'Malley drew her into his arms and pressed his lips to hers. "Ye nearly broke me heart when ye left Wyndmere Hall."

"It broke mine to leave you."

"Why didn't ye say goodbye?"

"I would not have been able to leave you, Eamon. And I did not know how to tell you about my past."

"If ye had only asked, I could have told ye that I already knew all about it."

"I was not as strong as I am now."

"Life challenges us, lass. 'Tis how we meet those challenges that shapes us. We're better for it…stronger."

"I know *I* am." She rose on her toes and kissed his cheek. "Thank you for not giving up on me."

"Thank ye for not being able to resist me manly charms."

Helen laughed. "Do you think you'll be too tired for another lesson in love tonight?"

"Lass, I'll never be too tired to make love to ye."

"Is that a promise?"

"Aye, lass. Pucker up, and I'll seal me promise with a kiss that'll curl yer toes." Lord love her, she gave as good as she got, and kissed him until his eyes crossed. "If ye're after distracting me, ye've succeeded, but I must warn ye that the penalty will have the both of us back in that bed and me brother and cousins banging on our door."

Helen's lovely lips curved into a smile that warmed the cockles of his heart and sent a bolt of heat straight to his bollocks, which had his shaft again making its presence known.

"Ah, lass, are ye after killing me dead?"

"No, Eamon, I'm after getting you back in that bed."

He swept her into his arms, carried her over to the bed, and knelt on it, placing her gently in the middle. The tangled sheets told the story of their first time making love. "Well now, here we are, lass. What did ye have in mind?"

The heavy pounding on the door was his reminder that making love to Helen would have to wait.

"Bollocks!"

"Get up, Eamon! Yer party of four is ready to leave now."

"Go away, Flaherty!"

"I was thinking about something Lady Phoebe mentioned…about lips and teeth and tongues," Helen murmured.

His attention caught, he slowly smiled. "And what did she say about them?"

"That's just it—she never gave specifics, but the mention of it had Caro and Prudence sighing."

"Well now, I know exactly what she had in mind. Would ye care for me to show ye?"

"Open the bloody door, Eamon!"

"Go *feck* yerself, Flaherty!"

"Is this what the rest of our lives will be like?" Helen asked.

O'Malley snorted. "I'm tempted to stretch the truth and tell ye that it'll never happen again, but I cannot lie."

"From this moment forward, there'll be no secrets, and we'll only tell one another the truth."

"Aye, lass." He lowered his forehead to rest on hers. "If ye must know, the truth of it is that me family is a royal pain in me arse, but they'll be there to stand beside us, to hold us up when we need it. We'll be there for them, too."

"They love you, Eamon."

"Open the bloody door!" Flaherty growled as he hammered the wood with his fist.

"He'll be singing a different tune when a lass falls into his path and turns life upside down," O'Malley said.

"Have I turned yours upside down, Eamon?" Helen asked.

"Aye, lass, and I wouldn't change one moment of it." His lips met hers in a kiss that promised a lifetime of ups and downs, highs and lows. "Let's get started living the rest of our lives."

"I thought you'd never ask."

"What in the bloody hell is keeping ye, Flaherty?"

O'Malley chuckled. "Sounds like me brother's patience is spent."

"'Tisn't me," they heard Flaherty reply. "'Tis yer randy brother!"

Helen's eyes were filled with laughter. She leaned close and whispered, "Do you think you'll be *randy* again tonight?"

"Depend upon it, lass." He winked at her, stood, and held out his hand. "Ye carriage awaits, lass. Are ye ready to face me irritated cousin and brother?"

"With you by my side, Eamon, I'm ready for anything."

# EPILOGUE

*Two months later...*

O'MALLEY RUBBED HIS wife's back, wondering what in the bloody hell he could say that would make her feel better.

"I love ye, lass."

The sound of her retching had his stomach muscles tightening.

"There cannot be anything left inside yer belly."

He should have kept his comments to himself—the poor woman heaved again.

Still leaning over the chamber pot, she held out her hand for the damp cloth. He placed it in her hand and watched as she swiped it over her mouth, folded it, and handed it back to him. O'Malley's strong constitution weakened with each successive day that his wife puked up her guts. He tossed the cloth into one of the spare chamber pots he'd insisted they have on hand after the first time he witnessed what Helen went through upon rising.

As God was his witness, he vowed he'd never plant another babe in her belly!

She held out her hand again. This time he gave her one of his handkerchiefs. The lass promptly blew her nose, folded it, and handed it back to him. He tossed it into the pot with the cloth.

Finally...*finally*, she sat back on her heels—his cue to let go of her hair. "Do you want to know what I think, O'Malley?"

It was telling that she called him O'Malley and not Eamon. "Aye, love, tell me what do ye think."

"Our babe will be a boy. Your son will grow up to be just like his father: a man who faces down death with a smile, whose body is riddled with scars, and who irritates the life out of me every time he tries to tell me what to do."

He gently pulled her onto his lap and eased her into the shelter of his arms. With her cheek leaning against his heart, he rasped, *"Mo ghrá*, if the Lord blesses us with a healthy babe, who are we to question whether or not our babe has some of me best qualities or yers?"

Helen groaned, and he braced himself for another round of holding back her hair while she puked up the lining of her stomach.

O'Malley wasn't prepared when she jabbed him in the gut with her elbow. "I'm praying we have a little girl, who will be sweet as sugar, with a temperament as soft as a morning in May."

*Seven months later, their prayers were answered...*

"YE'RE BRAVE, BEAUTIFUL, and I promise to never—ever—make ye pregnant again."

Helen smoothed her hand over the ebony peach fuzz on their daughter's head. "See that ye keep that promise, O'Malley."

He used the tip of his finger to trace the pale-as-moonlight silk atop their son's head. "Do ye think ye'll be calling me Eamon again anytime soon?"

"Mayhap when our daughter is sitting in the garden serving us tea from the tiny tea set Their Graces gave us."

"And just what do ye think our son will be doing? Having tea with his sister?"

She snickered. "He'll be tossing rocks at a bottle on top of the fence post, pretending he was shooting at it with your rifle."

*Seven years later...*

"ROISIN! HAVEN'T YE heard yer ma calling? She wants ye to finish yer chores."

The miniature version of his wife never ceased to amaze O'Malley. Her slashing dark brows over violet faery eyes would bedevil some poor man a decade from now. *Lord, don't let it be sooner than that!*

"But I can't stop now," Roisin protested. "Eamon and I are even. All I need is to knock off this last bottle and I win!"

"You won't win. I'm stronger, bigger, and have better aim," young Eamon said.

"Someday, lad, ye'll learn that 'tis the women who are stronger," his father replied.

"In battle?" Eamon asked.

"Aye, son…in the battle to give birth."

His twins tossed the rest of their rocks on the small pile by the back of the stable where they'd been having their morning competition. They rushed over to his side. Roisin grabbed his left hand. Eamon grabbed the right, and tugged on it until O'Malley glanced down at him. "Do ye think if we're really quiet, Ma will let us hold Finola? She said once the babe was a few weeks old that we could."

"Ye'll need to wash yer hands until they sparkle, lad."

Roisin yanked on his other hand. O'Malley grinned. The stubborn lass was always trying to prove she was stronger than her twin. "I want to hold her too."

"We'll see. First ye'll wash yer hands and finish yer chores."

She pouted. "I folded a few things."

"Ah, but ye need to fold the rest. Yer brother did his half of the folding. 'Tis no skin off me nose if ye don't finish yer chores. I'm certain Eamon won't mind eating yer share of the teacakes Constance sent over this morning."

Her eyes narrowed. "The iced ones?"

"Aye. When ye finish yer chores, Constance was hoping ye'd help pick berries."

"Berry tarts," Eamon murmured.

"Jam," Roisin replied.

"She said Deidre would be helping her too. I'm thinking between the three of ye helping pick the berries, ye'll gather enough for Constance to bake tarts *and* cook up a pot of jam."

Roisin grinned. "You'll have to make sure Uncle Patrick doesn't find out where she hides the jars of jam."

"Deidre will tell her da," Eamon grumbled. "She always does."

"Does not!" Roisin cried out.

"Does too!" Eamon let go of O'Malley's hand and ran toward the back of the cottage.

"Does not!" Roisin yelled, chasing after her brother.

If O'Malley and Helen's babe wasn't already awake and nursing, Finola was sure to be by the time the twin terrors reached the cottage.

Taking a moment to watch them racing and laughing, O'Malley felt his heart overflow with gratitude. "Lord, it's Eamon again. Thank ye for the gifts in me life. Me wife, our twins, and our new babe. Ye know I didn't want Helen to suffer through all-day sickness again. The lass suffered for nine months the last time, and it broke me heart."

He remembered how tiny their babes had been and how he worried that the birth would be too much for Helen to handle. But he'd be damned if she did not bounce back, and start putting the bug in his ear every time another one of his cousins' wives gave birth to another babe.

O'Malley had faith enough to trust that the Lord knew what he was doing. He added a prayer that little Finola would be the mild-tempered, sweet-as-sugar daughter the lass had prayed for the first time.


*Three years later…*


"LORD, IT'S EAMON again. I'm thinking 'twill be me last prayer, as ye've stopped listening to me entirely! The lass is as big as our cottage—though I'll never tell her that—and she wasn't supposed to have any more children. She puked up her guts every morning for nine months…again!

"Our little Finola sneaks out of the house every morning, following after her older brother and sister. Lord, have pity on me. They're teaching her how to knock bottles off the fence post with a handful of rocks!"

*Two years later…*

"LORD, 'TIS OBVIOUS that ye only answer me wife's prayers." He kicked at a clump of dirt with his boot and sighed. "Forgive me. Ye did answer me prayers when Helen only puked up her guts for the first three months this time. She's still glowing, Lord, even after giving birth just three days past. Our new daughter, Brigid, is healthy. And just like the other three, she has ten fingers, ten toes, two eyes, two ears, and a nose.

"Thank ye, Lord, for the gift of me wife and blessing us with a family to love."

Halfway back to the cottage, he paused to add, "Thank ye, Lord, for the gift of life, and the gift of one more day."

# About the Author

*If we have not met yet, I'm delighted to meet you. Here's a little bit about me...*

I have been writing romance novels for almost half my life—well, at least for the last thirty years. I'm a die-hard romantic and have to confess the broad shoulders and wicked glint in the brilliant green eyes of a stranger had my breath snagging in my breast, my heart beating madly, and my future flashing before my eyes. At the age of seventeen, I'd met the man I knew I was going to spend the rest of my life with.

I write Historical & Contemporary Romance featuring characters that I know so well: hardheaded heroes and feisty heroines! They rarely listen to me and in fact, I think they enjoy messing with my plans for them. Over the years I have learned to listen to them. I have always used family names in my books and love adding bits and pieces of my ancestors and ancestry in them, too! Visit my website to learn more about my books.

*Sláinte!*
*CH*